DEADLY
DISTRUST

DEADLY
DISTRUST

MARY SCHALLER

ISBN: Hardcover   978-1-6641-4210-7
           Softcover   978-1-6641-4208-4
           eBook   978-1-6641-4209-1

Print information available on the last page.

Rev. date: 11/09/2020

To order additional copies of this book, contact:
Xlibris
844-714-8691
www.Xlibris.com
Orders@Xlibris.com
771245

Dedicated to
the memory of my father,
who first introduced me to
Amanita ocreata.
And
to my husband, Don,
who gave me encouragement
to write this story.

CHAPTER 1

September 1979

I n a small apartment in the hills of San Francisco, it was early morning in August. Gina was having a phone conversation with her best friend, Elly. Their conversation had been about their classes coming up, when it quickly changed.

"Gina, you didn't answer my question! Why are you so silent?" Elly was beginning to sound frantic on the other end of the phone.

"Shush-someone is at my door, and they're using a key!" Gina's voice trembled as she whispered into the receiver, "Hang on, I'm going to see who it is." She didn't wait for an acknowledgment.

Gina only had time to lay down the receiver. Crashing through the bedroom door, a man flung himself at Gina. Muffled by his hand, she could let only a guttural gasp escaped her lips. Pinning her to the bed with his knee, he reached for the dangling receiver and hung it up. He smiled evilly down upon his squirming victim.

"I've come to get a piece of ass, you stupid woman! You can't deny what a husband is due," he growled.

Raising her knee, Gina strained to ram it into Gary's groin. The initial aim missed its intended mark but threw him off balance. Freed and scrambling off the bed, Gina made a desperate attempt to reach the bathroom. Gary was right on her heels. His sweaty hand caught her by the throat. He spun her around and then backed her into a corner, where she couldn't escape. She tried to scream, but his thumb pressing on her trachea silenced her. She struggled to gasp for breath to no avail. At first stunned by his actions, she didn't fight.

Then she realized the crashing earthquake of his intention to kill her. Squirming and fighting against his overpowering strength, she clawed for her life.

Then as suddenly as it had started, it was over.

Gina sardonically watched as Gary burst into tears. "Why do you drive me to do this?" she heard him wail as he collapsed onto the edge of the bathtub.

Her hand went to her throat and gently touched her neck to see if it was still in one piece. "Get out!" she screeched hoarsely. "I hate you! I want this divorce as soon as possible, and I am going to get a restraining order! Give me the key! Coming in and abusing me like you just did is against the law."

"If you tell the police, I will plead insanity!" he mumbled, barely coherent.

"Just go!" Gina screamed. "If you get out *right now*, I won't call the police, or my brother, or anyone. *Out! Now!*"

Later in September

Gina and Elly found an apartment within blocks of the university. They were second-year nursing students, and this new apartment was perfect for them with two bedrooms, a small living area, and a kitchen. Gina was unpacking some boxes.

"Murder and political scandal. That's all they can write about in these stupid newspapers!" announced the red-haired Gina while she unpacked some plates wrapped in old newsprint.

"If you read less and unpack faster, you will not be bummed out by the news and will get done faster so we can play!" soothed Elly, who was gazing around the nearly empty room.

In the middle of this vacant Victorian apartment, Gina thought about how she appreciated her newfound friend. *We study so well together. Elly is a bit more sophisticated than I am. Routinely, Elly catches the eye of virtually any man. Her sleek athletic figure, wavy dark hair, and stunning lavender eyes are captivating, and her patients love her. She is going to be a great nurse.*

"This place is going to take a lot of work!" Elly sighed.

"I'll help. I'm so grateful that you want to room with me," Gina gushed. "The guys should be here with the furniture soon, so let's pile everything into a corner and start painting as soon as possible."

"That's a good plan. Before the furniture arrives, we need to look at the bedrooms. Neither has a window with a view, so you can choose because it's all the same to me," Elly said.

Suddenly they heard pounding and the banging of boxes outside the door. Elly leaped over the cartons she was working on and tore open the door. "Hi. Oh, I know that box. It must be breaking your back! Let me help you."

Gina grinned with pride at her tall, lean, blond-headed brother in his early forties who held a large box. An open box with a microwave oven was at his feet. "Sorry. I was trying to carry both of them, but they slipped when I banged on the door," Todd said sheepishly to his sister and her friend. "I hope nothing is broken."

"This is my big brother Todd, Elly. Todd, this is my roommate and friend, Elinor, but call her Elly. Everyone else does," Gina announced.

Another man ran up the stairs while carrying a lighter box with kitchen tools hanging out of it. "Why don't you two worthless women get off your asses and help us?" Gary growled.

Gina looked at him with daggers. "And this is my uncultured ex-husband!" she said.

The next couple of hours flew by as the four brought all the household items into the apartment. When Todd had brought the last box up, Gina went to the refrigerator and brought out a six-pack of beer. As she gave it to him, she expressed her gratitude and told him to share the beer with Gary so she didn't have to deal with him herself.

"Also, just between you and me, Todd, Elly and I are going to Stinson Beach to catch some rays and relax. Would you like to join us? By the way, please don't tell Gary."

Todd laughed at her. "Some of us, little sister, have to work. But you have fun. I won't breathe a word to Gary."

Soon the men were gone, and once again Gina and Elly were alone. Gina stood in the bay window, nervously watching Gary, making certain that he drove away.

San Francisco's streets were awash in sunlight. The fog had been driven far out to sea as it often was in the late summer days with an easterly wind. It was gorgeous outside. Gina called to Elly, "It's beautiful! Let's get out in that sunshine. We start classes on Monday, and playing in the sun is good for us. This is the best day we've had all summer!"

Happily they took the stairs two at a time until they reached the street. Gina's older car sat patiently at the curb. The cooler, the towels, and the picnic gear were thrown in the trunk, and off they went.

As the two women drove north, the Golden Gate Bridge sparkled in the afternoon sun. It was busy with pedestrians strolling while they watched the sailboats on the bay. There seemed to be more bicyclists than usual. Gina was excited by all the activity. Silently, she admonished herself to watch her driving.

"See? It is such a wonderful day that we just couldn't miss out on enjoying it!" remarked Gina.

The hills of Marin were dry and yellow from the summer drought. Stinson Beach was reached by a winding narrow road over the hills and down to the point where the land met the Pacific Ocean. As they drew close to the sea, they could hear the crashing of the surf and catch the seductive odor of the salty air. The parking lot was crowded with cars, but Gina was usually lucky at finding a spot, and this time was no exception.

Burdened down with a cooler, blankets, and other picnic gear, they struggled to the top of the dunes to survey the beach. They settled on a place near the water, a site where they could watch the action right in front of them. Gina looked around to see if she knew anyone, but she didn't. Oh well. In all her thirty years, no one had ever said she was shy. Not knowing anyone meant she just needed to get out there and meet someone. She just loved to flirt.

Down by the water's edge, some young men were playing Frisbee. It looked like an enticing challenge.

"Do you think those guys would let us join them?" Gina asked Elly.

Elly, who was four years older, had just made herself comfortable with her pillows and the book she had brought. In addition, she had no interest in playing Frisbee or meeting young men, so Gina was not surprised when Elly answered, "Go ahead. I bet they would love to play with you, but I am going to relax here."

Striding off toward the Frisbee game, Gina turned many heads. Her firm, curvaceous figure in a two-piece suit with her wild hair flying freely in the breeze was certain to attract attention.

The men stopped their game and huddled around her. Gina loved the attention and had no trouble convincing the guys that she could play their game as well as they played it.

One man who was also watching Gina was not necessarily friendly. He was clad in swim shorts as he sat on a dune watching with binoculars the mini drama below. He was getting aroused watching the bitch. Out of the corner of his eye he saw a distraction. But he was concentrating on the flame-colored hair and her generous breasts, which he wanted in his mouth. But then he heard footsteps behind him and turned. An addict, a guy he'd supplied for a long time, approached him.

Tentatively, the other man crept up to him and flashed a card with the queen of hearts on one side and an angel on the other. The pusher acknowledged the newcomer with a nod, and the latter sat down near him. Continuing to look through the binoculars, the pusher asked, "Do you have the dough?"

The addict moved closer and whispered hoarsely, "No. You said that there was another way. Please, I can't cope without—"

The pusher smiled maliciously and whispered, "See that slut down there, the sexy broad in the two-piece suit playing Frisbee? I want …" He gestured by rubbing his heel in the sand. "Get her high and overdose her or something. Make it look like an accident. Okay? Now leave me alone," he growled.

Down on the beach, Gina eventually grew tired of the young men she was playing with and returned to share the blanket with Elly to do some serious sunbathing. Elly was glad to have Gina's company as her book was no longer holding her attention. Gina poured the sunscreen into her hand while explaining that her fair skin was vulnerable.

"Did you notice the cute buns on that one guy?" Gina gushed. "If he weren't so young, I would make a pass at him," she said with a wink.

Their conversation rambled on, covering the nursing program they were in and the men in their lives. Gina finally asked, "What did you think of Todd?"

"He's kind of quiet, but he seems to be nice," Elly said without raising her hat, which she had positioned over her face.

"You should get to know him better. He works too hard—really drives himself," Gina said. "He needs someone to distract him so he doesn't work so many hours."

"Oh, what does he do for a living?" Elly responded, mildly interested.

"He's a detective with the San Francisco PD," Gina said proudly.

"Does he have any women in his life?" Elly nonchalantly asked.

"No, silly, that's why I want you to get interested in him. And I think he is your type." Gina was getting mildly annoyed.

Rolling onto her side, pushing her hat down onto her head, then resting her head on her hand, Elly faced Gina and said, "Well, tell me more. Was he ever married? Children? Hobbies? Tell me all."

"I'm glad I finally got your attention!" Gina exclaimed. "He was married. It was a fairy-tale marriage. They were so happy together, but one day it all ended. He came home and found that she had been raped and brutally beaten to death. It was awful. And what made it far worse was that the man who had killed her was a man Todd had arrested and later convicted but who was released on parole. Ever since, he has been obsessed with catching murderers. He can be absolutely compulsive.

"He never talks about her or what happened. When someone asks him about his marriage, he just tells them she died in an auto accident. She was pregnant at the time, and he mourned both of them for years. I think he occasionally dates, but they usually turn out to be one-night stands.

"Todd needs someone who will really understand him. Under all his cool professionalism, he is a real sweet guy. I think he would really like you."

"Me?" Elly exclaimed in surprise.

"Yes, you, silly. I thought we would invite him over for dinner sometime after the apartment is fixed up. Say, speaking of food, let's have that lunch we packed." And with that she started to rifle through the cooler. "Oh, silly me, I forgot the fucking drinks!" Gina said with a scowl.

Elly gazed at Gina sympathetically. "That's okay. We can get something to drink from the vendor in the parking lot. I need the exercise. I'll go and get the drinks, and you can guard the goodies from the seagulls," she said as she tossed on a shirt over her bathing suit. "Do you want anything special?"

"Anything low in calories is fine. Thanks. You're great!" she said as she stretched out on the blanket to expose another portion of herself to the sun.

In Elly's absence, the roar of the ocean seemed louder, and the ebb and flow of the surf was mesmerizing, lulling Gina into a stupor. Warm sunshine caressed her body, until a shadow fell across her face and the sour odor of sweat stung her nostrils. Gina's eyes flew open.

"Hello, beautiful," Gary said in a low voice.

Gina's body stiffened with foreboding and suspicious attention. She lifted her downcast eyes to see Gary standing over her with a pair of binoculars hanging around his neck. The sharp jutting nose, receding chin, and sun-browned skin gave him the appearance of an overfed Doberman. It shocked her to realize she had once thought him ruggedly attractive.

"You followed us here!" she snapped in defense.

"Followed you? How you flatter yourself! It is a free beach, and as you know I come here often. In fact, I was the first to bring you here," he boasted as he sat down on the blanket beside her. "I saw you here alone and thought it would be a good time to have a talk."

Sitting up and reaching for her shirt, she glared at him. Her fiery curls coiled around her face like flames. She was tense with anxiety.

Gary was barefoot but fully dressed in jeans and a plaid shirt that was open wide at the throat to reveal his hairy chest.

"What do *we* have to talk about? If it isn't the alimony I am going to get, then you can stuff it!" Gina demanded with her eyes blazing.

"I was thinking the other day what fun we had when you and I went hunting this time of the year. Do you remember those times?"

As Gary talked, Gina became more upset by his droning on as if he had memorized his lines. His stiff body language and his gruff mannerisms were sending a darker message that made her anxious.

"Take Todd hunting with you. He would be good company!" Gina blurted out in her effort to calm him down and remind him of her protection. In her mind she was admonishing herself for not having gotten that restraining order.

He abruptly turned his whole body toward her and yelled, "It's you I want, not Todd!" He ranted on, but she could not understand him.

Suddenly she thought of a way to turn him cold. When she could get a word in, she dropped her head and said in a low, controlled voice, "I want you to know that after putting up with all your abuse, I have decided to become a lesbian!" There was a heavy silence after that.

Finally Gary recovered. A chill came over Gina as he clenched and unclenched his fists. Abruptly he stood up and snarled, "I would rather see you dead than a dirty dyke!" With that he skulked away like a wounded animal.

Gina was relieved to see Elly coming over the dunes with the drinks.

Sometime Later in October

It was Friday. Gina and Elly were in their mycology class at the university. The lecture was finished for the day, and Dr. Mark Jacobs was giving some closing remarks.

"With that, I conclude my lecture on *Amanita ocreata* for today. As you exit class, please sign up for the mushroom field trip to Marin coming up this Saturday. If you can provide transportation, please indicate that as we need more drivers. We will meet at the student union at ten. Bring a lunch and plenty to drink. We are going to be doing a lot of hiking, and I don't want anyone to get dehydrated. Any questions?" Professor Jacobs said in an inviting way. He always had the full attention of his students because there was never a dull moment during his lectures.

Mark Jacobs answered questions that ranged in topic from his subject matter to the field trip. When no more questions were forthcoming, Mark announced, "I would like to meet with Gina Williams after class, please."

The classroom was in the style of a small semicircular theater. Gina and her pal Elly came down the stairs of the auditorium with the other students and approached the demonstration table at the front of the room. Several other students were gathering around Dr. Jacobs, asking questions and sharing experiences. When they had all finished and the last one had filtered out of the room, Dr. Jacobs turned to Elly. She explained that she was just waiting to get a ride from Gina. "So if you don't mind, I would like to stay."

"Oh, it's okay. I'm just going to ask Gina if she would be interested in working a few hours in the lab on Wednesdays. Well, Gina, are you interested?" Dr. Jacobs asked in a congenial tone.

Gina's bright eyes lit up, but then she dropped her head. "I would love to, but I have taken a part-time job with a cardiology clinic, and with my studying, I don't think there is time." She coyly tilted her head in a flirtatious way and sweetly said. "I wish I hadn't made this other commitment."

Mark couldn't help but be captivated by her look of innocence. Her big brown eyes were like reflective pools of emotion that were filled with playfulness and vulnerability.

"I'm sorry too. How about you, Elinor? Can you spare us some of your valuable time?" Dr. Jacobs asked with interest that was now directed toward Elly.

"Let me check my schedule, and I'll call your office tomorrow. Would that be all right?" There was an air of quiet control about Elly.

"Sure. I'll keep the position open for another week. I must go now. I've got to get to my next lecture. I hope to see both of you on Saturday," he said as he walked briskly to the exit.

Gina and Elly walked in the opposite direction, but Gina called over her shoulder, "Bye. We'll see you Saturday."

The Following Friday

The day had emerged from a cloudy night with rapturous sunshine and clear skies as can only come after a few hours of rain. Gina loved mornings like this; they were made for adventure. Standing in front of the mirror, she combed her long unruly hair and tried to tame it into a braid at the nape of her neck. When her crown of golden-red hair was neat, she tied it up with a colorful scarf that coordinated with her form-fitting sweater. Then she carefully reviewed her image in the long mirror. Today it was important to look her best. However, as she turned in the mirror, she noticed that her jeans were getting a little too tight. There was no time to deal with unwanted bulges; the gym would have to wait for another day.

Her good-looking boss, Dr. Pace, had generously invited her to go with him to Napa Valley to pick up a couple of cases of wine. She had never been to the wine growing area just north of San Francisco, and she was excited by the opportunity.

The very thought of Allen Pace made her knees wobble. His sharply carved features were very powerful. Those eyes, luminescent blue, had a gaze that seemed to penetrate one's soul and undress one's body. Gina loved every innocent moment when his hands touched her. It sent tingles through her and made her want more.

The silver Alfa Romeo drove up to Gina's door twenty minutes late, but weren't doctors always supposed to be late? She fairly flew down the stairs to meet him.

Gina's effervescent enthusiasm always brightened a room when she entered it. *Allen Pace seems to have taken an interest in me, and he is so handsome. Dealing with ailing heart patients must get depressing at times. There is also his wife, who he had told me is always needling him. Yes, I want a powerful man in my life, and he galvanizes me with his sexy gaze. This makes me feel beautiful and sensuous as well. Oh, those muscles! I can imagine my legs wrapped around him! This trip has potential beyond the wine he will purchase. Such an exciting man!*

They drove north, crossing the Golden Gate, ambling through Marin County. The hills were just showing a little green after the dry summer. It reminded Gina of spring in Michigan, but this was fall in California.

Their conversation encompassed what Gina was learning in her nursing program, what she was doing at the cardiology clinic, and what her plans were for the future. She was thrilled that Allen purposely kept the conversation on her and her world. Gina naively thought he wanted her as a woman, not just as a plaything.

When they reached the Napa Valley area, they turned off the main road onto a narrow road that wandered into the hills. They headed for a small family-owned winery called Lark Hill. As they drove, Allen explained to Gina why he liked this little winery better than the more well-known ones in the valley below.

"They make the smoothest-tasting Chardonnay in this area. We'll go to the tasting room. I'm sure you will be delighted with their wines if they are as good as they were the last time I was here. If the latest is still good, we will buy a case plus a bottle for us. I know of a sweet place with a view in these hills where we can have bread, brie, and wine. Does that sound good to you?"

Gina had told him that she had never been to a winery before, and he was amused that she couldn't pronounce Chardonnay very well. He liked teaching her about new things like wine. As they drove through the Napa Valley, he told her all about the wines and their growers. Allen smiled to himself. He found Gina's lack of experience refreshing, and it made him feel important.

Soon they were out of the car and climbing the short way to Allen's exclusive spot he had promised. The view stretched for miles. There wasn't a house or anything in sight, just grass, trees, bread, and wine. It was a perfectly lovely place for romance.

Allen spread out a blanket. From a paper bag he produced a baguette of French bread and a small round of brie. Then he reached into the pockets of his jacket for wine glasses. The two sat down on the blanket and shared the feast.

As the afternoon rolled along, Gina's cheeks became flushed with wine. She loosened the scarf that held her hair and liberated her wild mane. Lying down on the blanket with her inhibitions suspended in time, she spoke more freely. "It's funny, but the office people warned me about coming with you today." She giggled. "They told me to be careful, but you are a perfect gentleman, and you have been so sweet to me."

"There is one who likes to play Mother Superior in the office. What could be harmful about this?" he asked seriously. "Tell me more about what she said."

"Oh, she thought I shouldn't go off for the day with a married man. But I am technically married as well, although separated from my husband. I felt she was treating me like a child." She pouted. "Would you mind telling me about your wife?"

Allen sat beside Gina's outstretched body. He was gently stroking her red hair and following the tendrils of hair down to her full breasts. Every touch of his hand was like fire. It was all she could do to keep her hands off him. She wanted to be tantalizing with naive, sweet ways. Gina let her hair flow wildly and seductively around her face, and she puckered her lush full lips to bait him. She heard him slowly begin his story.

"My marriage has been emotionally dead for years. We live parallel lives. The problem is that we have different interests. She has her friends, and I have mine. As you can see, I don't have much of a marriage. In a way you and I have similar situations, but you are legally separated and I am not." She had heard it all before, but she felt that this time she was falling for him.

It was a reasonable story, although Gina didn't listen carefully; she was too distracted by the hunger in his eyes. Her breasts longed to have his touch, and her lips desired his tongue. She encouraged his closeness and shivered with delight with him lying down next to her. The warmth of his body near her was more intoxicating than the wine. She rolled over and kissed his neck. She traveled down, kissing his chest. He reached out and drew her closer to him. Then he kissed her sensuously on the lips as he took her into his arms. Gina's body responded to his with delight as she arched up to meet him in an effort to show she was famished for more. He accommodated her by fondling her breasts and unbuttoning her sweater. It wasn't long before her body was as exposed as a forest nymph. She tore at his slacks to release his member so she could play with it. He shuddered in her embrace and his need for the intimacy of love.

They were on a common plane now. He was no longer the sole expert and she the naïve ingenue. And so when dusk unwrapped the night, it found them locked in a sensuous embrace.

***

Two weeks passed. Gina was writing in her diary.

Dear Diary,

Allen thinks I'm falling in love with him and told me I should date other men as well! Truthfully there weren't any other opportunities until today. Dr. Jacobs, I really mean Mark, asked me for a dinner date with him tonight, and it was a super date. He is so kind, and we had a wonderful time.

Gary, the husband who won't give me a divorce, is still trying to get me to come back to him! He called a record number of times today: nine. Sometimes I wish he would just jump off the bridge.

—Gina

***

Late one night in October, the man with a drug addiction paced back and forth in his sparsely furnished home. He expected the phone to ring any minute. It was excruciating as he waited. "Oh, why doesn't he call? I can't stand much more." He sobbed and held his head in his hands.

When the phone rang, the tortured addict picked it up before the first ring had finished. "Hello?" he said impatiently.

There was a long, agonizing pause, and then a deep voice said, "You sound a little desperate. That could be dangerous."

"Is this my source? Don't you have a name?" The addict was doing his best to sound calm. "I'll have the money as soon as the banks open tomorrow, but please, I need the … stuff. I shake uncontrollably. I can't function." His voice trembled.

"No deal without the money. You haven't kept your promise about the target. So what makes you think I can swing a deal without hard currency?"

"I have a plan; in fact, that is why I ran down my supply so fast. I got her turned on, and that is how the accident will happen!"

"Damn you!" the pusher interrupted. "Be more careful about what you say on the phone! It could be bugged. I'll meet you at the usual place in the morning at eleven." There was a *clunk*, and then the drone of the dial tone sounded.

CHAPTER 2

Sunday, November 12

M ark Jacobs was standing outside her house in the hills of San Francisco. He was talking at the door, which was ajar, to the home of his favorite friend, Annette Pace.

"Hi, Annie, I've had a change in plans. I was wondering if you would be interested in going with me over to Marin to do some mushroom gathering?" Mark Jacobs said in his usual nonchalant way.

Annette listened while she held the door to her home slightly open. "Okay, Mark. I just got up, and it will take me some time, but I will be ready as soon as I am decent. Come in and make yourself comfortable. I will be down in a few minutes."

Mark urged the door open slowly when he heard the rustle of Annette's flowing robe as she scurried away to get dressed. He decided the best place to wait for Annette was in her breakfast nook off the kitchen.

He looked anxiously at his watch. It was almost noon. The morning sunlight was shining in through the windows. Mark felt tense; looking out the window helped calm him. He knew worrying was a waste of energy, but being alone always brought on the gloom. *What have I recently read? "Success is failure turned inside out." I hope success is just around the corner.*

A few minutes later, Annette bounced down the stairs and entered the kitchen, looking for Mark. "Oh, here you are. Why didn't you fix yourself a cup of coffee while you were waiting?" she asked rhetorically as she reached for the coffee pot and poured him a cup.

Annette's smile was radiant and strong enough to chase the clouds of doubt from Mark's mind.

"You are so thoughtful," he said as he took the cup from her outstretched hand. *And beautiful,* he thought as he eyed her pleasantly full but trim figure decked out in jeans, a turtleneck sweater, and hiking boots.

"So, you had a change of plans. Is there anything you want to talk to me about?" she asked as she sat down on a chair opposite him.

"Nothing I want to bore you with. But it is too good a day to waste when we could have a productive time collecting wonderful morsels for one of your delectable creations. I saw some impressive areas for gathering specimens on the Marin hillsides last week when I was there with my students. I want to take you there because I know you will like it."

"It sounds like a wonderful idea. It just happens that I had nothing planned, and I am basically ready to go. We can have dinner here this evening," Annette offered.

Mark led Annette to his car, which was parked at the curb outside her house. It was a short distance to the road connections to the bridge. He was a careful driver most of the time, but this morning his mood made him aggressive as a driver.

However, it was a magical day. The clouds were just lifting off the bay, and they seemed to be playing peekaboo with the towers of the Golden Gate Bridge. The beautiful day was lost on Annette, who looked wistfully out the car window and wondered if her husband was really at the meeting he was supposed to be at or if he was off with his latest clandestine paramour, using drugs as he often did. The sun had come through the clouds and was dancing on the hills of Marin. It was gorgeous like a Chinese painting. The view was captivating. Annette couldn't avoid noticing it. She decided she must put Allen out of her mind and just enjoy the day.

Mark drove to Mill Valley and up the road past Muir Woods Park. When they came to a dirt road leading off to the right, he turned on to it and drove another hundred yards. Here large evergreen black oaks surrounded them. The air smelled of decaying vegetation in the moist afternoon air. "With the rain last night, we have the perfect conditions for *Amanita ocreata*," Mark said as he parked the car.

"Why do we want to collect *A. ocreata*, today? Didn't we get a box full last week? I would like to be looking for something we can eat tonight," Annette suggested.

"I need some specimens for the lab. I have some students working on the toxin to find an antidote for it," Mark explained.

He opened the trunk. They pulled out their day packs, hoisted them on, and set out on a narrow deer trail that led up the slope. Suddenly Mark stopped by a spreading oak tree and whispered as if it would move if he talked too loud. "There's a beaut," he described as he knelt down to get a better look at it. Before him clustered the delicate pure white deadly poisonous *Amanita ocreata*. "That is why they call them 'the angel of death'; they are so lovely to look at, but so deadly to touch." The spores must be kept off of the hands, so gloves were essential. If the spores were to get on one's hands, then they could be ingested. From his pack, Mark extracted a box in which to transport the mushrooms and a trowel. Setting to work, he carefully dug up the delicate fungi and placed them upright in the box. Then he took out a card and recorded the name of the mushroom, the approximate location where they were found, the date, and the time.

When he had taken off his soiled gloves and disposed of them in a plastic bag and then put on clean gloves, he said, "Let's try our luck over there in that stand of pole-sized redwood saplings and see what we can find."

The young redwood trees stood in a tightly knit clump like a family of siblings huddled against the elements. In the soft, well-mulched ground around the trees, miniature waxy caps raised their bright little red heads.

"Oh, look, *Hygrocybe miniata*. They are great as a garnish for salads," Annette cooed as she crouched to empty her day pack of the tools she had brought. "You don't suppose they could be *H. punicea*, do you?"

Mark leaned over her shoulder to take a closer look at the specimens she held in her gloved hand. "No, I don't think so. *Hygrocybe punicea* is found late in winter, and it is much redder."

Their path continued up the narrowing canyon. A trickling spring oozed among the ferns, and the tan oak limbs reached out to touch the visitors. Along the path *Coprinus comatus* (shaggy mane) grew like tiny sentinels guarding the wonderful world of fungi. Annette picked several of the freshest as she loved their delicate delicious flavor—and they were perfect for sauces. On one of the tan oaks they found the overlapped rows of *Peurotus ostreatus* or oyster mushrooms. "We are so fortunate to find them so fresh and young," Annette observed with wonder in her voice.

"I grow them on a log in the lab at the university," Mark responded. "We can take them to your house and prepare them by breading and frying," Mark continued.

Backtracking out of the canyon, they found another path that led up the hill. They climbed in silence to listen to the forest branches swaying in the breeze with birds fluttering with a flash of blue, green, and gray everywhere, singing in the forest's highest branches. Here and there they could hear the twittering of insects, and far away down the canyon the occasional frog croaked. It was heavenly peaceful.

They climbed a second hill and discovered many delectable mushrooms for Annette's palate. Later, as they grew tired, they stopped on a knoll with a breathtaking view of the ocean on one side and the sequoia grove nestled in a valley on the east side. Flopping down under a tired old cypress, they pulled out their bottled drinks, cheese, and crackers. "I get so thirsty doing all this," Annette exclaimed as she eagerly drank some water.

Mark too was thirsty. As Annette passed him a bottled drink, he put his hand around Annette's hand as he looked into the deep pools of her eyes. He said, "Thank you for coming with me today. I really needed your company."

"I was feeling lonely too," Annette admitted. She was captivated by the touch of his hand. It was a delicate hand for a man, smooth and soft like a woman's hand. To break the spell of the moment, Annette turned toward the west and appraised the view. She said, "The fog's gentle touch on the hills with the ocean peeking through reminds me of a Japanese screen painting. It is just lovely."

Mark, however, only had eyes for Annette. He marveled at the shape of her finely chiseled aristocratic nose, her moss-green eyes, her sensitive dimpled chin, and her flowing golden hair. He wanted so much to caress her, but all he could do was admire her from afar. Then, realizing that time had passed, he blurted out, "Yes, I always like to come up here for the view."

The hours slipped by. Gradually Mark and Annette felt recovered and keen for more exploration. The packs needed to be repacked and organized. Care was needed to get all the specimens back to San Francisco in prime condition. Standing up, they surveyed their options. Mark suggested, "If we walked back to the car along that pasture up ahead, we will probably find some *Agaricus osecanus*. You know them as giant horse mushrooms, and they are delightful served many ways." With her agreement, he took her hand and led her down the hill.

They found their prizes in an open grassy area. The broad rounded heads peaked out from between grass clumps. Each specimen was tested for its odor. If an individual was too musty, it was discarded as past its prime. When they had collected several, they moved on toward an oak, madrone, and bay laurel forest. In the forest they found some butter bolete with butter-yellow stalks. "This, darling, will be excellent in soup. That makes our meal complete. We'll have mushrooms for hors d'oeuvres, soup, salad, and the entrée," Annette announced. She loved to cook elegant dinners.

***

It was late afternoon as Elly scrambled from the bus. She slung her heavy backpack onto her back and, with heavy feet, headed up the sidewalk to 421 Ocean View Street. It was a nineteenth-century house converted into three apartments, which were labeled A, B, and C. As she entered the main door, the stale odors of bygone meals, pets, and wet diapers filled her nostrils. It was hard to find beauty in this place, but it had a purpose. It was cheap, and once you were out of the common hall and into the apartment, it wasn't so bad. Elly trudged up the short flight to apartment B and unlatched the dead bolt with one key. A second key opened the lower lock. She pushed open the door and was enveloped by her sanctuary. The original Victorian open structure was not completely lost when they turned it into apartments. Elinor had painted the walls white and covered the bay window with handmade roman shades with a spring print. The overstuffed furniture from the thrift store was slipcovered with a plaid fabric in the same colors. The overall feeling was clean with a light airiness.

Slinging off the book-laden backpack, Elly dumped it unceremoniously on a nearby chair and went into the kitchen to brew some tea. It was then that she noticed the phone answering machine was flashing for attention. She decided to ignore it. She wasn't ready to encounter another message from Gary or even other students. To be completely mindless after studying all afternoon was her deepest wish. The orange spice tea smelled wonderful, and the hot liquid seemed to revive her.

The telephone suddenly sprang to life. Elly reluctantly picked up the receiver. "Hello?"

"Oh, Elly, it such a relief to hear your voice. I have been trying to get you all afternoon," Gina said in a tortured, scratchy voice.

"I just got in the door," Elly admitted apologetically. "Are you okay? I have been studying in the library all afternoon."

"I think I have the flu, but I can't talk long 'cause I don't have the strength, and it is long distance." Gina paused to catch her breath and then continued. "I'm up in Amador County." She stopped again to take a breath. "I came up with the love of my life, and then I got sick and I've been vomiting all afternoon." Gina rested for a third time because of her shortness of breath. "We didn't have a very romantic time!"

Elly found herself holding her breath in sympathy. Then she gasped. "You sound really sick. Are you going to be alright?"

"I think if I lie low and rest, I'll be better tomorrow," Gina stammered weakly. "I just wanted to let you know that I won't be home tonight and I'll miss classes tomorrow."

There was a pause. "Don't worry, I will take notes for you tomorrow. This is a short week with Thanksgiving coming up, and midterms aren't until next week."

The line suddenly went dead. Elly was very worried because Gina hadn't said where in Amador County she was, nor had she given her a phone number. Staring at the receiver as the silence engulfed her, Elly abruptly had a feeling of dread.

For the last three months, Gina Williams had been Elly's roommate and best friend. They certainly had experienced some difficulties. Two people never agree totally all the time, but they had worked out the adjustments. Gina's light, bubbly personality was a nice contrast to the intense discipline of school. It was becoming increasingly clear to Elly that Gina's effervescent demeanor was a mask to cover her troubled personal life. Her estranged husband, Gary, called daily to beg and moan for Gina to take him back. He was a real damper on Gina's daily routine, but Elly was secretly a little envious. She would like Jerry, her ex, to be a little remorseful after having lost her.

She prepared her humble meal of leftovers, when the phone rang. She hoped that it was Gina again, but it was Gary.

"Well, finally. It is about time you decided to answer your phone! I want to talk to Gina," he growled.

"Gary?" Elly asked. She knew full well who it was, but she resented his lack of manners.

"Yeah, and don't keep me waiting!" he retorted.

"Gina is not here. She called and said she is sick and won't be here until tomorrow. I'm sorry. I'm worried about her, but I'll tell her you called."

"Where is she?" he asked in a calmer tone.

"I really don't know, exactly," Elly confessed. "Somewhere in Amador County. She went up to a cabin with … some friends, caught a flu bug, and decided not to come home until she feels better."

"Do ya have a phone numba for her?" His voice was once again tense.

"That is what concerns me the most. She didn't give me a phone number," Elly truthfully stated. Why don't you go up there and find her if you care about her? You would be a real hero if you did that!" Elly blurted out. Then she wished she had not said it.

The silence was only seconds long, but it seemed like an eternity. Abruptly Gary said reluctantly, "Okay, I will think about it. I'll call tomorrow. Bye!"

Elly sighed as she hung up, murmuring under her breath, "I'll bet you will!"

She ate her simple bowl of soup, her thoughts troubled.

***

In another part of San Francisco, in a neighborhood of elegant houses built in the 1920s with beautiful landscaped gardens nestled in a cove at the entrance to San Francisco's bay, a different sort of evening meal was taking place.

Annette loved to decorate with expensive furnishings like Chippendale antiques and old oriental carpets. A fire blazed in the marble fireplace topped with a cherry wood mantel. The table was set for two with candles and a large flower arrangement. In the kitchen the hostess was creating one of her favorite dishes. The professional stove was her "friend," and it was roaring with activity. The cutting board had numerous little piles of precisely sliced and chopped vegetables, including a complex collection of wild mushrooms.

"May I pour you some wine, Annie?" Mark suggested to his hostess.

"My goblet is ready. Let us make a toast to ourselves, that we may have many more wonderful mushroom hunts!" Annette said with a little drama and music in her voice and a lovely smile on her face.

Mark's happy face reflected his love for Annie's happiness. Her life was not an easy one.

They sat down to their exquisite meal complete with exotic sauces and delicious mushrooms. The conversation revolved around the day they had spent in the Marin hills searching for their prizes.

Finally, when they had exhausted all the neutral topics, Mark ventured into the obvious. "When do you expect Allen back?"

"Late, I presume. He said he had a meeting in Sacramento, but that could mean anything," Annette said as she seemed to be examining her plate as if it had a specimen on it. Then abruptly she said, "Excuse me, I think I'll clear the table. You go and sit by the fire, and I'll bring you some brandy." With that she rushed from the table.

Mark rose from the table feeling like a cloud had descended on his friend. He had never married, and now that he was pushing fifty, he wasn't sure that had been one of his smarter moves. He decided to create a conversation to bring Annie back from the doldrums.

The antique silver tray had a linen doily on it. The Waterford crystal decanter held an aged brandy. A delicate china plate gently held fresh ladyfingers. Two cut-crystal brandy snifters completed the offering Annette carefully placed on the little table between them.

Mark began, "There is a project I've been planning, and I want your opinion on it."

Annette smiled and nodded her head, encouraging him.

"I would like to take a group of students to Australia next April to study the indigenous mushrooms. Would you consider joining us?"

Annette's face took on a glow as he went on to describe some tentative plans. He wasn't sure if the pink in her cheeks was the result of his project or the brandy, but he liked it.

The evening hummed along with their conversation. When the mantel clock struck ten, Annette suggested that they adjourn to the kitchen and put things in order. Mark was happy to help her. Their exchange turned to investments, a subject that Annette was very keen on.

"What do you find in the market to invest in these days with the economy so crazy?" Mark asked.

"Actually, I've made a financial move that is radical for me. You know how I feel about investing too close to home, and you are well aware of the reservations I've had about a large investment in one place. Well, I've put a large sum of money into Allen's new cardiology clinic, and recently they made me a silent partner." She went on before Mark could offer comment. "But I am deeply concerned that Allen will do something foolish and jeopardize my investment, so when Allen requested the funding, I was very wary of it, as you know. I made him promise me something. If there ever was a scandal involving him and some other woman, like a pregnancy or a paternity suit, I would withdraw my funding and divorce him.

"Lately his behavior has gotten—I don't know how to describe it. His actions are sometimes so bizarre that I don't know what to make of them. I'm worried, Mark, and I don't know what to make of him," Annette said softly.

Mark realized he was seeing a different side to her. It left him momentarily speechless. Annie had never confided in him in such a meaningful way.

Annette apologized: "I'm sorry I'm burdening you with the family tensions, but I needed to talk to some neutral person, and there is no one I trust more than you, Mark."

They were suddenly aware that someone was at the front door. A moment later, in walked Allen.

"Well, isn't this a cozy domestic scene!" Allen said with sarcasm.

His height and sturdy frame engulfed the room. His otherwise handsome face was taut with emotion, and his icy blue eyes flashed.

"It is nice you could get home early," Mark said dryly. "Did you have a nice trip?" he added.

"If you call boring professional meetings *nice*, then the answer is yes. If you consider I would rather be doing something else, then the answer is no," Allen replied.

Mark felt uncomfortable and out of place like a third wheel. He tactfully said the polite niceties to his host and hostess and saw himself to the door.

A silent tension filled the room and was almost palpable. Allen went to the cupboard, chose a brandy snifter, and poured himself a jigger or two. Annette stood quietly, waiting; she didn't want to be the next one to speak.

Finally, Allen said, "My guess is that you don't believe I was at a professional meeting all weekend!"

She knew he was sparring with her, and she wasn't sure she wanted to play, so the silence continued and the tension mounted.

Allen came closer. He lifted her face to his. Her silky fair hair fell away from her face, and she looked up at him with large, intensely green eyes.

"My angel doesn't trust me! You think I was out—how would you put it? Ah yes, you would call it adultery. That isn't what I would call it. Adultery is where you love someone else outside of the marriage. And, you see, that isn't me. I love only you. You are part of my soul, and you know it. Those other women I screw are like so much meat to me!"

Annette felt her composure slipping. Allen sensed the power he had over her, so he continued. "Now one could establish a powerful argument that you commit intellectual adultery with that slimy friend of yours *Mark*. Weren't you out with him all day pawing the dirt looking for toadstools? And then my sweet angel brings him home and makes him one of her sensational dinners! All day and all evening you are lovingly discussing your favorite subjects. You see, I don't like him getting so much attention from my soul mate."

The words cut through Annette like a cleaver. "Maybe you should stay home more," she muttered.

Allen heard her but continued to torture her. "And when her poor, tired husband drags himself home, he has to pour his own brandy!"

With that, he threw the remaining brandy in her face.

CHAPTER 3

November 22

Elly was jolted awake by the shriek of the telephone. She tumbled out of bed and ran to the kitchen phone. "Hello?"

The answer came as a coarse gurgle and a squawk: "Help!" Elly softly replied, "Gina, is that you?"

"Yes, please call ... my ... brother." Every word was labored. "He works for the ... police ... department. They'll ... find him." Her coarse breathing was as loud as the words.

It was impossible for Elly to find something to write on in the darkened room. Carefully, she felt along the wall for the switch. The light blinded her for a second, but she fumbled with the pencil and paper anyway. "Your brother's name is Todd? And what is his last name?"

"Markam," Gina squeaked.

The effort of her breathing was painfully audible in Gina's voice. Elly made an extra attempt to write the message carefully. Elly asked Gina to give her a simple address and phone number, but each syllable was work as Gina replied. Then Elly offered, "Shouldn't you call 9-1-1 up there and have them take you to the hospital?"

"I'm not that bad!" Gina retorted with some effort. "And if ... you ... can't get ... Todd, then get ... Gary."

"Okay, I understand. I hope you feel better. I wish I had a car to come to your rescue," she responded softly and hung up.

Elly's brain was awhirl with urgent plans. She grabbed the phone book to find the police non emergency phone number, and once she'd found it, she dialed it.

"San Francisco Police Department. Is this an emergency call?" the woman answered.

Elinor took a deep breath and announced, "I am Elinor DeMartini, and I need to talk to Todd Markam. There is a family emergency, and he must be told about it right away!"

The operator responded coolly, "I'll ring Lieutenant Markam's office, but I doubt if he is in at this hour."

Click! Somewhere in the police department a phone rang and rang again, and then the answering machine came on. Elly reluctantly left a message, giving her phone number, and hung up.

Frantically Elly started opening drawers trying to find Gina's personal address book. It was then that she noticed the clock. It read 4:20 a.m. *It's going to be hard to find anyone at this hour,* she thought. When she finally found the book, she looked up Markam's home number. Thankfully there was a number for him. She dialed it. Another answering machine greeted her. *"How frustrating!"* she said to herself. Then she left one more message with a plea to call as soon as possible.

Under the name Williams, Elly found Gary's number. Now it was decision time. *Should I wait for Todd to call, or should I call Gary now? I prefer talking to Todd, but if he doesn't call and Gina's situation is life-threatening, she could die before anyone is able to get to her. The vision of Gina's suffering is driving me to the conclusion that I have to call Gary.* She dialed. Gary answered on the third ring.

"Grunt. Why da fuck is some jerk calling me at dis hour?!"

"This is Elly calling, and I wouldn't bother the devil at this hour if I didn't think it was absolutely necessary!"

"Sorry, I'm not very nice when I am dragged out of a deep sleep."

Elly told him the story and gave him directions to the cabin. Gary actually sounded grateful that he was needed and promised to call Elly when he got up there. He planned to leave as soon as he could get dressed and drink some black coffee.

Talking to Gary seemed to lift Elly's spirits. *Like dumping my books on the couch,* she thought, chuckling. *Maybe he isn't the bad person I think he is. The problem isn't solved, but at least there is someone with whom to share it.*

It was almost 5:00 a.m. by now, and Elly was much too awake to go back to bed. The gym opened at five thirty. She could get there when they opened and work off her frustration. The brightly patterned leotard slid over her body effortlessly like a second skin. At thirty-four, Elly had the trim, flexible figure of a woman ten years younger. Over her leotard she pulled on sweatpants and a jacket to keep herself warm. A firm bushing of her gently wavy brown hair untangled it and made it shine. She grabbed her keys and was ready to leave. Then she realized it might be wise to put a new message on the answering machine about Gina being ill and unavailable, in case Todd called.

With that accomplished, Elly left the apartment. She locked the door and faced the street. The moist, cold air assaulted her face, and a spasm of loneliness engulfed her. Normally the two-block jog to the gym was a delight. She and Gina had never feared for their safety as they ran the gauntlet each morning together. It was sort of the illusion of strength in numbers. This morning the two blocks seemed like a mile. Finally, Elly ran up the steps and into the safety of the gym.

An hour and a half later, Elly plunged back into the security of the apartment. Quietly the answering machine sat without any calls quite yet. Elly consoled herself with a quick shower and gobbled down her oatmeal. Finally she was ready for her world and was off to her eight o'clock class.

**

Across the bay in Tiburon, Mark Jacobs stood pensively brooding while staring out the filthy widows of his lavish home. He had a panoramic view of the bay. However, his home was sparsely furnished with only an old worn leather couch and a moth-eaten brown hassock. Both had been inherited from a recently departed relative. Now he was so in need of money that everything of real value had been sold or pawned. He was facing a balloon payment on a loan coming due soon, and he had no way of refinancing it. If only he could bring himself to ask Annette for a loan. The pusher was getting very nasty about the money he owed, too. That was really scary—almost as frightening as being without the drugs. Surely his fortunes were about to change.

The time was flying by. He had to teach a nine o'clock class at the university on Mondays. Why had he given himself such a demanding schedule?

In the bathroom while shaving, Mark inspected his face. Along his hairline the scars of his numerous face-lifts seemed more obvious this morning. Yes, he was forty-seven and abhorring the day when he would turn fifty! But with a little help from makeup, he could look thirty-nine or even thirty-seven on a good day. Carefully he parted his dark brown wavy hair, looking for bald areas and any gray hairs that he plucked from their moorings. Each bloodshot eye got a drop of a medication that would make both his eyes sparkle.

"I think I'm ready to clothe my beautiful body," he cooed to the mirror. He chose a white silk turtleneck sweater, gray wool trousers, and a black tweed jacket, which was his favorite combination of clothes. He approved of the image in the mirror and, at last, was ready for his public.

***

The long drive to the cabin in Amador County was almost coming to an end. Dawn was just breaking as Gary's truck with Williams's Construction Company printed on it approached Jackson. The cabin was only fifteen miles or so beyond this cozy town nestled in the foothills of the Sierra. Gary drove slowly, looking for the critical turnoff. He passed it once. Realizing his mistake, he turned his truck around and found it on the second pass. The cabin was dark as he drove up the drive. Gina's small compact yellow car was parked outside. He recognized it.

The nearest neighbor was out of sight, but Gary still felt nervous approaching a strange house, even though he was certain the car outside was familiar. The license plate was also identifiable now that he was closer. He honked his horn, but the lights didn't go on in the house. He had many anxieties, but he pulled himself together and went to the door. At the door, he was worried about what he would do if he could get in and then what he would find inside. First he gently knocked, and then he banged on the door. To his surprise, the latch yielded and the door fell open. With that the stench of vomit and the putrid smell of shit hit him like a bomb. "Gina!" he cried out. Only silence answered him. "Gina, Gina, are you here!?" he yelled as he plunged in. To the right, he heard a muffled cry and responded to it.

On a rumpled bed, lying in her filth, a woman lay in a fetal position. "Gina?" asked Gary softly as he was holding a part of his shirt over his mouth and nose to ward off the odor. Creeping up to the bed, he barely recognized Gina. Her hair was matted with vomit, her cheeks were sunken, and she was as pale as plaster, but it was Gina.

Her breath was coming in short gulping motions as he sprang into action. He got the cleanest blanket he could find and wrapped her in it. Then he scooped her up and carried her to the truck. "Please, God, don't let her die in my arms," he mumbled.

The drive back to Jackson took less than twenty minutes as the truck careened around the corners and lurched into the hospital parking lot. Gary screeched to a stop at the emergency dock.

"Help!" Gary yelled in desperation.

Several people in white responded with a gurney. They loaded up Gina and disappeared inside the double doors. An older woman grabbed Gary's arm to prevent him from following.

"Come with me, sir. We need some information," the woman said as she pulled Gary to another entrance.

The questioning seemed endless, and the following wait in a chair, alone in an empty waiting room, was maddening.

***

It was noon before Elly returned to the apartment and answered the calls on the answering machine. "This is Gary. Gina is at Amador Community Hospital, phone 216-437-5000. The doc says she is critical. They have her on life-support equipment. He says her liver isn't working and her kidneys are in trouble. I'm just praying like I have never done." *Beep.* "Todd Markam calling back. I'm catching the first plane home this afternoon if I don't hear from you by noon. The number is—. Honolulu, Hawaii." *Beep.* "Thanks for the message about Gina's illness. This is the cardiology clinic. Call us when you have news." *Beep.*

Elly transcribed each message carefully and then reran them to make sure she had the information correctly written down. The time difference between Hawaii and California was three or four hours, so she should be able to call Todd before noon in Hawaii. Carefully she dialed the number. An exchange answered first. Elly requested her party, then there was a pause and Todd came on the line.

"Hello, Elinor. I remember meeting you last September when I helped Gina move into the apartment you are sharing. What is this about Gina being ill and its being a big emergency?"

"I'm so sorry to interrupt your vacation—or is it a business trip? Gina is critically ill and in a hospital in Jackson, which is in Amador County. She needs you very much," Elly responded.

"It's okay; I was getting tired of lying around on the beach anyway." He was trying to make light of the situation. "I've got a flight home scheduled for tomorrow. I will try to get an earlier flight. I will call you when I get into SF. Have you been to visit her? If not, maybe we can go together."

"No, I haven't seen her. I don't have a car. I had to enlist Gary's help. He was the one who called me to tell me she was in the hospital on life-support equipment. I would be very happy to go with you. I am worried about her."

"Sure. I'm sorry. I'm so worried that I am not thinking straight. You are welcome to come. It will be nice to have some company at such a terrible time. Our parents are no longer living, and I feel quite alone with this tragedy. You have been such an asset, and I think Gina would like to see you, too. See you soon," Todd replied.

"Thank you. Bye," Elly responded.

Elly was aware that her stomach was growling. With so much going on, it was hard to concentrate on her studies, and yet if she was going to be away tomorrow, she would have to get a lot done.

***

Dr. Allen Pace swaggered down the hall of the San Francisco Hospital. His rounds were completed or at least under control, and he had just gotten off the phone with Annette. *Making up is such an exciting and satisfying experience. We are going to dine out, and then*

I am planning to punch her number. I should not think about it here because I might get aroused!

As Allen turned a corner in the hall, he met Dr. Darrell Minix, who was one of the partners at the cardiology clinic.

"Hello, Darrel. What gives you such a hound dog face?" Allen said tongue in cheek.

"I just had a wrenching encounter with Dr. Shirley MacKay. May I have a word with you in private?"

"Okay, we can just duck into the lounge down the hall. I will tell you how to handle Ms. MacKay with style."

The lounge they chose was empty except for Dr. George Carpenter, who was the third partner at the cardiology clinic. George's round, middle-aged body was slumped down in an overstuffed reclining chair. It appeared that he had fallen asleep while reading the paper as the newspaper was strewn across his lap and his glasses were hanging precariously off his nose. Allen and Darrel's noisy entrance startled George. He clumsily tried to sit up as the other two entered.

Allen was impeccably dressed as usual in a navy pinstripe suit with a fresh white shirt and a conservative blue tie. Darrel, on the other hand, was in green scrubs and was looking a little ruffled.

"Hi, George. We're sorry to disturb your nap. Darrell had a mini run-in with one of our illustrious colleagues and needs some support," Allen announced.

"Not a problem; I'll just go on reading the news. You can forget I am here," George said as he fumbled with his glasses and tried to find wherever it was he had left off in the paper.

Allen and Darrell poured cups of coffee and settled down on the couch that stretched across the lounge.

"Okay, keep me in suspense no longer, Darrell. What happened?"

"Dr. MacKay has this patient. We'll call him Mr. Jones. Anyway, Mr. Jones has serious heart problems, and he really needed me to do a catheterization. Shirley wouldn't hear of it. She wanted to run some tests first. I waited three hours, and when I saw the patient again, he was worse. This really upset me, and Shirley was unavailable for a consult. All the tests she had ordered had been done. The heart cath looked to me to be absolutely necessary, so I did it. Shirley walked in just as I was finishing, and she blew her top. She ranted and raved that I was stealing her patient. It was very embarrassing in front of all the staff."

There was a long silence. Allen took a sip of coffee and said, "Confidentially, all Shirley needs is a good fuck!"

They both laughed nervously.

Allen took another sip of coffee and said in a conspiratorial way, "All you need to do is treat these so-called liberated women right. You know, wine them, dine them, and say all the nice complimentary things to them, and soon you will find they are slurping and salivating. You won't have to wait long. Shortly, they are wetting their pants trying to get them off for you!"

***

It was 10:00 p.m. when Annette and Allen returned from their dinner. Annette shimmered in the low-lit room. She wore a silver-gray silk jumpsuit with a plunging neckline that showed off her full breasts. Her jacket and matching belt were an emerald-green Chinese silk with silver embroidery. At her throat was a priceless green-apple jade and diamond necklace that was a family heirloom.

Allen made a fire in the fireplace and gently urged Annette to sit near the warm fire. He went to the kitchen and made them each a hot buttered rum drink, which he brought on a tray with a flask of warm massage oil.

Returning to the living room laden down with his offering to assuage his guilt, he was disappointed that Annette was not waiting eagerly for him. She was curled up on the love seat with a book and hadn't even noticed his grand entrance.

"Could I interest my sweet angel in some lovemaking?" he asked in a low, soft voice.

"Thank you for the hot drink. That was very considerate of you. Don't be silly and just stand there like a lost puppy. You haven't had a chance to read the mail or the newspaper. Sit down and let's read awhile before we turn in," Annette said nonchalantly.

Choosing the chair that faced her, he scowled at the fire. "Look, Annette, you complain that I don't spend enough time at home, and then when I am here, you either want to have guests in or you have your pretty snout in a book. I wanted to make love to you in front of the fire. It is a cold night, and it sounds romantic and sweet to me." His voice was full of hurt, and it trailed off at the end.

The crackling fire dominated the otherwise silent room. Annette lowered her book and gazed at him. "We gave up screwing in front of the fireplace a few years ago when we got the new carpets and the brocade furniture. Now, if you demand that I do my wifely duty, I will, but let's retire to the bedroom."

He could only look at her with big, sad eyes. "I had something else in mind, thank you." Hiding behind his newspaper, his thoughts strayed to Gina and her spontaneity. The comparison was painful. Maybe another tactic would work better. Carefully he lowered his paper and asked, "Are you mad at me?"

"You acted preposterously last night. You embarrassed me. Your numerous affairs take their toll after a while, you know. Can't you have affairs without making them so public, so that I can be spared hearing all about them?"

"Sneak around like a criminal? Dishonesty is not my style," he sneered with arrogance.

"You make it sound so gallant. Do you realize how your behavior makes me feel?" She sniffed defiantly.

"Half the time you don't display any warmth for me. When I am treated like a servant boy, it is easy to come to the conclusion that you don't give a damn," he objected.

"Blatant betrayal is what I call your behavior, and I can't help it if I can't be loving to you when I rarely see you and I know you are out with a paramour half the time. It is a real turnoff! We no longer take trips together, and I have to bribe you into staying at home. You are always cultivating some other woman, and when you are here, you expect me to fall all over you. Well, I'm sorry I can't change sheets that fast." Her voice shook with feeling, and she was near tears.

"Okay, I am not the perfect loving husband anymore, but you have changed too. At one time you were quite the fox. Remember when we would go to restaurants and you would wear those sexy short skirts and no panties? You took my breath away. How you would tease me, taunt me, and tear me up with your sweet charms. I get aroused just thinking about it. I have never loved another woman as much as I love you." No longer able to stay away from Annette, he moved to her side. "Please," he implored, "I need you."

Turning to grasp him with her moist green eyes, she said, "Your affairs are tearing up this marriage." She looked at him for a long moment and then asked, "Why is it so difficult to be faithful to me? Is that too much to ask?"

"Yes, I will make an effort to. I'll do anything to make you happy," he lied. "Just let me have you and hold you because I can't live without the center of my universe." He gently took her in his arms and kissed her neck, her cheeks, and then that sweet, sensuous mouth. Then he held her close to him and purred, "I am going to show you in many ways how sorry I am that we had our little spat last night. I'll make up for all my other sins, too."

With a triumphant, glorious smile, she turned away from him ever so slightly and sipped her drink slowly. "No matter how mad I am at you, I can't resist you."

He moved closer to nibble on her ear. "You can't resist me because you know how crazy I am about you. If I lay a love nest of pillows for my angel beside the fire, would my darling join me on the floor?" he whispered.

Like a siren she turned to him with her eyes glittering in the fire light. "Surely your ardor can wait long enough to get upstairs. I really do not want to soil those expensive pillows. Besides, you need to shave, and I would like to get into something sexy, loose, and comfortable," she whispered. Then she kissed him, running her tongue seductively around his mouth.

"Ah, now you are sounding more like my baby." He sighed as he tried to pick her up, but her weight was too great for him. Setting her gently down, and laughing in his embarrassment, he offered, "You make me weak, sweetheart."

They walked hand in hand up the stairs to their bedroom.

CHAPTER 4

Wednesday, November 23

A vision of a young woman in white gossamer robes floated in front of him. Her hands were outstretched, beseeching him. A sea of mist lay between them. Gary saw himself trying to stumble toward the figure, but with each footfall he sank deeper into the mist. The more he tried to reach her, the more distant she became. "Gina, Gina!" he cried out.

"Mr. Williams, Mr. Williams, wake up. You are having a bad dream. Wake up!"

Gary awoke with a nurse hovering over him. "Mr. Williams, Dr. Lovejoy would like to speak with you. May I take you to his office?" Her professional manner was coolly efficient.

He shook himself and answered, "S-sure … but could I get a cup of coffee first?"

"Of course you can. We'll pick you up some on our way to Dr. Lovejoy's office," she offered more compassionately. The coffee machine was down the hall. Once Gary had his cup in his hand, they walked down the hall, passing several doors to get to the doctor's office.

Dr. Lovejoy's office was a small room near the emergency room. Martin Lovejoy stood up to greet Gary as the latter entered the room. After they shook hands, the doctor motioned Gary to a chair next to his desk and asked the nurse to close the door as she left. Dr. Lovejoy looked at Gary directly and said, "I'm sorry we had to wake you, but your wife has taken a turn for the worse, and you wanted to know when there was a change in her status. We are having difficulty maintaining her blood pressure, and she is desperately in need of a liver transplant. I have been calling all the major hospitals in Northern California that do the surgery that is required, as well as trying to locate a donor with her blood type. Without a liver transplant, I don't give Gina more than a few hours to live."

Gary clung to his coffee cup and nodded to show that he understood. Tears brimmed in his eyes, but he fought to hide them. With a weak, halting voice, Gary asked, "May I see her?"

"Yes, of course. I'll call the intensive care unit and make sure they are ready for you," the doctor responded. Dr. Lovejoy made his phone call while Gary concentrated on drinking the coffee. When the arrangements had been made, Dr. Lovejoy escorted Gary to see Gina.

The hallway seemed endless. Gary felt the sweat run down his face. He had no idea what to expect, and he feared the worst. They turned a corner, went up a flight of stairs, and entered some huge double doors on the right. Fluorescent lights gave the intensive care room an eerie glow. There were strange noises of buzzing and the whirring of alarms. The sounds were oppressive to Gary. He wanted to hold his hands over his ears, but he didn't want to look weird. Dr. Lovejoy led Gary to a long desk-like work area where several nurses in light blue scrubs sat writing notes in charts. Dr. Lovejoy presented Gary to one of the nurses with, "Betty, this is Gina Williams's husband. I have brought him to visit Mrs. Williams."

Betty was a rather plump, round-faced woman with soulful eyes. After the doctor had introduced her to Gary, he thanked her and left by way of another door. Betty stood up and came around the workstation to greet Gary. "Would you like a refill on that cup of coffee?" she asked.

Gary was unusually mute. All he could do was nod his head in the affirmative and hold out his cup to her like a beggar.

"Come this way. I'll get you settled, and then I'll get you a nice cup of hot coffee. Do you take cream or sugar?"

The bed was surrounded by a gray curtain and was a short distance from the nursing station. It was the major source of whirring, buzzing, and whooshing sounds. Gary's first sight of Gina took his breath away. He stopped at the entrance and looked confused.

Betty assertively took Gary's arm and steadied him. "She has lots of tubes in her. It is all part of a life-support system. You can sit on that chair by her bed and hold her hand," Betty assured him as she maneuvered him toward the chair. When she had him safely in the chair, she advised him, "Take her hand. That will comfort her. She can hear you, but she can't speak because of that tube in her mouth helping her to breathe." She pointed to the tube between Gina's purple lips. "Tell her how much you love her," she suggested. "She can most likely hear you, and it will give her hope to receive your words of encouragement."

Gary sat uneasily. Gina lay on her back with tubes in her mouth and nose. There were tubes in her arms and in her neck. The many machines droned, and lights flashed on and off. One large machine was the source of the whooshing sound. There were bottles of liquids hanging like so much fruit. Were they the pods of life or of death?

Gingerly touching her hand, he was reassured that it was warm even though it did not respond to him when he squeezed it. He came close to her ear and whispered apprehensively, "Gina, this is Gary." He swallowed hard and then softly said, "I dreamt you were calling me."

The nurse, Betty, returned with a steaming cup of coffee and handed it to Gary. "Do you have any questions?"

"No, thank you," Gary mumbled.

"Well then, you are welcome to stay for thirty more minutes. Then we will ask you to step out of the room for a few minutes while we do our job. You might like to go and get some breakfast later, too." To Gary, Betty sounded positive and friendly.

***

A small blue sedan entered the empty lot and parked under a tree. Kat was always the first one to open the office. She extracted her large frame with painful difficulty from the small compact car. Kat McKinney had been Dr. Carpenter's nurse for over twenty years, and in that time she almost always opened his office to get everything going before he arrived. Now that he had joined offices with Doctors

Pace and Minix, she felt more responsibility to get to work early and get the day started right.

The new modern building wasn't in the style and taste that Kat liked best, but she would make do. As she opened the door, the light in the office was blinding. Annette Pace was responsible for the decor. She had enlisted one of her designer friends who didn't know a blooming thing about heart patients. He must have grown up in a jungle because the place looked like the arboretum in Golden Gate Park with the high-vaulted ceilings, stark white walls, white wicker furniture, and potted palms everywhere. In the middle of the room was a bubbling fountain. It was supposed to relax the patients, but Kat thought that they would be lucky if no one fell in it or tripped over it. She just didn't think a fountain belonged in a doctor's office.

Her first job of the day was to make coffee and transcribe the phone messages. Kat attacked her responsibilities with earnestness. By eight thirty, most of the office staff had arrived. As usual, George Carpenter arrived before the other two doctors because they came when their rounds at the hospital were complete. Kat hurried to settle him in his office and brought him a cup of coffee.

"There was a disturbing message on the voice mail about our Gina. It was a Gary Williams who called to say she won't live very long if she doesn't get a liver transplant. He wants to know if we can help. Here is a phone number and a doctor's name," Kat announced in a professional way.

***

Elly was working in the kitchen, busily preparing lunch, when the knock came at the door. Hastily she washed her hands. To save time, she took the hand towel with her as she went to answer the door.

Todd stood in the doorway. He was obviously tanned as he had just come from a tropical beach. His very short sandy hair was bleached by the sun. He had the same wide-spaced brown eyes as Gina, and there was something about his chin and cheekbones that reminded Elly of her.

"Forgive me for staring, but I never realized how much you and Gina look alike. Please come in."

Todd looked as if he felt a little uncomfortable, and he said very little beside the pleasantries. Elly ushered him to the couch and sat herself in a chair opposite him.

"I had a rather depressing message from Gary on the answering machine when I got back from school this afternoon. Gary said that Gina was worse, and they are looking for a liver donor. He doesn't think she will last until we get there. I called the hospital, and she is still critical, but because I am not family, they wouldn't give me more information. I made a lunch that we can eat while you drive. I am all ready to go."

Todd looked at her and said in a quiet voice, "I find it so hard to comprehend that my little sister is dying!" He stood up and continued, "I'm so glad you are coming with me. It was so nice of you to make a lunch, Elly. I don't eat well when I am under a lot of stress, and it was very thoughtful of you. Yes, let's get going."

After they had put everything in the car and locked the apartment, they drove across the bridge and left the traffic behind. Neither of them spoke until the city was just a distant vision on the horizon and they were finally on a long stretch of freeway. Elly passed a sandwich to Todd and munched on one herself. It was only after he had eaten that Todd began to talk.

"I am seven years older than Gina. My parents doted on her. She was rather spoiled by all of us. My dad died when she was only fourteen, and I guess I was her father figure after that. I think I have botched that job. I was only twenty, and I was trying to get my own life in order. I was in school, and I had my own private life, which consumed me. I just didn't have enough time for her. If I had only prevented them from getting hitched, some problems may never have occurred. Gary and I got along well enough, but I should have counseled both of them. However, I didn't. Our mom died two years ago, and that hit Gina like a ton of bricks. That is when she decided Gary was not what she wanted in her life. I should have been there for Gina, but I was too busy. Today is another event that I am late to. What kind of a cop am I when I can't even save my little sister's life?"

Elly responded with compassion, "Oh dear, you can't take all that on yourself. You can't help it that you were off on a vacation. She is over thirty, an adult, and she is capable of making her own decisions and helping herself most of the time. I'm also not ready to accept that she is so sick and could die!"

Silence lasted a mile or so. Todd decided to change the subject. "Tell me about you, Elly. I understand you want to be a nurse."

"I needed to make something of my life. That is what Gina and I had in common. We were both searching. I'm a couple of years older than Gina, and sometimes I felt I was mothering her. I tried hard not to do that because she needed to grow on her own. There is an ex-husband in my life, too. However, I have two teenage boys, and that is something of which Gina was envious. She wanted to be a mother more than anything, but she never got pregnant and that was what tore her marriage apart more than any other issue.

"I got married when I was merely nineteen, just a baby. My former husband was a student at the time, and I put him through school. It's the old story of a wife who educates hubby and then one day he feels he has outgrown her and trades her in for a woman who is more his speed. It is all pretty boring. Nursing is my salvation. It will give me independence and plenty of people who need me. Now it is your turn. Were you ever married, and do you have children?"

"First, I need another of those wonderful cookies." He continued after he had swallowed the last crumb. "When I was twenty-five, I married my high school sweetheart, but she was killed by ... I mean ... in an auto accident two years later. She was pregnant at the time with our first child. It took me ten years to get over it to the point that I felt like dating again. By the way, is it possible to have another cookie?"

"Sure, here. Eat all you want." Elly offered them with a warm smile.

"We are going to be in Jackson in about ten minutes. I hope I haven't been boring you. I am not the best conversationalist, but our talking has made the time fly by. Thank you for listening to me," Todd added.

"You are wonderful to talk to. I'll try to have cookies available for all those painfully quiet moments in the future."

The hospital was located in the eastern part of town on a hill overlooking the valley. It was almost dusk as they drove into the parking lot.

They were each lost in their own thoughts as they walked in the door. The hospital was quiet, and there were a few people milling around the entrance, smoking. The lobby smelled like a hospital, very antiseptic. Todd went to the booth labeled "Information" and asked for his sister, using her full name.

"Are you family members?"

"Yes, I am her brother, and this is her best friend."

"One moment please." The clerk turned from them and made a phone call.

A few painful minutes passed. Then they heard the *tap, tap* of leather shoes on the hall floor. A woman in a black suit came over to Todd and Elly. She said, "Please come with me."

The woman in black escorted them down a hall. She turned and walked down another hall to a door marked "Lounge," and she ushered them in.

Gary stood up as they entered. His face was streaked with tears as he stammered, "She, Gina, is dead ... She took her last breath just a few minutes ago."

"My God!" Todd exclaimed as he clumsily flopped down on the closest chair. "I can't believe I just missed her. My poor little Gina." He looked utterly dejected.

"Did she die peacefully?" Elly asked, trying to find something reassuring to say, but there was no answer from Gary. She couldn't think of anything consoling, so feeling self-conscious, she found a chair and sat down. The chair was close to Gary, but not too close. She took out some tissues and blew her nose and mopped her face. Then she offered the tissues to the men. They nodded in appreciation.

Todd turned to Gary and asked, "Did they say what caused her illness, Gary?" Todd was recovering. Leaning on his professional training, he was starting to take control.

Before Gary could reply, Dr. Lovejoy came in the room and introduced himself as the doctor who had been treating Gina. "I want to express our profound sympathies to you on behalf of myself and our staff. I am sure you have lots of questions, and that is why I came to talk with you." Dr. Lovejoy turned to Todd and asked, "Are you Gina's brother?"

"Yes, I'm Todd Markam, and this is Elinor DeMartini, Gina's best friend. Also, I am a police officer. I want to know why my sister died when last week she was in the best of health."

Martin Lovejoy sat down and leaned forward, bracing his elbows on his knees. "She is a coroner's case. We did everything we could to save her. We searched all over the state looking for a donor for her because her liver was compromised. The transplant was her only hope. There was nothing we could do to save her life without it. I'm very sorry."

Todd stood up and demanded, "Are you telling me you don't know what caused Gina's liver to fail and you are suspicious of foul play? When is the autopsy?"

"We will have more information for you tonight. Also, we did extensive toxicology tests while she was living. Those will shed some light on the cause of her death."

"Thank you," Todd said briskly.

Dr. Lovejoy said, "Since the meeting tonight is late, may I suggest that you three get dinner before nine o'clock?" Then he excused himself and left.

It was almost eight o'clock in the evening by the time Elly, Gary, and Todd returned from dinner. They had had a meal at a local Chinese restaurant. They had largely eaten in silence. Only Todd kept asking the same questions to no one in particular: "Why was Gina up here in a cabin?" and "Who came up here with her?"

Elly reached out to him. "She softly said that she came here with the love of her life, but she never gave me his name."

Dr. Lovejoy and Hank Simons, the coroner, were waiting for them. The three were taken to a room with a large table, at which they were seated. The room had a chalkboard at one end with a television and a VCR. Hank Simons sat next to the TV. He was a large powerful man whose dark hair was graying at the temples. He spoke precisely with a deep voice. He began, "We brought you to this room because this is a very complicated case to discuss. I understand that one of your party is with the San Francisco Police Department."

"That's me. Here are my credentials," Todd said, displaying his badge and identification.

"Hmm, you are Lieutenant Markam, and you are a detective with the homicide division. Sheriff Krammer will be interested in your opinions. He will be here within the hour. Now let's get to the important information. Gina died of cardiac arrest due to liver and kidney failure, but there is more. It was discovered that she was about six weeks' pregnant, and she has track marks on both arms. The poisoning that caused her liver failure and subsequent death was either self-induced or introduced by a second party. The poison has some complex chemicals called phallotoxins and amanitins. We have sent these specimens to UC Davis for further study."

Elly suddenly felt claustrophobic. A hot wave of nausea washed over her. Abruptly she got up and ran for the door. Once out the door, she ran down the halls and out into the fresh air. Desperately she gulped the air, trying to control her nausea. A cold breeze cooled her trembling body, and gradually her mind cleared.

Poor Gina, why didn't you talk more about the really important stuff? Pregnant! Track marks! These are mind-blowing subjects, but you never gave me any clues as to what was going on. There must be someone you confided in. You only talked about safe subjects like school, the lab ... The mycology lab—that's it. We worked with all those chemicals! Suddenly, Elly realized something that needed to be shared. She ran back into the hospital and into the meeting room.

Hank Simons was still addressing his audience. He glared at Elly for the interruption.

"I'm sorry if I caused a disturbance. I felt nauseated, but I'm better now."

"I was just explaining the possible source of the poisons that killed Mrs. Williams. The common source of these chemicals is to ingest them by eating poisonous mushrooms." Hank Simons seemed a little impatient when he saw Elly's hand shot up.

She didn't know any other way of getting some recognition. "Excuse me, I'm sorry if I am speaking out of turn, but Gina and I are, or were, taking mycology at the university where we are studying, and we just covered the family of *Amanita*, which is the source of those polypeptides you mentioned. The important fact I want to bring up is that phallotoxins are destroyed in the gastric tract if ingested.

The only way they could get into Gina's bloodstream is if they were intravenously injected." With this revelation, Elly went on to say that Gina was the happiest of friends. She could not have been suicidal. Elly clamped her hand over her mouth in horror as she realized that she had pointed a bloody finger at *murder!*

***

The evening was still young for Mark Jacobs. Standing in front of his mirror, he held up various garments, trying to decide which outfit he would wear tonight. *Should I dress like a sensuous yellow-haired beauty like Annette or a voluptuous strawberry lollipop like Gina? Hmm. Or maybe a luscious female from my fertile imagination.* He chuckled to the mirror image. *My therapist wanted me to get a hobby. So now I have one.* He giggled again, thinking of what his therapist would think of his new hobby. *Yes, a little drag. What harm could come from that?*

In the bathroom, Mark opened a drawer and took out a black case. There were four sets of contact lenses in each of the small sections of the box. *Let's see, shall I be a blue-eyed hussy? No, I'm going to choose dark brown exotic eyes.* After applying the lenses, he applied a pair of false lashes, and then he shaved. As he smeared the makeup on, he thought back to his short career as a drag queen.

It was last Halloween; Annette was throwing a big costume bash of a party. She had dared everyone to come in a costume that would be so complete that no one could recognize one another. There was a prize for the most enigmatic costume.

I had seen an ad in the paper of a person named Joey who could make you look like anyone you wanted to. He had a little shop over on Clement Street, and I went to see him. Joey promised to dress me so that I would get the prize. On the day of the party, I spent two hours with Joey, being made to look like Elizabeth Taylor.

At the party, no one guessed who I was. Allen had even flirted with me. It was all I could do to suppress my giggles. And I won the prize! It was a dinner out at an elegant, foxy restaurant in town. I took Gina there, and what fun we had.

He looked in the mirror at his finished image. He was transformed! He wore an auburn pageboy wig, he had brown smoldering eyes with long, sexy lashes, and he was wearing a low-cut green blouse and a tight-fitting black miniskirt. He adorned his long legs in black sheer stockings, and his all but dainty feet were crammed into a pair of four-inch black pumps.

There was one last touch. Mark went back to the dressing room and rummaged in a drawer. Aha, he found it, and now the little pink pill lay innocently in his palm. *The magical drug of choice. Eclipse, a designer drug to give me just the right kind of confidence I need to go to one of the most popular nightclubs in the city and flirt with the male tourists.*

Abruptly the vision of Gina was before him. *Yes, she liked Eclipse too. Hadn't she complained to me of feeling nervous? I had offered my little pink pills. Wasn't that kind of me? Later, I had bragged to her about how wonderful sex was when sniffing coke. Ooh, was she a handful when she was under the influence of that one.*

I can see her now, rolling and moaning for more. She was an insatiable nympho. That wild red hair of hers was all over the place. She would do anything I wanted and then some. She certainly had her kinky side, and the coke really brought it out.

It was so easy to get her hooked, but was that a cost-effective way to sell drugs. It took too much energy to keep up with Gina. I had to find another way.

CHAPTER 5

November 24, Thanksgiving

It was a cozy little kitchen with a small gatelegged table, opened out, and two small chairs. The faded and yellowed wallpaper looked as if it had graced these walls for the last thirty years. A naked sixty-watt bulb hung from the ceiling. At the table, a middle-aged, gray-haired man in a brown uniform bent over his steaming cup of coffee with a day-old doughnut.

Sheriff Krammer was up early that morning. It was a cloudy, gloomy dawn. The coffee he held tightly in his two hands was comforting. He'd had difficulty sleeping last night. *It was only been the decent thing to do to invite the widower and the brother to come to my modest cabin to spend the night. They had both had a bitch of a day. They were a sullen pair. I guess that was due to the tragedy,* he thought. *Today is another beginning … They're okay fellas. They know fishin' and huntin'.*

There was a rustle and footsteps, and in walked a sleepy, bedraggled Gary. "Is there more coffee where that came from?" Gary asked dryly.

"Halp yo'self, buddy," Brian Krammer drawled.

Nervously, Gary poured himself a cup of coffee and took the remaining chair by the window. After several moments of silence, Gary spoke. "I was wondering if you had any more questions for me? And if you don't, I will move on. I'm supposed to be at my aunt's house at noon for a Thanksgiving pig-out."

Brian Krammer took a long look at Gary. Then he said, "I'll git ma notes and see if dar is anyt'ing else I need to know f'om you."

With that he got up and went to his desk and got out a well-worn black notebook. He read it over and then said, "Wall, I ha' your phone numba. Can I reach yo at this numba easy?" He added, "Let's see, you said dat you's goin' to your aunt's house. Den I's need dat numba, don't I?"

Gary tried not to look too startled. "I … I don't have it just now. That's why I have to show up. What I can do, though, is call your office when I get there and give you the number."

"Whar is dis aunt's huse?" Krammer was showing some irritation as he glared at Gary.

"Concord. It will take me about three hours to drive there."

Krammer considered Gary's role in the murder and decided he wasn't going so far that the law couldn't catch up to him. Finally he said, "Okay, yo' can go. We will find yo' if we need to."

Relieved, Gary's voice lightened up. "Thanks. And thank you for putting us up for the night. I know how much I appreciate it."

Hastily, Gary gathered up his belongings and left by the back door. His exit was just a little too fast for Brian. He wondered what was going on in that fella's head.

***

There was no traffic. Gary sped along as if he could outdistance the apparitions that plagued him. He didn't slow down until he got to Stockton. There was a small truck stop near the highway that he remembered. He thought it would be a good place for breakfast. The long skinny diner was fairly deserted. He moved to the back corner of the room and slid into a seat at the counter. Ham and eggs appealed to him. The order came without a hitch.

While he ate his breakfast, he thought about this man who was supposedly with her. *Could my addict be the love of her life? I can't imagine Mark humping Gina.*

It was only after he had satisfied his gnawing stomach that he could even begin to review the dream he had had that night. *There was Gina, her belly swollen with her bastard child, and she was angry. Now that she is dead, I can collect the life insurance. She was demanding a share! I need the money, and I am not going to share it*

*with that drug-taking whore! What craziness am I thinking? I don't
have to share that money with anyone! I do have to be careful, though.
Someone might get suspicious. After all, I only took out the policy six
months ago.*

***

Todd awoke with a start. At first he was disoriented and couldn't
remember where he was. Then in the twilight of the early dawn, the
room became more visible. He heard the low mumble of Gary's voice
and the sound of a door opening and closing. Gary's truck started
up before Todd could get his trousers on and walk into the kitchen.

"Wall, good mornen' to ya!" Sheriff Krammer greeted him.

"Where is Gary going?" Todd demanded.

"Sit yo'self down and hav' som' java and I'll tell yo'." Sheriff
Krammer was sitting bolt upright now. He had no intention of being
intimidated by a city slicker detective.

Todd did not want to irritate the sheriff, so he carefully said, "I'm
sorry, I guess I was a little rude. I'm just concerned for Gary. He was
so upset last night."

"He tol' me he ha' a Thanksgiven' date with his'n aunt in Concord."

Todd's eyebrows shot up. "This is the first I've heard of him having
any relatives in that part of California!"

There was a long pause while each man gazed at nothing, each
collecting his thoughts. The phone rang, pulling them from their
reverie.

"'Allo. Brian Krammer here. … Oh ya, he's ra' here." Brian passed
the receiver to Todd.

"Todd? This is Elly. I wanted to propose that Gary, you, and I have
breakfast and commiserate together."

"Gary has already left, but I would like to go somewhere for
breakfast. I could use someone to talk to. I'll pick you up. Where
are you?"

"I spent the night at Dr. Lovejoy's house. He has a lovely family.
Dr. Lovejoy is leaving for the hospital now, so he offered to take me
there. If it is alright with you, we can meet there."

"Okay, see you soon."

It was 9:00 a.m. by the time Todd drove up to the hospital to pick up Elinor. She looked very refreshed. He was wondering how she did it. Maybe she had had a better bed to sleep last night.

"Hi. Where do you want to go for breakfast?" Elly asked.

"I saw a place as I was driving here that looked halfway decent. Are you game to try it?" he suggested in a friendly way.

As they drove to the restaurant, they each shared what the last night's accommodations were like.

Elly decided to tell Todd about her experience in a way to cheer him up. "I shared a room with the Lovejoys' eighteen-month-old son. He was so cute this morning. You see, he wasn't awake when I went to bed last night, and this morning he was very surprised to see a stranger in the extra bed. At first he wasn't sure if he should call for help or coo at me. So I cooed and played peekaboo with him, and soon he was laughing. We were old friends by the time his mother came to fetch him. And what was your night like?"

Todd turned to her and forced a smile. "Not at all like that, unfortunately. The great sheriff of Amador County is very kind, but his bed is like a sack of potatoes. I don't think my back will be the same again. As for Gary, I guess his mattress was so bad he got up as soon as possible and left town." There was a note of sarcasm at the end of his speech.

It was a small, sleepy café in Jackson's midtown area. The waitress was cheerful and seated them in the back, where the sign read No Smoking. They took very little time deciding on their selections. While they waited for their order, Todd and Elinor discussed the weather and other safe subjects. Their orders arrived, and they realized how famished they were. Several minutes passed as they ate. As their appetites were satiated, they relaxed and felt more comfortable with each other.

Finally, Todd asked, "Do you need to get back to the Bay Area for a Thanksgiving celebration?"

"I called my sons already this morning. We had previously planned for them to spend Thanksgiving with their father, but I just wanted to make sure they were happy and having a good holiday. As for my holiday, Gina and I had plans, but ..." She trailed off and looked very sad and teary. She took a moment to wipe her tears. When she had regained her composure, she said with conviction, "I want to see Gina's murderer caught!"

Todd looked at her for a long moment and then said, "We have to get those tests back to thoroughly substantiate a murder. By the way, I was very impressed with your knowledge of the matter last night."

"You mean the mushrooms. 'The angel of death' is its common name; the poison was either given to her or forced on her. If she was using drugs, it could have been offered as something new, or—" She paused and said, "Gina wasn't suicidal. She was thrilled to be with whomever it was she was with."

"I want you to get a special notebook just for this case, and I want you to write down everything that you can remember concerning the last several days. For instance, did you happen to keep all those messages from Gina on the tape recorder?"

"Oh, I wish I did," Elly said in a small voice, "but I transcribed them and I have the notes at home. I know she didn't mention who she came up here with her, but she considered him the love of her life. And maybe he is the father of her child? Some of the message was that she came up with this lover, but it wasn't a romantic time because she got sick. She thought she had a flu bug. I don't have a clue about who this man is because Gina didn't confide in me very much. I don't know why she was so closed off from me, but maybe it's because we hadn't known each other very long. Or maybe she was embarrassed by what she was doing or something."

"If it is murder, then we are going to need suspects and motives," Todd asserted professionally.

"What about Gary? He must have at least one motive. He was furious when he learned of Gina's pregnancy and that it wasn't his! He didn't want to pay alimony, and he had threatened her many times. On top of that, he was the last person to see her alive," Elly energetically offered.

"We will know more when we go out to visit that cabin today. I think we should get going," Todd said as he stood up. "Breakfast is on me!"

Elly and Todd drove out to the cabin where Gina had been found. They parked next to the sheriff's department cars. Todd turned to Elly and said, "I'm sorry, you cannot get out of the car. This is an official visit, and we must protect any evidence, so until everything is covered and compiled, it is off-limits to all but the professionals."

"That's fine with me. I have tons of homework to do. I will be happy here in the car for hours. You just go and do whatever you must do and don't worry about me."

The cabin stood in a stand of pine trees. It had cedar siding and a green metal roof. The two window frames and the door were also green. The door was unlocked, so Todd walked in.

Several officers were working the rooms over. Todd recognized Brian Krammer's tousled gray hair and found him in the bedroom. He asked, "Have you found anything yet?"

"We hav' fo'nd syringes and needles, and da' have good fi'gerprints on 'em. The cabin wa' rented to an Allen Pace. I've put in a call to a numbe' I foun' on a business curd we foun' unter da bed," he said as he rummaged for the card in a plastic bag marked Evidence with a serial number. Once he had it, he handed it to Todd. "Da person who picked up dem key wa' a woman mit a vague desc'ption that sound' lik' Gina. I's need a picter of her, if ya hav' one," Brian said.

Todd nodded and took out his wallet to look for a photo of his sister. "This one is really old; I will send you one when I get to my home base. Is there anything else?"

Brian thought a second. "Ya. Dey got de blood type of the fetus. It is O-positive, which is the most common blood type de doc say, but da moder's blood type is mo' rare, AB-positive. All we ha' do is match the O-positive to haf the male population."

Todd considered the information for a moment and then said, "I'm going back to San Francisco to call that cardiology clinic and ask them some probing questions. I will let you know what I learn."

"Good. I'll han'le everything here, and yo' tak' care of the invest'gadion ther'. And wil' wo'k together. Sta' in tuch," Brian said as he shook Todd's hand.

***

Annette was just putting the last touches on the hors d'oeuvres, when the guests started to arrive. She left the hired help in charge of the kitchen and went to help Allen greet the guests.

She watched Allen doing the greeting. "Hello, Mark. How nice that you could come," Allen said in as polite a singsong tone as he could muster.

Behind Mark came Darrell and Clair Minix, and then several members of the office staff. Soon the house was buzzing with conversation. Clair Minix was discussing her new job as an office manager for an architect, which Annette knew. "You know, after I sat down and worked out the office procedures, he started to actually see a profit! I think I could be a big help over at the cardiology clinic, but I can't get Allen to agree to discuss it with me. Do you think you could put in a good word for me, Annette?"

Before Annette could answer, the doorbell rang again. Clair followed Annette at a discreet distance to the door. The new arrivals were George and his wheelchair-bound wife, Beth Carpenter.

"Ah, Grim and Bear have just arrived," Clair mumbled under her breath as she turned and decided the hors d'oeuvres looked more interesting.

"It was good of you to invite us, Annette," George said. "I'm taking call today, and I hope my beeper won't be too distracting."

"This crowd will be graciously happy that you are curing everyone today!" said Annette genuinely. "Can I get you some wine and canapés, Beth?"

"How nice to see you, Beth," said Kat McKinney between mouthfuls of stuffed mushrooms. Try these. They are out of this world."

Annette listened to everyone. "I'm embarrassed that we were so late. It looks like everyone is here," Beth said to no one in particular.

"Everyone except Gina! Have you heard that she is very ill and in a hospital in Amador County?" Kat informed her.

"That is simply awful. I dread being bedridden on a holiday. That is the worst part about my situation. I never know when I'm going to be too ill to come and enjoy everyone." Beth seemed to be talking to the flower arrangement.

"Dinner is served. Everyone is here. Let's all sit at the table. The place cards will help you find your spot." Annette directed them to the huge, well-appointed table.

Annette was very adept at managing people for a large dinner. George was positioned so that he could get to the phone easily. Beth and her wheelchair needed turning space. In addition she needed to be near her husband. Also, Annette was sensitive to the various personality conflicts and adroitly avoided them.

They were well into eating turkey and the trimmings when George's beeper came to life. "Well, at least they let me get halfway through my meal. Excuse me, please," George said as he rose from the table to answer the call.

Many guests didn't notice this little disturbance, they were so absorbed in their conversations. When George came back to the table, he looked very grim and drawn.

Heavily he sat down at his place and did not seem to be interested in the meal anymore. Annette noticed George's consternation and leaned across the table to ask, "What is it, George? Tell us if we can help."

The room became painfully silent. George cleared his throat and announced, "The call was from Gina's brother, who is a detective. He says that Gina died last night, and they think it is a murder case! The police are going to call in most of us around this table for questioning."

Beth reached for her husband's hand. "How very sad. I feel for her family. God rest that poor girl's soul."

Allen hung his head over his plate to hide his tears and his distraught face.

Annette was staring vacantly at her plate. Her right hand was manipulating the wedding ring on her left hand with erratic harsh movements that seemed out of place.

Mark Jacobs was pushing food around on his plate as if it were bumper cars. Across from him was Clair Minix, with a look of utter disgust on her otherwise pretty face.

Kat McKinney finally said, "May Gina rest in peace!" Several other guests joined in with their amens.

Allen tried to change the subject and even dared to bring up politics, but only Mark was half interested in the subject.

The dinner guests left shortly after the dessert was served. Each one had a different reason why they had to leave so soon.

Clair took Annette aside. "It is so unfortunate that that terrible call spoiled your lovely dinner, Annette."

Annette looked at her for a moment. "How kind of you to worry about me. I'm sorry I can't control my world ..." Her voice trailed off. "I mean, it is an unfortunate situation beyond our control. I only wish for a pleasant end to it."

The guests were gone. There was just the murmur of voices of the extra help and Annette supervising the kitchen staff's cleanup. Allen sat morosely in the living room by the now dead fire. He clutched a half-empty brandy snifter.

When the chores were done and the helpers sent home, Annette joined him and sat in a chair opposite him. Quietly she asked, "Was Gina important to you?"

"She was just part of the office staff and nothing more," he said firmly.

Annette persisted. "I meant what I said about any scandals! I will not stand for it if you have any involvement of any sort in this steamy affair!" She glared at him across the space between them.

His eyes could not meet hers. Many moments passed, then without another word she loudly stomped from the room. Over her shoulder she said, "I do not want to share my bed with you tonight. Go to sleep in the office."

***

The rain drizzled down on the car as it sped along the highway, heading home. Elly offered to help with the driving as Todd looked exhausted, but he said he liked driving and he would be fine.

Silence followed them as they were each lost in their thoughts. Elly was reviewing her homework for school, and she was sure that Todd was rehearsing his investigation. Elly broke the silence with, "I have been going over my mycology notes. To distill that poison that Gina was given, someone would need a lot of equipment and knowledge.

They would have to have a familiarity with the mushrooms and the chemistry involved. I don't think Gary has any knowledge of that kind. It would take a scientist who is an expert in mycology. Do you think Dr. Pace could have that capability and a motive?"

"Very good, Elly. You are becoming a real detective! I can't speculate about Dr. Pace until I question him, but your logic gives me material to ask him. Your mycology teacher might be a good expert witness. I'm sure you mentioned his name before, but I would like his name written down in a notebook for future reference," Todd said.

"Why, yes, I would be happy to do that. His name is Professor Mark Jacobs, and he has extensive knowledge of mushrooms." It pleased Elly that Todd was so supportive of her contribution to the solving of this crime, even though her information was limited.

"Another issue is that I need to review Gina's personal effects soon. I'm really sorry I have to impose on your time, but would you ..." He didn't seem to want to ask, which was funny to Elly.

"Of course. Gina kept a diary, and she has a personal phone book. I'm sure you want those quickly. The rest I'll pack up for you. I know where the phone book is but not the diary. Do you need this done this week?"

"I'll pick up the diary, if we can find it, and phone book tonight, if that is okay with you. However, the rest is less important. When do you have exams?"

"Next week. If I got it all together by the first of December, would that be early enough?" Elly responded.

"That would be great. Thank you so much." His smile was genuine. Elly felt she had removed a weight off his shoulders.

Todd continued, "We will get to SF about seven. What do you want to do about dinner?"

"If you don't mind chicken instead of turkey and a thrown-together dinner, then you are very welcome at my place. You have to drop me off anyway."

"Sounds perfect!" he said with appreciation.

CHAPTER 6

November 25

E lly, freaking out over a dream, sat bolt upright in bed. The scenes continued in her head, flashing before her inner eyes with disturbing images of Gina. There she was pleading for Elly's help. But how could she help her now? She burst into tears thinking about the fact that Gina was now gone and she would never see her again.

Looking around her, Elly saw that the room was small and that most of her personal things were still packed in boxes. The petite dresser was opposite her single bed. When they first moved into the apartment, she had offered Gina the choice of bedrooms, and Elinor had gotten the smaller of the two rooms by default. Now she had a choice, but could she really put aside grief and guilt just to have more space?

Reproaching herself, Elly resolved to be positive and respectful. These thoughts were so confusing. What did the dream mean anyway? After much confusion, Elly decided to concentrate on constructive reality.

If she put in four hours of study, she would still have time to work on Gina's room. She drew her knees up to her chin and wrapped her arms around her knees. It puzzled her that she was using a less than pleasing activity as a reward for studying. Maybe in the process of packing up Gina's personal effects, she would find something important. "Silly. You will be believing in ghosts next!" she exclaimed out loud as she bounced out of bed.

Music dispelled the loneliness, and the shower felt very refreshing. Returning to her bedroom, Elly passed the closed door to Gina's room. Her first impulse was to hurry past, but something drew her to it. She put her hand on the doorknob and paused before she opened the door.

The room was just as Gina had left it. Gina's beloved teddy was sprightly perched, and the bed was neatly made. The books were in organized rows on the bookshelf. The thought came to her that the room was a symbol of Gina's driving ambition. It meant freedom from Gary and a sense of independence she had never experienced before in her life. Now she never would experience anything again!

Elly ran from the room and slammed the door shut behind her. Hot tears ran down her face. Was she haunted, or was this just a normal part of bereavement?

Maybe after breakfast and some studying she would treat herself with a phone call to her boys. She could plan to see them and take them somewhere on Saturday. Yes, that sounded much more positive than wallowing in grief.

***

Todd arrived at his office at police headquarters early that morning. He hadn't slept well, and he needed to work off energy. The office staff was surprised to see him because they thought he was still on his vacation.

"Hey, you're supposed to be in Hawaii!" said a tall, imposing black officer.

"Yeah, a family difficulty brought me back. By the way, Jim, I need to ask a favor of you."

Lieutenant James Collins and Todd had worked together on many homicide cases in the past. Jim's easygoing but efficient manner made him an indispensable partner.

"I need you to question some suspects in a homicide case," Todd said matter-of-factly.

"That sounds simple enough, but something about you tells me there is more to this than just a routine interrogation," Jim said as he lowered himself into the chair next to Todd's desk. "What's up, buddy?"

"My sister was poisoned, and this list of people may have some information we need," Todd said as he passed the list to Jim.

"Jesus Christ! That's rough! I'm not very good at expressing my … my … sympathies, but you can count on all of the guys to be getting the flowers and such. By the way, shouldn't you be off on bereavement leave? You just leave it to me, champ. I'll get your man. Tell me what you know."

Todd looked noticeably relieved. "Actually I want to be part of the investigation. It's a way to wade through the grief. I just need to be on the sidelines. I'm sure the chief will think I am too close to the situation if I get in too deep. I'll tell you what happened."

The two officers discussed the case facts for over an hour. Jim left with his notes to make calls and arrangements, and he urged Todd to take it easy.

Alone in the office, Todd remembered that he should check back with Sheriff Krammer. He quickly dialed the number. His call went through several exchanges before he reached Brian Krammer.

"Hello, Brian. This is Todd Markam in San Francisco. I was wondering if you have any more information on the Williams case yet?"

"Ya, just happen to ha' da report'n front of me. Dose finga'prints we foun' in da cabin are disappoint' in da' mo' of dem are Mrs. Williams's. Yo' can com' up and pic' up dat car of hern' an' time. Wir finis' wit' it. Da corone' estima' da Williams wa' given da poison o' mush'oom o'bot on F'iday even'. Dis poison taist a long time to d'da job. It's ma opinion da' Gary Williams 'accident'ly' dest'oy much of da eviden' wen he move' her to da hospital. H'needs mo' question' as to h' wer'abou' on da' F'iday, Novemba 19. Da' ist all," Brian drawled in his heavy Southern accent.

"Thanks for the info. We might as well question Gary Williams here for convenience, if you like. I'll have a recording sent to you. Is this agreeable to you? We are in the process of calling suspects and witnesses here. I'll try to come up on Sunday to pick up the car. I'll let you know later."

It was almost noon when Jim returned to Todd's office. "Here is a schedule of when these folks are coming in for questioning. I had to schedule Dr. Pace late because he is bringing his attorney with him. The lawyer's name is Frank Decker. Have you worked with him?"

"No, he's a new one. Dr. Pace probably has enough dough to hire the best. Don't let him snow you."

***

Somewhere in the Bay Area, the following phone conversation was taking place:

"Ya, I'm d'man," a gruff male voice said.

"This is me, your needy one," answered a nervous, squeaky male voice.

"You son of a bitch, you did the job, but I thought you were going to make it look more like an accident!" the pusher said angrily.

"I couldn't help it. Things got out of control. I did my best to make it look, er, good. I mean accidental. They won't figure it out," the addict whined back.

"They had better not come looking. Now, let's talk about you. Since you screwed up, I'm giving you another week to get the money to me!" he yelled into the receiver. "I need it by the second week in December. December eleventh. Do you get the point? So to speak." He chuckled to himself.

The addict spluttered and stammered, "I'll come up with it. I promise that!"

***

Later, in the afternoon, Todd decided to call Elly. They greeted each other warmly. Then Todd explained why he had called. "I want to thank you for all the moral support you gave me at this difficult time. And I have one more thing to ask from you. I need you to go back up to Jackson with me to get Gina's car. I was wondering if you would like to have it."

"Oh, what a wonderful offer, but does Gary have any claim to that car?" Elly responded.

"The registration is just in Gina's name. I haven't consulted an attorney on this, but I would like to see *you* have it."

"Oh, how nice of you. Let me think about it. If you need help bringing it down from the mountains, I'm happy to help you with that. It will give me a chance to try it out and see if I like it," Elly said with enthusiasm. "Have you thought about the timing for Gina's funeral?"

"I have to talk to Gary first. On a related topic, he will probably want to come over and pick up some of Gina's things soon, but first I need to send over a team to gather evidence."

"Darn, I'm not looking forward to that. You see, I was studying and I needed one of Gina's reference books, so I went in her room, and when I lifted the book out, there was part of a diary stuffed behind the books. I'm sorry, I couldn't resist looking at it—and it covers this year up to October," she said, carefully choosing her words.

"It's okay, Elly," Todd reassured her. "Tell me what you read."

"Well, there is a lot about her relationships with the men in her life. The baby's possible father could be Allen Pace. But there is also a lot in there about Gary abusing her."

"It sounds like I need to get that diary as soon as possible. I'm coming right over. Don't open the door for anyone until I get there. Okay?" Todd hurriedly hung up the phone, grabbed his coat, and headed for the door. Jim saw him leaving.

"Hey, Todd, what's happening?"

"I'm going to pick up some evidence that will help you with your interrogation this afternoon. I won't be long."

It was a ten-minute drive to Elly's. The nearest parking space was almost two blocks away. Oh well, he rationalized, he needed the exercise anyway. The distance wasn't very far, but by the time he'd jogged to the building and ran up the stairs, he was breathing heavily as he rang Elly's bell. Elly peered through the peephole and then unbolted the lock.

"That was fast. Come in," she welcomed.

"I'm sorry if I frightened you when I warned you not to open your door to anyone. Some think this occupation makes us a little paranoid. I like to think we are just extra cautious."

"It's okay. I'm a little edgy about Gary coming around here after reading this," she said as she handed him the diary.

Todd scanned several pages of the little book, looking at dates and specific names. After a few minutes he said, "I think I need to send a team over fast to go through Gina's things. It is crucial that we find the missing part of this diary. I hope that won't be too awkward for you."

"No, quite the contrary. I find it hard to go in that room, and I can hole up in my bedroom studying while they work. This way I can put off Gary for a while, too. Also I have something I would like to discuss with you."

"Yes, what is it?" Todd encouraged as he sat down on the couch.

"I've been giving this plan a great deal of thought. In fact, it is getting in the way of my studying, but that is another story. What my plan is, er, is to look into the steps she went through to get into drugs and all the rest. The cardiology clinic is somehow at the center of Gina's mysterious death. On Monday I'm going to apply for Gina's former job."

"Are you sure you want to do this? It sounds risky to me. You quite possibly will be putting yourself in danger," Todd said carefully.

"I think I'm a bit more mature and experienced than Gina. I have a lot to gain in knowledge and experience in cardiology, as well as being sort of a spy. I also need the money. I have to do it for Gina!"

"But it could be hazardous! People who commit murder aren't always predictable. You could be seen as a threat, and then you may become a victim."

Elly gave a sigh. "Yes, I see your point. But somebody needs to see what is going on in that place, and I am your best candidate."

He rummaged in his pocket, and when he found a card, he gave it to her. "This has an emergency number. I will show you how to page me yourself." After he was sure she understood and was willing to memorize the number, he felt more relieved. "Call me anytime. Your life may depend on it."

***

Taking the diary with him, Todd left. This time he walked to his car. A light drizzle fell on his face and cooled the heat he felt inside. He always felt like this at the beginning of a case. The emerging energy of the chase building in his mind and body totally possessed him.

Dear Elly wants to solve this one as much as I, but she doesn't know what she is getting into, and that makes the problem much more complicated. His thoughts were in turmoil, which was strange for him and unnerving. *I'm glad Jim is doing the questioning today. I don't think I could keep my temper in place.*

Jim was waiting for Todd when he returned. "This diary is loaded with facts. Let's go over it together before you question Allen Pace," Todd began.

The two sat together in Todd's office reading the diary and taking notes. When they were done, they had the diary secured in the vault.

Allen Pace arrived twenty minutes late for his questioning session. His attorney rushed in ten minutes later. As they arrived, Sergeant Fuentes led them to a room used for questioning.

This room was well designed for its purpose. The cold cement walls were painted a pale blue. High up on the walls were three small windows with bars on them. Cameras with sound recorders were positioned so that it gave a full view of the suspects. Four chairs and a table were the only furnishings. At one end of the room there was a smoked panel where the observers could watch the proceedings unseen through the one-way glass.

Quietly, Pace and his attorney waited for the inquisitor. The room was obviously bugged, and they knew it.

Sergeant Maria Fuentes found Lieutenant Collins in Markam's office. She was a sturdily built woman in her thirties with short black hair and flashing dark eyes. Her neat blue uniform looked poured on, and she wore a holster complete with handgun. She briskly said, "Allen Pace and his attorney are waiting in room B, sir."

"Thank you, Maria. I'll be right there," Jim answered politely.

"I think we are ready for them, Jim. Feel free to consult if you think it is necessary," Todd said after Maria had left.

"Yeah, they have the nerve to be thirty minutes late. I think sitting there a few minutes more and sweating over what I'm going to ask will be good for them!" Jim said as he leaned back in his chair and took a long drink from his soft drink bottle.

"Sure, enjoy your soda. Your throat will appreciate it, and you've had a busy schedule today," Todd assured him as he rearranged the papers on his desk.

Together they walked to the elevator for the ride down to the investigation area and interrogation rooms, where they met Maria Fuentes again. Todd went into the anteroom, where he could observe unseen. Jim and Maria entered room B by the main door. Lieutenant Collins's tall football linebacker presence seemed to fill the small room and suck all the oxygen out. "Let me introduce myself. I'm Lieutenant James Collins, and this is Sergeant Maria Fuentes. She is here to observe. I am in charge of the investigation into the death of Gina Williams," Jim announced as he walked to the table and took a chair opposite the suspect. "Would you please introduce yourselves?"

"I am Frank Decker, and I represent Dr. Pace. I want you to know that Dr. Pace is a prominent cardiologist with critically ill patients, and this is a gross inconvenience for him to take time away from them to talk to the likes of you! His time is too valuable to be sitting around waiting for you to ask a few trivial questions," Frank retorted in a caustic manner.

"Excuse me, but I am here to save lives by stopping a person who has committed murder and may do it again. It is possible that I have evidence that implicates Dr. Pace in a way he hasn't explained to you, and you have something to learn here as well. Now, we will save ourselves both time if we just get on with the business at hand," Jim answered. Turning toward Allen Pace, he continued, "Dr. Pace, please introduce yourself."

"Allen David Pace." Allen mouthed the words, sparing as few as possible.

Jim proceeded to read Allen Pace his rights. After that, he started with the first question. "Tell me about your relationship with the victim, Gina Williams."

"She was an employee at the cardiology clinic that I and my partners own," Allen said coolly.

"Dr. Pace, I want you to tell me about your personal relationship with this woman," countered Jim.

"I had only a professional interest in this *woman*," Pace said with conviction.

Jim retorted with, "But in fact you took Mrs. Williams on trips, dined with her, and had sexual relations with her. You call this professional?"

Allen looked disturbed. Whereas he had sat back in a relaxed pose before, he was now bolt upright with dilated pupils and beads of sweat forming on his brow. He hoarsely said, "I deny that!"

"Mrs. Williams kept a very detailed diary, and she was six weeks pregnant when she died. We are conducting DNA tests on the fetus. We can subpoena a DNA sample from you too. Yes, Dr. Pace, you, in fact, had a very involved relationship with Mrs. Williams. Your genes will testify for you. Now, I think you had better start telling me about it."

Allen gave in and reluctantly related his encounters with Gina. He denied any knowledge of her pregnancy. "Women don't always know when they are only six weeks pregnant that gestation has commenced. She had other lovers, and I was under the impression that she was using some form of birth control. I never dreamed that she would be so irresponsible."

Jim decided that subject had been developed sufficiently, so he launched into the next topic. "Dr. Pace, do you use any mind-altering drugs?"

Allen relaxed a bit and primly responded, "Nothing stronger than coffee or an occasional social drink."

"Would you submit to showing me your arms and having a urine test?"

"Certainly not!" Allen turned to Frank Decker, silently beseeching him to respond.

"We must protest against such invasions of privacy without due process," Frank asserted.

"Do you have any knowledge of Gina Williams's use of illegal drugs?" Jim rejoined, leaning toward Allen aggressively.

"I deny any knowledge of Mrs. Williams's use of drugs," Allen responded, looking pale and tired.

"Mrs. Williams had track marks on her arms. Wouldn't you notice that in an act of sex?" Jim continued, "The same diary that I mentioned before gives evidence that you offered and shared illegal substances with her. And may I remind you that you are obstructing the law by falsely denying and withholding information."

"I am no longer using those substances, and I regret introducing them to Gina because I loved her. But I did not kill her," Allen said contritely. He continued to divulge information about the subject.

"Tell me about your knowledge of poisonous mushrooms."

"I eat mushrooms when my wife cooks them, but otherwise I can't tell one mushroom from another."

When Jim felt he had the information he needed, he started asking questions about another topic on his list. "Can you give me a detailed accounting of your actions and whereabouts on the nineteenth to the twentieth of November? I have a form here to assist you. I need times and contact persons who will vouch for those times. Give me names, addresses, and phone numbers. We need to call these contacts who are willing to testify on your behalf."

Allen appeared drained. He picked up the form Jim had given him and pondered it. "I was on call at the hospital that Friday until 4:00 p.m. I don't recall where I was or who I was with that evening. Saturday I went to a medical conference in Sacramento. My lodgings were at the Capitol Hotel, where the conference was held. There were a lot of people I talked to, but I don't remember their names right now. Sunday I was still at the conference. It was a bore, and I was upset because I wasn't asked to speak at it. I kept to myself most of that day and got home at about 10:00 p.m. My wife can testify to that." He opened his briefcase and took out a brochure of the conference and a name tag with his name on it.

Jim sat patiently and let Allen labor over the form. His very silence had an impact, and he knew it.

After a few minutes of the silent treatment, Jim held up a plastic bag with a card in it. "Dr. Pace, can you identify this card?"

"Of course I can. It is my business card. My name is clearly printed on it."

"I am aware that your name is printed on it, but this particular card was found at the scene of the crime," Jim retorted.

Frank asserted himself with, "But Mrs. Williams worked for the cardiology clinic. I'm sure she must have carried my client's cards on her person regularly. She most likely brought it with her on this occasion too. It in no way indicates that my client was ever at the scene of the crime."

After some closing statements cautioning Allen not to leave San Francisco had been made, Jim thanked both Allen and Frank for their cooperation. As he showed them to the door, Sergeant Maria Fuentes made some calls, then she got their attention. "If you are parked in the back of the building, I will escort you to a less used exit because the regular entrance has a crowd of media reporters. If you want to avoid them, come this way and I'll get you out with fewer reporters."

Jim left Maria to get Allen and Frank out of the building. He looked for Todd. He found Todd at the coffee machine refreshing his cup. "Well, that was the last one today. Do you want to discuss the interview tonight, or can it wait for morning?" Jim asked.

"We can talk on my way to the office. What is your overall impression?" Todd began.

As they walked to the elevator and took it back up to Todd's floor, they discussed the interview. "The evidence is circumstantial. The DA's office would never go for an arrest at this time. My gut feeling is that Allen Pace has a lot he is hiding," Jim stated.

Todd added, "We need more information. Krammer, the sheriff in Amador, may have a witness somewhere. I'll look into that. We can go over the diary with meticulous care. Maybe we are missing something."

They got off the elevator and stopped at Todd's office. "It's frustrating that the diary is not complete. She didn't write in it consistently. It seems she was seeing several men, and any one of them could be guilty. I just remembered something I need to complete. I've got to go. We can get back to this tomorrow," Jim offered as he turned to leave.

"I'll be here early as usual. See you then," Todd yelled after Jim as he unlocked the office door.

CHAPTER 7

Saturday, November 26

As the year moved toward the winter solstice, the sun rose later in the day. This was only part of the reason Mark Jacobs was up before dawn. He had been up most of the night.

So much had taken place the day before. There was an interview with the police. He had approached it with such trepidation, yet it was a breeze. All he had to do was document where he was that Friday, answer a lot of technical questions about *Amanita ocreata*, and agree to be an expert witness. What a joke that would be! Imagine, he would get to testify against, of all people, Allen! The police hadn't mentioned Allen's name specifically, but who else would they be talking about? The late night news was full of it. "I wonder if Annette and Allen were watching it?" he blurted out loud.

He thought, *The morning newspaper should be here any minute.* He was looking forward to reading about the downfall of the haughty Allen Pace. The paper was one thing he knew Annette would read. She may not have watched TV, but she always read the paper with breakfast. Hadn't she confessed that once?

With Allen out of the way, I will have a better chance at Annette's money. Ah, my Annie, you must be mine soon! I've wanted that woman for so long! It has been at least ten years since we met at the Mycological Association meeting. She seemed to be lonely, he remembered, and looking for a way to meet people. Mark was more than willing to teach her about mushrooms, and she was generous with her culinary skills. It was when they were out on a mushroom trip that he first felt a longing to hold, caress, and devour her. Like one of her luscious desserts, she was created to be sensuously experienced.

There was a large thump of the newspaper hitting the pavement outside the door. Mark waited until the paper person drove off before he ran out in his bare feet to fetch it.

***

Annette was also up early this morning. She was in her kitchen joyfully making cinnamon sticky buns for her husband. He had been so sweet the night before. The roses he had bought for her were her favorite. They had dined at her favorite restaurant, and Allen had called ahead, arranging for the chef to create something wonderful for her. After dinner he had taken her home and made great passionate love. The very thought sent goose pimples of excitement down her spine. Her breasts ached to have him once again caress them. The vision of him kissing and sucking her breasts made her writhe with desire. Smiling to herself, she decided she had better concentrate on breakfast or else they would never eat. Fruit compote would be a nice complement. She combined the mangos, kiwis, and papayas and arranged them in crystal compote dishes. Then she put a cold sabayon sauce in a small crystal bowl with a sprinkle of shredded coconut and topped it off with a fresh mint leaf. They were picture-perfect. She squeezed the fresh oranges for juice and added champagne for smoothness. She arranged everything carefully on the large silver tray. She was starting up the stairs with the tray when it dawned on her that it would be nice to get the morning newspaper and include it with the breakfast.

Allen was upstairs taking a shower. He was feeling rather smug about the sweet way he had pulled off the night before. *It is so easy to win over Annette. She is so gullible to lovemaking.*

He dried himself and opened the shower door. There stood Annette, fuming with anger, fire in her eyes. Holding the newspaper, she forced it in his face. "Look! It is all over the front page!" she shrieked with fury.

"But, angel, I can explain. Just give me a chance," he said, trying to soothe. He reached out in an attempt to take her into his arms, but she slapped his face instead.

"Get dressed. We are going to talk business, and I don't want you confusing things by trying to seduce me." She turned brusquely and stomped out of the bathroom.

When he emerged from the dressing room, he was in a gray leisure suit. He was worried, looking around the bedroom. Annette was gone, the bed was made, and there was no breakfast in sight. The smell of brewing coffee was usually comforting, but not this morning. He decided to take a few more minutes to carefully shave and put on his shoes.

Annette had dressed in jeans and a cream-colored silk shirt with a cardigan of amber wool slung over her shoulders. She sat at the head of the dining table, looking like the chairman of the board. She motioned him to a chair.

"We cannot continue to play this stupid charade of a marriage any longer!" she said emphatically. "I will give you a choice: either get some therapy, or I want a divorce."

"I will not see that Dr. Denman of yours for anything!" he said with derision.

A silent tension hung over the table as they picked at their food. After a hesitant few bites, he decided to try again. "I'm sorry I can't be your knight in shining armor, but that doesn't mean I need therapy." His voice was soft and pleading.

Annette cut in, "All that I've ever asked for was your love and your *loyalty*—in that order. I don't get either. I can't trust you! Oh, you are *very* good at making love; you get plenty of practice. But that isn't really all there is to loving someone. Do you respect me? No! Are you truthful to me? No! Do you give me more than the symbols of love? No, no, and no!" She pounded the table with each *no*, and tears ran down her face. Then in anger she said bitterly, "I don't even get loyalty. I asked you not to embarrass me by creating a scandal. But here it is on the front page of the paper! I cannot tolerate this! Do I make myself clear?"

"I think you ought to stop being so theatrical and look more carefully at yourself, my angel. Aren't you being a fair-weather wife?

It looks to me that you are kicking a man when he is down. And don't play your holier-than-thou card with me, babe!"

"This is not a game of cards! I don't make you look like a fool in public. We had a very nice time last night. You were so attentive, but for what? To buy me off. You knew the newspapers would tell all, and you wanted to soften me up." She was no longer crying.

"Did you ever consider that I might have had a lousy day and I wanted an evening with you to recharge my batteries? You are just like your father, quick to judge others and ruthless in your assessment. And if you think your sainted father didn't have other women in his life, you can think again," Allen said angrily.

"You have no right to bring up my father. He may have had other women in his life, but he never embarrassed my mother or me. His affairs were never in the papers, and none of his women had an inconvenient death. Let's get back to the problem at hand. Are you going to get some therapy, or are you going to leave?"

"I reject the idea of seeing your shrink. Can't you come up with a better choice?" he growled sarcastically.

Annette took out a tissue and wiped her face. She took a sip of coffee and thought a moment. Then she said in a quiet, controlled voice, "Okay, you give me no choice. I want you to leave. Yes, that's it, just move out!"

***

Elly was busily assembling sandwiches in the kitchen. Ted and David, her boys, were going to be dropped off by their father so that they could spend some time with their mother. The thought of being with her sons again, even if it was only for a few hours, was sheer delight. She was just finishing the last details when the doorbell rang.

Running to the door, she set all caution aside and threw open the door. "Oh, I was expecting someone else," she said, trying to shut the door again.

"Not so fast," Gary said gruffly. Beside him were two burly-looking men, and they all stank of alcohol and sweat. "Who were you expecting?"

"My former husband is bringing over my boys to visit me. They will be here any minute. You really should go. Please," she pleaded as she leaned against the door with all the force she could muster.

Gary's strength forced the door further open with an explosive push. He came in. "I brought these friends with me to help move Gina's furniture and things."

"But the police are coming anytime to go through her personal things and look for evidence. They won't like it if you take anything or make a mess of it," she said, beseeching them as she was forced to back up and give them more room.

"That sounds like Todd's idea. He is my brother-in-law, a basic good guy, but he has some screwy ideas at times," he said to his henchmen. Turning back to Elly, he said, "Look here, I've got rights too. This here"—he gestured by pointing a muscular arm attached to a calloused hand toward Gina's room—"is considered community property, and I'm her husband. I demand my rights!"

Spinning through her limited options, Elly's mind was caught on a carousel going nowhere. How could she stop them? All she could do was try to delay them. "Yes, it was Todd's order. I think you should discuss it with him before you touch anything."

"Nah, that's a waste of time," he grumbled at her. Turning to his two comrades, he said, "Let's get on with it." Again he waved his hand in the air angrily, indicating he meant Gina's bedroom door.

The two helpers showed some reluctance, and the three engaged in a loud, animated discussion on the subject. The men seemed almost out of control, and this frightened Elly more. At this point the phone rang.

Elly rushed to the phone. "Hello!" she said in a hysterical voice.

"Elly? This is Todd. Are you okay?"

The room got quiet. The three men were watching her. She said, "Hi, boys. Are you on your way over?" Elly hoped Todd would understand.

"Huh? What's wrong?" Todd asked.

"Yes, er ... no. You won't be too late if you come now. But please don't be any later," Elly said in code.

"You want me to come over now?" Todd ventured.

"Yes, come as soon as possible. The lunch is all ready. I've packed all your favorites. Please don't be late." Elly could feel Gary's eyes on her back. "Bye!"

Placing the receiver carefully back on the base, Elly turned to face the men. "That was my kids; their dad is bringing them here in just a few minutes. You had better go."

"You can take your brats off to a movie or something, and we will work here. You just leave it to me; you would be in the way here anyway. Give me your extra key, and I'll lock up when we leave," Gary advised.

"Well, let's sit down and talk about it." Elly motioned them to the couch and chairs. "I'll make some coffee, and I have a treat for you, something really good. Would you like that?"

"We didn't come for a *kaffeeklatsch*!" Gary snarled.

"Hey, I'd go for some java," said the larger of the other men. The smaller fellow agreed.

The aroma of coffee was just starting to be noticeable when the doorbell rang. Elly said a silent prayer that is was Todd and not her children.

To her surprise three police officers dressed in street clothes stood in front of her. Todd had brought help. They all looked very serious. Elly greeted them, saying, "Hello. What a surprise!"

"This is Lieutenant James Collins and Sergeant Maria Fuentes," Todd said to Elly. Then turning to his companions, he introduced Elly DeMartini, the roommate of Gina Williams. When the introductions were complete, he announced, "We have a warrant to search Gina's personal effects. May we come in?"

The door was held wide open, and Elly happily made them welcome. Her transformed demeanor was observed by Gary.

Gary and his two helpers were introduced to the police officers, and Elinor explained Gary's presence. There was a strained conversation between Gary and Todd. Elly excused herself to serve coffee. The small room filled with so many people, and the tense emotional atmosphere was giving her a throbbing headache.

Cookies accompanied the coffee. Soon the guests were more relaxed, all except Gary. There wasn't anything Gary could do to assert his rights above the warrant that the police had obtained, and he grudgingly conceded that. His attitude was still hostile, however, and it took a lot of quarreling between Todd and Gary before he would leave. Gary glared at Elly as he left and told her he would be back, saying that next time no one would stop him.

As Elly closed the door behind Gary and his henchmen, she felt a great sense of relief. "Thank you all for coming so fast," she said to the officers.

"You were very clever at getting that message to me," Todd commented.

"I was so lucky that you called. If you hadn't I would have had to wait until they were working or run over to the neighbors' to make a call. Meanwhile they would be ransacking Gina's room," Elly replied.

"I called because we had the warrant and were ready to come over. I was just checking with you as to the timing. You know he's going to be back. And there is no guarantee he is going to be any more cooperative," Todd warned her.

"We can post a guard if you file a complaint, Elly," Jim Collins offered.

"Do you think it is that serious?" asked Elly.

"No. I'll talk to Gary again. I've known him for a long time. I think I can reason with him," Todd said.

Again the doorbell rang. This time Elly approached the door with some restraint, but it was a happy experience. Her two boys were excited to see their mother. They all laughingly hugged and kissed each other. Then she brought them into the room to meet the police officers. Ted and David were thrilled to meet officers investigating a crime, and they volunteered to help the officers search Gina's room. Todd laughed and told them that they could help later, but now their mother had other plans for them.

"Ah, let us stay. We have never watched real detectives work. I bet it isn't anything like we see on TV," Ted, the sixteen-year-old, said in his defense.

"Unlike the TV cops and robbers shows, we can't watch the real police. Sorry. Besides, I made all your favorite goodies, and I am taking you to that new sci-fi movie. You will love it," Elly explained as she urged them toward the door.

Todd followed Elly and the boys. Elly gave Todd her extra key. "Everything will be locked up tight when we leave. I'll call you this evening, Elly. Have a good time," Todd assured her with a smile.

***

As soon as Annette was sure Allen was gone, she drew herself a bath and slipped into it. Pretty Passion was the name of the new bath salts, and even though she didn't feel passionate, she did long for something to wash away the pain of the morning.

Why can't I find a man like my father? Someone I can depend on emotionally. Someone, I can love who will be a sweet lover, whose dearest desire is to please me. Is that too selfish a wish? Was Dr. Denman right that I have a "Daddy's girl" complex?

Suddenly, Annette remembered that Mark would be there in an hour. Her first impulse was to call and cancel their meeting, but it was probably too late. She could hear Dr. Denman's admonition to her not to isolate herself when she felt depressed.

When the long soak was completed and the water was getting cold, Annette got out and wrapped herself in a luscious warm towel then walked to her dressing room. Only boring neutral colors appealed to her, so she emerged in jeans and an old white fisherman knit sweater that she had picked up in Scotland years ago. Brushing her damp hair, she pulled it back and secured it at the nape of her neck with a black ribbon. Sitting at her makeup table, she looked at her reflection. "Gad, you look old today!" she grumbled to herself. Then she remembered that Mark would be at the door any minute. Choosing some waterproof mascara in case of tears, she made up her eyes.

Mark was a little late, but when he came he brought a beautiful bouquet and greeted her with, "Roses for the rose, my pet! I thought you would need some cheering after I saw the morning paper." He bowed gallantly as he presented his love offering.

"Oh, they are so lovely! Please come in. You are so welcome," Annette said genuinely. "I've had a very distressing morning, and I needed these roses in the worst way."

The morning's events were rehashed over the preparations for their picnic. When the basket was filled, Annette added one of Allen's prized Chardonnays. "I feel a little like a thief," Annette admitted.

The crocodile smile on Mark's face was conspiratorial. He wanted to hug and hold Annette so much, but the time was not ripe yet.

It was a dreary, cloudy day, not a good day for a picnic but a wonderful day to hunt down the elusive fungi. Their drive took them across the Golden Gate and into the woodlands of Marin. While they drove, Annette quizzed Mark on what had killed Gina.

"She was one of my students. I told them that there is a possibility that she accidentally poisoned herself. Many amateur mushroom enthusiasts poison themselves every year. So it is reasonable that Gina could have done that. The police could be wrong about the murder," Mark explained.

"I hope you are right. Did the police call you in for questioning?"

"Yes, they did. If it goes to trial, they want me to be an expert witness."

Mark parked the car on the side of the road. They gathered their equipment and headed up the hill to the path.

The woodlands and open areas near Mount Tamalpais were rich with hundreds of varieties of mushrooms. Each find was discussed and identified. The time passed quickly as the two friends relaxed and gave in to the hunt.

It was almost 1:30 p.m. when they sat down by a rock with a view of the ocean for lunch. "Thank you, Mark. Thank you so much for bringing me here. The view is wonderful, and I feel much better. I'm afraid if I was home alone, I would have wallowed in my stew, and I would have ended up calling Allen and making up!" Annette confessed.

She heard Mark say, "You can always tell your problems to me, Annie. My shoulder is always available. I want to be closer to you." But when he cautiously tried to put his arm around her as he spoke, her body tensed and then relaxed.

"Allen and I had such a terrible argument this morning. He can be so manipulative. Sometimes I just don't know right from wrong.

He actually told me that I was being a fair-weather wife and kicking him when he was down," Annette lamented.

"Would you like some of his fine aged Chardonnay to ease your frustrations, my dear?" Mark suggested cynically as he pulled out the bottle and glasses.

"Yes. And in the basket are some smoked oysters, a fresh loaf of sourdough bread, and brie. Let's get those out too," Annette responded with a smile.

As they drank the wine, tore the bread into bite-sized pieces, and ate the treasures, she lost her reserved demeanor and began to share her concerns. "I have such a horrible time sleeping alone, and I just dread tonight. I won't sleep a wink, and that will depress me more. I would like to call my therapist and have him order me something, but on the weekend it is so hard to get him. He really keeps banker's hours, as if people's emotional problems did the same."

"Would you be interested in something to help you cope when life gets rough?"

"What are you suggesting?" Annette asked in surprise.

"It's like a mild tranquilizer, nothing wild. Like putting on rose-tinted glasses," Mark whispered in her ear.

"Will it help me sleep?" Annette asked timidly.

"Sure, and you won't have nightmares." He reached into his pocket and drew out a small box that contained the pink tablets. "You could take one now to try it out."

The small pills looked innocent enough. "Okay," she quietly murmured.

Washing the pill down with wine, Annette in a short time felt playful. "I think it is working already. I feel a little giddy." Actually the wine and the pill together accentuated the power of both to change the sensorium, and Annette became very groggy in less than thirty minutes. She lay on her back, and in her mind the scenery seemed to dizzily rotate around her. Mark leaned over her and tried to kiss her, but she just clumsily rolled away and giggled. When she attempted to sit up, he put his arms around her and hugged her. "Ooh, are you my teddy bear?" Her speech was slurred.

"No, Annie. I love you, and I want to show you how much I adore you." Mark panted while he fondled one of her breasts.

"Marky, you are my friend and I'm a married woman. I can't ..."

His hand slipped down and was unzipping her fly, but before he could reach into her pants, she rolled away from him. She attempted to rise up on her knees, but he pushed her down, pulling off the jeans. The cold air chilled her exposed rump, and the pants hobbled her. "No!" she blurted as she rolled again to escape him. He was suddenly on top of her, pinning her arms down. "Please, don't. You're hurting me! I want to go home." Her face, wet with tears, was also caked with dirt. Her golden hair was matted with grass and dirt.

Money. I need to borrow money from this woman. What am I doing? This painful thought caused his erection to go limp. "I'm sorry. I don't know what came over me," he mumbled as he brushed the debris from her hair. "I'll take you home."

Getting back to the car was not that easy. Mark helped Annette get presentable. She seemed unable to help herself. Ultimately, he was forced into carrying her. With several trips and much difficulty, everything was back in his car. Mark's mind was affected by the drug, but less so than Annette's. He had grown used to it. The effort, however, he put into getting Annette and the blanket, basket, and food into the car had taxed him a great deal.

The fog was rolling aggressively over the hills and into the bay when they reached Mark's house in Tiburon. Annette was fast asleep in the passenger seat. Mark tucked a rolled-up jacket under her head to make her more comfortable. He decided it was safe to leave her there after cautiously evaluating the street for witnesses.

Inside the house, Mark's brain charged into action. Running to his dressing room, he tore into the dresser where he kept his special outfits. Out came the makeup, dress, wig, and underwear. Quickly he transformed into his drag appearance. The strawberry blonde wig would work the best with the green dress. When the image in the mirror met his approval, he gathered up his syringes and other drug-related gear in his purse. After a thorough inventory of his person and effects, he returned to his car.

Annette appeared not to have moved in his absence. Her body was slumped in the seat just the way he had left her. Bending over her, he listened to her respirations. They were regular but shallow. He cooed in her ear in a falsetto, "We are going home now, my pet. And I am going to bathe you and put our little darling to bed."

The drive across the Golden Gate was uneventful. The man at the tollgate had remarked on how the passenger was really in a deep sleep, but Mark in a falsetto voice had explained how his friend had had too much to drink and he was giving her a ride home.

Mark cautiously approached the Pace residence. He did not want to be seen by the neighbors and especially Allen. A search of Annette's purse produced her house keys. This time he took Annette firmly under her shoulders and drag-walked her to the front door. Once she was in the door, he carried her upstairs to the master bedroom and laid her carefully on the huge king-sized bed.

"And now, my little darling, it is time for your bath." Mark chortled as he walked into the adjoining dressing room to look for Annette's best nightgown. He looked everywhere, and finally in one of the last drawers he found a suitable garment. It was a full-length pink silk gown embroidered with flowers and trimmed with lace. Mark was so excited with his find that he had to hold it up under his chin to see how it would look on him. He paraded in front of the mirror. "Perfect," he purred.

The bathroom was a generous size with an oversized sunken bathtub on one side of the wall. The tile wall had shower facilities with many shower nozzles. Mark turned the gold fixtures and tested the water temperature. Next he found some foaming bath oil and poured some in the tub. He debated whether he should bathe her from outside or inside the tub. It would be so much more sensuous to be in the tub with her, but his disguise could be compromised. The bubbles would help. And if she seemed too alert, he could always shoot her up with H.

Everything was set; now all he had to do was to undress Annie and get her into the tub. The vision of her naked body was maddening. He was determined to control himself. She was sprawled out on the bed in an ungainly fashion. Slowly he raised her sweater. It was not going to be easy to drag it over her head without arousing her too much. She moaned as he pulled it over her head. He kissed her tenderly on her cheek and left a lipstick mark. "It's all right, my darling; I have a fragrant bath drawn for you. You are going to love it!"

Carefully he unbuttoned her blouse and unzipped her jeans. His heart was pounding. Her bra had a front closure, which he struggled with. Deftly controlling his desire, he played with the bra until it fell open and Annette's voluminous breasts leaped out, free. There were her full, smooth breasts urging him to fondle them. His hand shook as he maneuvered her out of the blouse and bra. She sighed and mumbled something as he caressed her. He couldn't resist kissing her stomach and running his tongue in circles around the soft mound of pubic hair.

Now with this luscious female in front of him, he could no longer control his erection. He took off the green dress and couldn't help but fondle his own organ. Carrying her nude body to the tub, he carefully stepped into the tub and laid her tenderly in the warm water.

"Ooh, I love to bathe, Mama." She moaned and opened her eyes. "You're not my mama, and you aren't my nanny. Who are you?"

"I'm your guardian angel, sweetheart. You are going to be a good girl and take your bath," he said in his best falsetto.

She wrinkled her nose and played with the bubbles while Mark took the sponge and washed her face. With the utmost care, he applied shampoo to her matted hair and scrubbed the dirt and grass from it. She ran her hand over his body, and her touch was like fire to his taut, excited flesh. He took her hand and had her hold his shaft as he ran the sponge over her breasts.

"My goodness, you're a boy!" she said with a playful surprise.

But Mark could no longer control himself. Grabbing his throbbing organ, he ejaculated into the water. "Oh God, what you do to me!" he groaned, forgetting his falsetto.

He was both relieved and embarrassed, but he covered it up by continuing to bathe Annette. "Now my beautiful lady is all sparkling clean. It's time to put a gown on you and tuck you in."

Relieved of sexual tension, he could work better. He had to lift her out of the tub and then carry her to the bed. Exhaustion was taking its toll. She was unceremoniously dumped on the bed. Mark covered her with the bedspread and then took care of his own needs. Quickly he dressed himself back in the green dress and reapplied the makeup. Now he felt revived and returned to the bed. Soon he had Annette dressed in the lovely gown; her damp hair was combed and held with a bow. Gently he positioned her on the bed and tucked her in. As he hung over her, she opened her eyes. "Who are you? You can't be a ghost. Or are you?" Her voice was weak and slurred.

"Whose ghost could I be?" he playfully asked in his falsetto.

She seemed to be inspecting him, but her vision was blurred. He dimmed the lights.

"Oh, heaven help me. You are *Gina's* ghost! Oh God, have you come back to haunt me?"

CHAPTER 8

Sunday, November 27

E lly gazed at the rising sun as Todd's car headed east, ever deeper into the Sierra foothills, to retrieve Gina's car and ask questions. The sun was barely over the horizon, yet the golden rays provided enough soft light to make the rural locale look peaceful, almost like an impressionist painting. As they drove, Elly listened to Todd tell her about how the questioning of suspects was coming along. "The last of the office staff we interviewed was Dr. Allen Pace. We are still checking out his alibis. For instance, we have called Mrs. Pace several times for her to back up her husband's stories, but she doesn't answer, nor does she return our calls."

"Maybe she is away for the weekend or something," Elly offered.

"Oh yes, that is always a possibility. It is easy for your mind to imagine all sorts of sordid situations when you don't have the facts. Take Mark Jacobs for instance. There is something going on with that guy that is strange or doesn't quite fit, but I can't put my finger on it. And Gary is another one. He is acting rather too hostile for my liking. By the way, did you call the cardiology office where Pace hangs out yet?" Todd said.

"I will on Monday. I have to call them soon. I don't want that job to go to someone else. Back to Gary, I was amazed at all the tales of abuse that Gina had written about in her diary. Gary really beat her up at times. It was so painful to read about. Did she ever talk to you about how he treated her?"

"One time, about five years ago. Gina and Gary were up at Tahoe gambling. Some guy was flirting with Gina, and I guess she liked it too much. Anyway, Gary gave her two black eyes and dislocated her shoulder. Then he just took off, leaving her in the hotel room. She called me because she didn't have any money and had no way home. When I finally got to talk to Gary about it, my anger had dissipated a bit, so I didn't smash him like I had wanted to do at first. I warned him that if he ever did anything like that again, he would have to answer to me. Gina never called for help again, and I didn't know that he just kept it up until I read the diary." Todd related his story with sadness in his voice.

"I bet Gary threatened Gina with something awful to keep her quiet," Elinor said. She added, "Do you think he could know the killer? And that is why he took out a life insurance policy?"

"That is an interesting point. We will have to check that out," Todd replied, looking at Elly with added interest.

"Is this car we are picking up community property, and will Gary demand it?" Elly sounded more than just a little concerned.

"It might be a technical matter. According to the DMV, she purchased it after they separated, and it is registered in Gina's name. We need to look at the sales paperwork. If only her name is on all those papers, then the law will decide it is not community property. We may have to consult an attorney if Gary objects, but I don't think he has a leg to stand on."

They arrived in Jackson after lunch and went directly to the sheriff's office. Sheriff Krammer was waiting for them. They discussed the car and asked about the person who had rented the cabin where Gina was before she died. Todd wanted to talk to the cabin owner himself. Krammer assured them that that was possible, but the woman was very strict about business talk on the Sabbath being forbidden. He advised them to make it seem like a social call instead of a police interview. When Todd and Elly agreed, Krammer called Mildred Stevens and asked if they could come over and visit. It took him some moments to convince Mrs. Stevens to see them.

Outside the sheriff's office, Todd mumbled, "A social visit, huh?"

"Maybe I can help, Todd. We can both ask questions in a friendly manner. You need to tell me what to ask and how to ask it. Also, you aren't in uniform, and that should help. Just introduce yourself as Gina's brother."

"Yes." He chuckled. "I am beginning to really appreciate your logical thinking." Then he told her what the police needed to know.

***

Earlier that same morning, long crooked fingers of light crept across the elegant room. Annette was huddled in her bed, terror-stricken. She pulled the sheet over her head and cringed. Was she dreaming? Was it all a terrible dream? The idea that it wasn't a nightmare was too frightening to even consider. Peeking furtively above the sheet, she tried to focus on the room, but it would not stand still long enough. Then she passed out again.

Several hours passed, during which Annette tossed fitfully. The late morning light filtered in and around the drawn drapes. Annette seemed to be wrestling with her covers. "Help, I'm drowning!" she called out in her sleep.

In Annette's mind, the sea was churning surrounding her. Seaweed had her wrapped in a choke hold, and she was sinking. Frantically, she reached upward toward the light and called for help. She made one last thrust to the surface. Physically she sat up and became conscious.

The room was her familiar bedroom. Something was not right. She shook to rid herself of the constraining seaweed and discovered she was enveloped in a strange gown. When she took a good look at the gown, it freaked her out even more. "Ugh, I hate this thing!" she shrieked in horror, ripping it off and tossing it to the floor. She was not satisfied until it was out of sight. It was as if the very vision of it had the power to strike terror.

Panting and weeping, she reached for the phone. The phone number was one she had memorized as she called Dr. Denman often. There were three rings, and then Dr. Denman's exchange came on the line. "I'm desperate. I must talk to Dr. Denman as soon as possible." Annette sobbed uncontrollably. The exchange advised her to stay by the phone and said that Dr. Denman would call as soon as he was available.

Ten excruciatingly slow minutes passed. Annette cowered under the sheet, trying to sort out her thoughts. Then the phone rang. "Oh, bless you for calling," she said, whimpering.

"Mrs. Pace, how are you? This is Dr. Denman calling."

"I'm going crazy! I dreamt my mother was here—and other strange people. My mother forced me to wear an awful gown that I had stashed away long ago. Anyway, when I woke up this morning, I had it on!" Annette paused a moment to control herself and then continued. "I never sleep in anything, and the last thing I would do is choose this horrible gown of all things to wear. It was something my mother gave me years ago, and I never liked it. The colors are so gaudy and old-fashioned. The worst part of this is that it is symbolic of my mother, and I woke up with this gown choking me."

"Did you have a little too much to drink or other mind-altering substances last night?" he probed.

"I can't remember anything about yesterday," she confessed.

"Give me any memory that comes to mind," he said in a confidential tone.

"I made Allen move out, sort of temporarily. We had a terrible fight about what was in the papers about him, and then my friend Mark and I went over to Marin to hunt mushrooms. We had a picnic with some wine, but I can't remember much after that."

"Come, there is more," he prodded gently.

"I have these vague memories or dreams or something like that. There is my mother and a strange creature that was half man and half woman. I know he or she was half man because it came—you know, ejaculated—in the bath right in front of me!" Her voice trailed off at the end because it sounded so silly to be saying this to Dr. Denman.

"You might have been hallucinating. Are you sure you didn't have anything besides wine?"

"I have a fuzzy memory of a pink pill or some such color."

"Mrs. Pace, I want you to get a lot of rest today. Don't drink any alcoholic beverages or take mind-altering pills. You can have some tea or weak coffee, but I don't want you overly stimulated. I want you to come see me on Tuesday at 10:00 a.m., and we will talk about your marital separation. Okay?" He waited for her to answer. "You are going to be fine," he added when she didn't respond.

"So you think it was just the wine and that pill? ... Sure, I'll be there Tuesday. I guess I feel better. Thank you." She sounded weak but saner. Carefully she placed the receiver back on the cradle. She drew the covers up around her. *Hallucinations. That makes sense. But how did I choose that horrid gown and get it on? I need to talk to Mark.*

Again, she reached for the phone and dialed Mark's number. He answered in a few rings. "Good morning, Mark." Her voice was almost normal. She was feeling stronger.

"Hi. How nice to hear from you. Is everything okay?" he inquired.

"Not entirely. Just what happened yesterday?" She was upset.

"You were very drunk. It is my guess that the tranquilizer and the wine were too much for you, and you just needed to sleep it off."

"You must have brought me home. What did you do with me when we got here?" she inquired suspiciously.

"I helped you walk into the house, and then I left," he lied.

"Are you sure that is all?" she inquired, full of suspicion.

Mark hesitated; he didn't want to sound guilty. "Why do you ask? What is wrong?" he said, modulating is voice.

"Would the wine and that pill makes me hallucinate?" she persisted.

"It could. Did you have a bad night, Annie?" He was honestly compassionate.

"Oh, I had the worst night of my life. I imagined that my mother was here, and she made me put on this gaudy, ugly gown she had given me so long ago. Then I dreamt I was choking, and when I woke up I was strangling on that dreadful gown." Her voice trembled as she spoke.

He was taken aback that she didn't like the gown he had so carefully chosen for her, but he had to put that reaction aside. "Annie, it is so sad to hear about your miserable night. Would you like for me to come over and comfort you? I would be happy to do that for you."

"Yes. Yes, please. It frightens me to be alone."

Mark hung up the phone and thought carefully. *Annette might be remembering more about last night than is healthy. It could be disastrous if she knew the truth. I must be much more disciplined in my approach this time. The money issue must be broached in the most delicate manner. My cock has got to stay out of it. I wonder if there is something I can take to make myself impotent?*

The drive to Annette's house took less than an hour. Mark had carefully chosen his clothing. He wore a sweater that Annette had given him long ago. It was mauve, her favorite color.

Annette let him in. She was more subdued than usual. "Would you like some coffee?" she offered.

Mark followed her into the kitchen and assisted her in pouring cups of coffee. They sat in the little breakfast nook. Annette diluted her coffee with milk, which surprised Mark. "I'm sorry, I'm not myself today," she apologized. "What happened yesterday?"

Clearing his throat, he began. "I feel guilty for offering you that tranquilizer. I should have known that with the wine it could be much more volatile." Then he shifted to a cooing tone as he reached over and took her hand in his. "I want to make it up to you somehow."

The window held Annette's blank stare. She let go of Mark's hand and wrung her hands and played with her wedding rings. "I thought I was mad, stark raving mad, out-of-my-mind crazy. It was such an unnerving experience that I'm afraid of being alone." She paused and caught her breath. "I'm not going to be wonderful company, but please stay with me today."

Steady, he warned himself. This was fantastic news, but he must not be too fast with the enthusiasm. He caught both of her hands and held them. "I will stay as long as you like," he said with all the compassion he could invent. "I have offered my shoulder before. Tell me all about your pain."

"It is all about my mother. I thought she was here last night. She wasn't around much when I was growing up. Her social life took all of her time. All those beautiful dresses were too special, and I was never allowed to climb into her lap. It was like I was a doll that she would dress up and then set on a shelf. My grandfather really raised me. He was a big, generous man who loved to hold me and play with me. He would take me to his bank, and all his employees would let me 'help' them. They made it all so much fun, but I must have been a pest."

"How did you meet Allen?" Mark asked.

"It is something I don't like to talk about. Maybe I am ashamed. He came from a dirt-poor family, but he is very intelligent, and he got a scholarship to study in New York. I was visiting an aunt in New York at that time, and my cousin who is Allen's age came to dinner one night with Allen in tow. I was only sixteen, and I foolishly fell in love with Allen that night. We wrote to each other for a whole year, and then my mother sent me to school in London. Allen was just starting medical school and was working very hard. As a result, he didn't have much time to write to me. One day I got on the ferry to cross the Channel and ended up at a culinary academy in Paris. Later, my parents found out I had escaped England and made me come home.

"At that time, my grandfather was dying, and I nursed him during his last illness. Allen at this time was studying here in the Bay Area, and one day I introduced Allen to my grandfather. They instantly established a rapport. It was phenomenal because my grandfather was more or less a bastard in the way he related to most people who were outside of the family. That evening was so important to me, and it had a profound influence on my marrying Allen.

"Over half my grandfather's estate went to me in a trust when he died. My father and mother were both furious. I was thankful they were not the trustees.

"Meanwhile, Allen and I were having a love affair. I refused to 'shack up' with him, but we had a lively sex life. At this time I was the dessert chef at Au Mieux on Pine Street. One day my father was brought there by one of his friends. I created a special dessert for them. I called it 'Cloud Nine.' It had nine layers of pastry, chocolate, custard, raspberries, and such. *Outrageous* is not a strong enough word to describe it. My father and his friends loved it and asked to meet the chef. My father practically fell over backwards when I came out. His friends couldn't stop complimenting me about the dessert and everything about my person. It was the first time I really felt like a desirable woman.

"That experience was what led my father to talk me into starting my own restaurant. I think I have told you about that adventure. But what I haven't told you or anyone besides my shrink is how this house came about.

"Allen and I were married when I was twenty-two. He was a fully-fledged doctor by this time, and I was struggling with the restaurant business. We lived in a cute little apartment, and we were so happy. Then a few years later I got my inheritance from my grandfather. Allen was working on his fellowship to become a cardiologist, and I was bored. I sold the restaurant and bought this house. It is mine, all mine. Since I paid for it and all the upgrades to it with my inheritance, it is not community property. The furniture and all are bought with my money, not a dime of his. However, that is when Allen started having other women in his life.

"I did it all wrong. When I was trying to make a home for him that he could be proud of, he betrayed me. I set him up, my counselor told me, and took away his masculinity. I just drove him away." Annette sat back. Her sad eyes were gray-green with tears.

"Aren't you being rather hard on yourself? If Allen had a strong sense of his personal value and was emotionally mature, he would not have sought the company of these other women," Mark commented.

"You know, I think that way at times. If Allen was only strong like my grandfather or even my father, he would have understood my actions. I didn't know when I was twenty-five that he was so insecure. He is very smart, but his self-esteem is low. If I had known that, we might still be happy," she lamented.

"Annette, you are not his therapist. How would you go about convincing him that he really is all those things he pretends to be?"

A faint smile creased her sullen face. "You are right. Dear Mark, I am so grateful that you have let me talk to you."

"Let's get out in the sunlight and enjoy some exercise. The fresh air will lift your spirits. We could walk along the beach. Would you like that?" he suggested with eagerness.

It was only a few minutes later that they were walking the two blocks to the trail to the beach. The fog still shrouded the bay in gossamer curtains. Foghorns wailed forlornly in the distance. The misty cool air was stimulating. Mark held Annette's hand as they climbed down the steep, slippery trail. Annette's spirits lifted with the fog. She said, "I love to hear those foghorns. When I was a little girl, I thought they were talking together, and I would sit on a rock and fantasize about their conversation."

As they strolled along China Beach with the Golden Gate Bridge in the distance, it was a magical place in the fog. Annette talked aimlessly about her family and their various businesses. She was feeling much more in control of herself, but she noticed that Mark was looking like a lost puppy. He seemed to be distracted and a touch morose. "I'm sorry, I must be boring you. It is horrid of me to talk endlessly about myself. What have you been up to lately?"

"Oh, nothing much," he said with a note of dejection in his voice.

"Mark, if there is anything bothering you, I want you to tell me about it without hesitation. You have been so good to me. I am very indebted to you."

Mark stopped in his tracks. *Is this the opportunity I have been waiting for?* Slowly he laid out his problem at her feet. "I'm so worried that I'm going to lose my house."

"Good heavens, that's awful. Tell me about it," Annette urged him.

"A couple of years ago I got what I thought was a fantastically good deal on a loan for the house. The interest and other conditions were reasonable, and there was only one small hitch: A balloon payment was there waiting, which is now due. I went to my bank and to various lenders, and not one of them will loan me the money. I could go to a scalper, but I'm really afraid of that. Money is really tight right now, and I am frantic with worry."

"How much is outstanding on the present loan?" she asked with interest.

"Seven hundred thousand dollars," he said timidly.

Annette smiled and said, "Well, that *is* a hunk of change! Hmm, I would love to help you, but I have to talk with my accountant first. Also, I need more information before I decide whether or not to lend you the money, such as would I carry the first deed of trust, and have you had an appraisal done in the last three months?"

"You would carry the first deed, and if anything happened to me, it would all be yours. Also, I have an appraisal that more than supports the worth of the house loan. Annie, you give me the hope I need to make me want to go on living!" He was truthfully appreciative.

***

In Jackson, Todd and Elly were looking for the Stevens's home for their interview. They found it on one of the backstreets. The house was one of the older Victorian homes left over from the gold mining days. The paint had faded and was peeling. A wild garden sequestered the house from the street with its thick growth of weeds, untended shrubs, and trees. Each stair creaked as they climbed the stairs to the porch and the front door. A bell fastened to the wall next to the door had a long pull cord attached to the clapper.

"This must be the doorbell," Elly said as she rang it.

The door was opened by a sprightly, angular, white-haired old woman using a cane. "You must be the fella that Brian sent over. What's your name?" she asked.

"I am Todd Markam, and this is Elly DeMartini. May we come in?"

"Hmm, we have some DeMartinis in town. Do you know them?" Without giving them a chance to reply, she said, "Well, I guess I can't leave you out on the porch. Yes, you can come in." She reluctantly held the door open for them. Leading them down a dark-paneled hallway, she softly mumbled about strangers coming on the Sabbath. At the end of the corridor, the space opened to a well-lighted room with a high ceiling and a large bay window. This parlor seemed to have come from another century.

"To answer your question about the DeMartinis in Jackson, I'm sorry, I have never met them. Are they friends of yours, Mrs. Stevens?" Elly politely asked.

"They run the hardware store on Main Street. Please sit down. You both seem so big and overpowering standing there," she said as she motioned them toward the faded brocaded loveseat.

Elly sat down first. Todd looked around in puzzlement for another place to sit. Mrs. Stevens saw his consternation and commanded, "Oh, for heaven's sake, she won't bite. Sit next to her."

A neat tray with china coffee cups, coffee server, and a plate of cookies was placed before them on an ornately carved table. "Miss DeMartini, I want you to serve the coffee because my rheumatism is acting up today," Mrs. Stevens instructed.

Carefully pouring, Elly served a cup of hot steaming coffee to each of them and then passed the plate of homemade cookies.

They sipped their coffee in silence. Then Mrs. Stevens said, "You didn't come here to sample my coffee and cookies. Aren't you going to ask me some questions?"

Elly spoke first as she and Todd had planned. She explained their relationship to the dead woman, Gina, and why they were interested in more information. Then Todd brought out the picture he had brought of Gina. He asked, "Is this the person you gave the key to your cabin to a week ago Friday?"

Mrs. Stevens put on her glasses and held the picture up to the light. She looked at it for what seemed to be a long time and then said, "The hair is the same, but this here lady has nice fine features, and there is something about the eyes that is especially different. How tall was this lady?"

"Gina was five foot four inches. I would like to know what you can remember about the woman who came to get the key. How tall was she?" Todd asked.

"Oh, she was a huge one. I'd say she was as tall as you." She was pointing at Todd. "She had big shoulders, but it could have looked that way with the shoulder pads women wear these days. I remember she was wearing a green dress. I recollect the color so well because that real emerald color is my favorite. What I didn't like about her was that she had heavy makeup on her face. It was not attractive."

"If I could bring some pictures by, could you look at them and see if you recognize any of the people?" Todd asked discreetly.

"Yes, but next time don't come on a Sunday. That is not a proper day to talk about this sort of thing."

After thanking Mrs. Stevens for her hospitality, Todd and Elly walked to the car. Todd said, "I'm so glad you came with me, Elly. I don't think I would have gotten to first base without you."

Elly laughed softly. "She was a nice lady. I'm sure you would have managed it."

When they were safely in the car, Elly asked more questions. "What do you think about that person she described?"

"I don't think it was Gina who picked up that key. I think we can rule out Gary because he is shorter than me. It could be another woman. Maybe we are looking for two suspects, or this woman is a man or the lover in disguise." He paused and then continued, saying, "I'm going to take you back to the sheriff's parking lot for Gina's car and see if you can drive it. Then we had better head for home."

Gina's red Ford coupe sat forlornly in the back of the sheriff's lot. They got out of Todd's car and looked it over. Todd ritualistically kicked the tires. Then he opened the door. The odor of cleaning agents stung their noses. This caused them to open the windows to air it out.

Elly peered in and remarked, "They did a nice job cleaning it up." She then slid in and adjusted the driver's seat.

"It has an automatic transmission, so you should not have difficulty driving it home. I called before we left SF about the insurance to make sure you are covered." Todd stooped down to look inside. "They took lots of samples for evidence. I haven't evaluated it all for merit as of yet. What do you think? Can you drive it? Do you have any questions?" he asked.

"Sure, I can drive it. And if you don't mind, could I follow you so I don't get lost?" Elly asked.

"Yes, and I promise, I won't drive too fast," he assured her.

The long drive home seemed lonely without anyone to talk to. Elly realized she missed Todd's company. It had been a long time since she had had a problem being alone.

***

"Ah, how I love that face, those curves, and all that money!" Mark sang aloud as he drove home to Tiburon alone. "I can see her in pink and blue and best of all green, the green of money. She is so naive; it is this very childlike behavior I love. I love everything about her. My Annie, my sweet gullible Annie."

He was dancing up the walkway and humming to himself. The house was dark and gloomy, but he didn't notice. The dwelling had spectacular architecture with panoramic views, but it was a property that was suffering from deferred maintenance and was as devoid of cheer as one could imagine. Tonight, however, it was a wonderful place to Mark. He was seeing the world through the kaleidoscope of achievement or imagined success.

A hot steaming bath appealed to him. He poured scented oils into the water. Slipping into it, he couldn't help but remember the scene from the night before. How he wished he was back there. This time it would be different. She would be cooperative, and he would take her into his arms and pleasure her as she deserved. The very thought made his blood rise.

Maybe I should call her and propose to her my desires, he thought. *She can't refuse that. It could be a super mind trip.* The phone was by the tub. Mark impulsively called Annette's number. She answered after the third ring. "I hope I'm not calling too late. I wanted to thank you for a lovely day," he said, each word dripping in syrup.

"I also enjoyed today. It was so kind of you to listen to all my ramblings. And don't worry about losing your house. I'm going to look into it first thing in the morning."

"That is very wonderful of you. I really appreciate it. I was thinking as I was driving home that if you have trouble relaxing, a massage might help. I took a class in massage last summer, and I'm pretty good at it."

"That sounds interesting, but how do we arrange it?"

He was worried that she would ask too many questions, so he cut her off with, "It's easy. I'll start with your face. I'll ease out all the tension in your brow, cheeks, and jaw. I use special oils and work them into your neck, rubbing all the tautness out of every muscle. Moving on to the shoulders, I will knead the strain that you hold there into oblivion. Each arm will get special treatment. Every muscle will feel the caress of my fingertips. All the pain of stress will melt away like hot butter. A very important area is the back, where soothing fingers will coax each tendon into completely melted submission. Complete serenity and peacefulness will fill you with pleasure. My hands will comfort and pacify the taut muscles of your abdomen and turn them into jelly. Every fiber will relax, accepting the pleasure of the dance of the mesmerizing rhythm of my hands. Your thighs will call to me, and my hands will respond with tantalizing strokes with soothing oil, which warms the area for togetherness and bliss. Ecstasy—that is what your flower of pleasure will experience when my tongue caresses it. Oh yes, Annie, you will love every wet, sweet moment of it. Every fiber of your body will swoon with that sensual fire dance. I want to pleasure you, Annie. I want to be more than a friend to you." He stopped, breathless, to see if she would respond to his amorous solicitation.

"Mark, you can have the loan or possibly my body, but not both!"

CHAPTER 9

Monday, November 28

Elly was up early. She had a test and she needed to do some cramming to make up for the time she was in Amador County. The bus this morning was crowded; she had to stand all the way to the university. Pumped up, she ran to her class to take the exam. Tina, another nursing student, sat next to her. After the test, they had a short conversation.

"I thought that last question impossible. What did you think of it, Elly?" asked Tina.

"Gosh, I would love to discuss it with you later, Tina, but I have to make a phone call and then get to my next midterm now."

"Okay, I think it will wait. Bye, and good luck on the next one," Tina called out as Elly ran down the hallway to the public phone.

Putting down her books, Elly searched through her purse for the number of cardiology clinic. Finding it, she placed her call. There was a slight wait, and then her call was answered by one of the office staff. "Longacre Cardiology Clinic, this is Karin Walters. How may I help you?"

Elly explained that she was a fellow nursing student and a friend of Gina Williams and that she empathized with their loss of a valued employee. If that position was available, she would like to fill out an application and have an interview.

"We really haven't had time to adjust to the loss of Gina, but I think you can come in and talk to Dr. Pace about it. Let me get his appointment book and see when he is available." Karin put Elly on hold and then came back momentarily. "If you come in at 5:00 p.m. today, I can fit you in after he finishes with his patients. It might turn out to be later, depending on the patients. Would that work out for you?"

"That would be perfect. I'll be there. Thank you." Elly hung up, happy that she had called early.

***

Arriving late to work wasn't Todd's usual way of running his life, but he had left his apartment on time and had gotten in a terrible traffic snarl. "What is going on at Van Ness that the traffic is backed up to Sutter?" he asked no one in particular.

"They just started some repair work on Market, and it's got everything backed up. I think they thought all during the long holiday weekend about how they could foul up the commuter this morning," the dispatch officer commented.

"Very funny! If you hear from or see Jim Collins, tell him I need to talk to him when he has the time. I'll be in my office," Todd advised the dispatcher.

Todd picked up a cup of coffee before he entered his office. Turning on the lights, he found a heap of paperwork that needed attention stacked on his desk. He sat down and started to organize the paperwork so that he could attack it systematically.

It was almost 9:00 a.m. before Jim stuck his head in the door. "Hey, my hardworking friend, what's up?"

"Just doing the usual boring paper shuffle. Come in. I've got some ideas I want you to pursue."

Jim sat down, took out his notepad, and looked expectant. Todd told him about the trip to Jackson and the interview with Mrs. Stevens. "I want you to look in the files and get pictures and pertinent info on all transvestites in this city. Make that the whole Bay Area because this guy could come from anywhere," Todd suggested.

"You are positive this is a male we are looking for, huh?" Jim interjected.

"My mind is not closed on the subject. It's just the comment Gina made to Elinor about her 'romantic weekend' and the fact that she was pregnant. She didn't even hint at any lesbian relationships in her diary. Do you have anything to add to that?" Todd asked.

"Well, while you were away on Sunday, Fuentes and I went out to the Pace residence because we couldn't contact Mrs. Pace by phone. The door was answered by Mark Jacobs. They let us in, and they were not hostile, but they weren't very cooperative either. Evidently, Mrs. Pace separated from her husband on Saturday after an argument over what was in the papers Saturday morning about this case. She was cold and angry as if we had purposely leaked it all to the papers. Jacobs was very protective of her, and I almost got the feeling that there was something between them, like they were lovers. You don't suppose we are looking for a murderer and an accomplice? Could Mrs. Pace been the woman whom Mrs. Stevens was describing? She is reasonably tall for a woman." Jim sat back and let his news sink in.

"Mrs. Pace is interesting, but Mr. Jacobs interests me more because he has expert knowledge of poisonous mushrooms. I would like some plainclothes officers to dress as students and, unannounced, visit Dr. Jacobs on his own turf. Ask as many questions about this mushroom family as you can. I have some notes here somewhere," he advised. Todd opened his desk drawer to find the pieces of paper on which he had the names of the mushrooms that were in question. "Here they are. And find out about distillation of the mushroom's poison. We need to know if Mrs. Pace is an expert on mushrooms too," Todd added.

"I'll look into that. When you refer to Jacobs's turf, do you mean the university? I also asked Annette Pace to back up Dr. Pace's statements and to give an accounting of her own time."

"I'll be interested in seeing those reports. I see the DNA report marks Dr. Pace as the father of Gina's fetus. That could make Mrs. Pace upset if she knew of the pregnancy. There is something else I want you to look into. I want to know about any life insurance policies on my sister and who is the beneficiary."

Jim left to do the necessary research, and once more Todd was alone. He was no sooner engrossed in some reports than the phone rang. "Todd Markam speaking."

"Hi, Todd, this is Elly. Are you too busy to talk?"

"No. What's up?" Todd's voice was friendly.

"I've got an interview with Dr. Pace today at five o'clock," she announced.

"I wish I was free to take you over there. Please be careful," Todd warned her.

Elly had more to say. "Also, I've got tickets to the symphony for Friday night. Actually they are tickets Gina and I bought to celebrate the end of our midterms. There is no one I would rather take in her place than you."

"I'd feel honored. What is on the program?" Todd sounded genuinely interested.

"They are doing a Brahms concerto and a Tchaikovsky symphony."

"Sounds great. We'll talk later about the timing."

"Yes. I'm in a rush too. Bye."

***

This was one of Annette's select restaurants. The atmosphere was light and airy with lots of mirrors. She was acquainted with most of the staff. "Hello, Daniel, I have a reservation for two. I would prefer a table in the back, away from traffic areas, please." He led her to a quiet corner.

"Would madame like a glass of her favorite wine before lunch?" Daniel asked as he seated Annette.

"No, I'll have some of your peppermint tea instead," she said in a detached manner. "I'm expecting a young woman who will be dressed very stylishly. Would you look out for her and direct her to this table? Thank you, Daniel."

Clair Minix arrived a few minutes later. She was dressed in a chic black business suit trimmed in red with a low neckline. Her dark brunette hair was cut short in a bob, and her blue eyes were bright with interest. "And what brings you downtown? Did you need to do some shopping?" Clair asked mischievously.

Annette's eyebrows shot up. "No, I had an appointment with my therapist. And I specifically wanted to talk to you." Annette did her best not to sound defensive. To regain control, she asked, "If you would like a glass of wine before we order, I will get Daniel for you."

"If I have wine with lunch, my whole day is shot. No, let's order, and I'll have some coffee later."

They sat reading the menu in silence. The waiter arrived and took their orders.

"You mentioned on the phone that you wanted to talk about the cardiology clinic," Clair said as if it were a question.

"Yes, I want you to be the office manager. I thought that you and I could meet with the doctors on Wednesday at their weekly meeting and propose our plan," Annette announced.

"Have you talked to Allen, and is he in agreement?" Clair probed.

"Allen and I have separated, and I haven't said a word about this to him," Annette admitted ruefully.

"He will be more negative if we don't get his agreement or at least propose the plan to him in private before the meeting," Clair advised.

"I really don't care what his opinion is or what he wants. This is what I want, and I am going to have my way!" Annette had raised her voice more than she meant to. She adjusted the volume of her voice and continued. "Formerly, I threatened to sell the building or tear it down and build a shopping complex, and I will if he doesn't cooperate."

"Annette, I know you are angry and rightly so, but a hostile environment would never be productive. Are you trying to get revenge? If you are, you are going to hurt a lot of innocent people. What about George and his invalid wife, Beth? It costs thousands each month to keep her comfortable. And then did you think of the patients? Cardiac patients are delicate; they don't need more added stress," Clair pleaded. Before Annette could answer, she said in a more intimate voice, "If you want real revenge, then have an affair. You don't owe him anything, so what is good for him is just as delicious for you."

"I can't bring myself to lower my values to his standards. Besides, with venereal disease on the rise, it seems foolish to be sleeping around," Annette said defensively.

"I presumed you would do it in a ladylike way and not like Allen. Surely there is a clean man around whom you would like to know better, a man who will treat you like the desirable woman that you are," Clair suggested.

"I'm shocked that you know about Allen's activities. How long have you known?" Annette said in a hurt voice.

"Nobody wants to see you hurt. Darrel hasn't gossiped, but Allen spares no one when he talks about his women. He doesn't mind bragging about his conquests, and his partners are concerned about him. He is embarrassing everyone. Darrel and I think he needs therapy, and we have discussed how to talk him into it. I'm so sorry that it is now in the papers," Clair said, trying to empathize her compassion.

Their lunch arrived, and they ate in silence. Annette didn't have much of an appetite, but she needed to eat.

"It is so nice that you and Darrel talk together. I would like a man in my life with whom I could talk to with confidence. I would someday like to have a child or two, and I'm running out of time biologically," Annette confided.

"I am willing to support you if I can, but I think it is important for the clinic that we not force anything on Allen at the moment. I will try to talk to him, and I will ask Darrel to talk to him. However, I think it would be bad timing to have a meeting this week. It would be best for your investment as well as theirs to wait a bit," Clair recommended.

Their lunch had come to an end. "I must be leaving soon. There is another appointment on my schedule," Annette stated.

"Yes, I must get back to my job. I appreciate that you called and proposed lunch, Annette. I will get back to you when I have more information," Clair formally said.

They walked out to the street together. Annette offered Clair a lift, but she declined. Parting on a friendly basis was important.

***

The bus pulled up to the corner, spewing diesel exhaust. Elly jumped from the last step and ran to her apartment building. She was relieved to find the apartment as she had left it. At the back of her mind was the nagging fear that Gary had returned and broken in. It was nice that it had not happened.

There were two hours left to get ready for the interview. She would have to allow time for the bus. Gina's car was tempting, but she had not had time to transfer the registration or to insure it, so that option was out of the question.

The closet contained only a few nice outfits and only one suit, so it wasn't difficult to decide on what to wear. Elly showered, curled her hair, and gave special attention to her makeup. With skill, she accentuated her assets and played down the negatives. An hour had passed before she felt ready.

The bus stop was almost in front of her apartment. Elly trotted down the stairs and ran to the stop just in time for its arrival.

The bus let her off two blocks from the clinic. The walk helped Elly steady her nerves. All this time she had only been able to imagine what Dr. Pace looked like, and now she was going to meet him.

Elly's first impression of the cardiology clinic was a positive one. The fountain, the high ceilings, and the color scheme appealed to her. Karin Walters introduced herself and gave Elly information on heart disease and the clinic for her to read. The brochures on heart disease were interesting. When she had read and reread them, she looked around for magazines. There were several on health. The time dragged by. Some of the staff left, some of the lights were dimmed, and finally the last patient left. It was almost 6:00 p.m.

A tall, strikingly handsome man suddenly stood before her. "Miss DeMartini, I am Allen Pace. I am so sorry I was detained. Won't you come into my office?" he said in a voice as soft as velvet.

Said the spider to the fly, Elly thought, but she followed him.

The office was warmly furnished in tropical wood and leather furniture, and an interesting primitive carving of a nude woman stood in one corner. Several bronze statues of horses and large cats were used as bookends to support the books on medicine on the shelves. An aura of masculinity permeated the room. Elly was directed to one of the soft leather chairs.

"I understand that you were a friend or a fellow student in the same program as Gina."

"Yes. We all miss her, and I'm sure your office must miss her too. We have similar skills, and I thought your office may need some help," Elly said, hoping it came out right.

"It just so happens we do have a position open for the right person. Tell me about yourself," he said with a reassuring smile.

"I am a second-year nursing student at the university. I have a 3.5 grade point average, and I love what I am studying. I think I can offer you a person who takes an interest in your patients in a special way. Also, it would be such a privilege to work in your office and get some hands-on experience with heart disease patients."

"Let me show you around and tell you what your responsibilities would be." He turned on the lights and took her to the various examination rooms. He briefly demonstrated the EKG and echocardiogram machines. With each device he explained its use and said that he would teach her how to run them. He always enjoyed these little tours and showing off his knowledge. When they got back to his office, he said, "I think you are perfect for the position. Would you please fill out these forms?" He gave her an application and a W-2 form.

Elly filled out the forms as quickly as she could. She then returned them to Dr. Pace's side of the desk.

"Now that you are an employee, you can call me Allen," he said as he put on his glasses and read over the application. "Hmm, you are divorced and living by yourself. With your looks, I'm surprised you don't have a steady man in your life." He studied the application for another moment and said, "I'm dining alone tonight at a little restaurant around the corner, and I would like to suggest you join me. There we can discuss cardiology in depth, and we can celebrate your new employment."

Elinor was a little stunned by his offer, but she decided that it didn't sound dangerous, so why not? She responded, "Sure. I don't have any other plans. I would like to have dinner with you."

He was the perfect gentleman, and he led her out of the clinic and down several streets to Montgomery Street and then down an alley.

Allen chose an intimate little restaurant on a side street. The lighting seemed to be very dim to Elly, but then she thought maybe it was just that she had not been out to dinner at a nice place in so long that she had forgotten what it was like. Candles seemed to be the only source of power. Elly wished she had brought a flashlight.

"This restaurant is not one I recommend to my patients. Here they specialize in beef, mouthwatering, tender, juicy, rare *boeuf.* May I order for you?" Allen's eyes glittered in the candlelight.

Elly smiled radiantly. "What do you suggest?"

"The chateaubriand has a sauce that has mushrooms sautéed with cognac. It is superb. Would you like some wine to go with it?"

"It all sounds wonderful, but only a little wine for me. I have exams tomorrow, and wine hurts my performance." Elly had other concerns as well, but she buried them.

They discussed a little about the medical world and the hospitals in which Elly was doing her clinicals. Allen had many insights that interested her. She found him very easy to talk to, and he seemed very attentive to her description of her activities.

The wine arrived on a tray. The waiter showed the bottle to Allen for approval of the label. Using an elaborately carved corkscrew, the waiter expertly extracted the cork. A small amount of the ruby liquid was poured into a stemmed glass, and Allen tested it by rolling it around in the glass, inhaling its bouquet, and lastly running it over his tongue. A nod was all the waiter required for confirmation. He left the bottle on the table. Turning to Elinor, Allen said, "May I pour you a glass?"

After the wine ritual was completed, Allen spoke more confidently. "I am interested in the fact that you are divorced. I recently separated from my wife, and I was wondering if you had any wisdom on coping you could share."

It was hard not to be flattered that he was seeking knowledge from a lowly nursing student. Elly flushed and lowered her eyes. Slowly she began, "It will be a very painful time, and your friends will not be very helpful. They either are afraid to take sides or will stay away because they think divorce is contagious or something. The result is that you are shunned and left out. You basically have to start life all over and make new friends. It isn't easy."

Allen nodded his head in agreement. "It is very nice of you to have dinner with me tonight, Elly. I feel unpopular right now and eating alone is that much more painful," he said as he moved ever so much closer to Elly. "Let's make a toast to your new employment!"

Their dinner arrived. It was everything Allen had described. When it came time for dessert, they both declined as the dinner had been very rich and filling. Instead they had café au lait and some ladyfingers. Allen maneuvered himself so that his knee touched Elly's. When she felt the contact, she quickly moved to give him more space, but he moved with her.

To distract him gracefully, Elly asked, "Have you attempted to reconcile with your wife?"

He gave a great sigh and said, "Not yet. She doesn't answer my calls. Tell me about your former husband. Did he try to reconcile with you?"

"No. He was an abusive man, and he had other women he wanted to pursue. I was an inconvenience. I distrusted him, and I wanted out of the marriage as much as he did.

"My only concern was for my two sons, who are caught in the middle. It is very hard on them, and that is so sad." Elly hung her head as she reexperienced the sorrow.

Allen lifted her face gently with his large, powerful hand. When their eyes met, he softly said, "He did not appreciate your beauty and intelligence. His loss is my gain."

A shock of electricity shot through Elly. A mixture of pleasure and fear paralyzed her for a moment. Haltingly she said, "I can't stay out late. I have an exam at eight in the morning, and I really must be going."

***

A warm roaring fire blazed in the fireplace. Annette had candles burning on the table, too. They provided a feeling of warmth that she felt missing in her inner being.

She and Mark had spent most of the afternoon discussing his loan, and now Annette felt like an empty shell. Deep inside she loathed business transactions. They always made her feel inadequate. Her dearest wish was to have someone in her life she could trust enough to do it all for her. Her day had been exhausting. She did not feel comfortable about the lunch with Clair, and then all afternoon she had spent arguing with Mark about the terms of interest and points on the loan.

Mark was aware of her depression. His talk about his upcoming trip to Australia had not aroused her interest. The idea of a therapeutic massage had not gone over well at all. Now they both sat staring at the fire, each from an opposite side of the fireplace. He got brave and asked, "What does your therapist suggest when you get so far down?"

"He thinks I need to see more of my family and friends. My solution is a hot bath and a good book. I need to find an all-consuming novel right now. I should have spent my day looking in bookstores instead of arguing with you."

Sensing her despair and isolation, Mark moved to the place next to her and put his arm around her in a fraternal way. She didn't withdraw but seemed to melt into his arm. "I'm sorry this loan has you so bummed out. If that didn't stand between us, then I could really comfort you."

"It's me, I know. I'm tied to values that will kill me. I know I'm doing it to myself, but I'm terrified of changing."

"I meant what I said last night. I love you, Annette, and I want to be more to you than just a friend," he said quietly.

She sighed. "I'm sorry I was so abrupt with you after you gave me that very sensuous description of massage. It is hard for me to express what I felt. I was a little frightened by it. I didn't know how to react to it properly."

"Dear Annie, can you remember how fearful of sex you were before you lost your virginity? It was a push–pull emotional response. You wanted it, but you were afraid of it. Could that be what you feel with me?"

"Yes, something like that. Honestly, I've never had any other man besides Allen, and I'm afraid I don't know how to act."

"Let's just take one move at a time, and you can stop whenever you like or go as far as you like, but you are always in control."

Annette turned and faced him. Her large green eyes brimmed with tears. "I do want to trust you—more than anything."

He kissed her lightly on each eye, and then he kissed her trembling lips. He whispered, "Do you think you will have trouble sleeping tonight?"

She nodded her head and tried to snuggle closer.

She noticed that Mark was uneasy, but she didn't know that he was needing his heroin more than sex. Annette was too emotionally stressed out to worry about his discomfort.

"Let me make you some hot chocolate. That will help you sleep tonight," Mark said softly as he slid out of her grasp.

In the kitchen he found the makings for cocoa. From his pocket he withdrew a small box and took out a pill. Crushing it with a knife until it was powder, he mixed it with the cocoa powder and added a pinch of sugar to cover the bitterness. Lastly he added the hot milk. He topped it off with whipped cream from an aerosol can and a touch of cinnamon on top. His creation was complete, and he proudly served it to Annette.

"What a beautiful surprise. You are a dear," she said. Smiling, she added, "Are you going to tuck me in, too?"

"I would love to, you know. I have had a long day, and I have classes tomorrow too. I need to tuck myself in at home. Now I want you to go straight upstairs and crawl into bed with that hot chocolate. I'll see you tomorrow." He hadn't lost his desire for her. It was that he needed a fix, and he wasn't ready to introduce her to that.

**

Allen had been a perfect gentleman and had taken Elly home as soon as she had requested it. He waited until she was in the apartment and waved to him from the window.

Elly had found her phone answering machine flashing messages frantically. Just as she was approaching the phone unit to listen to and transcribe the messages, the phone rang. "I have been trying to get you all evening. Are you all right?" Todd sounded tired and irritable.

"I had my interview, and it ran very late, so Dr. Pace asked me to have dinner with him. I just arrived home. He gave me a lift. He was the most pleasant host."

"I was worried about you. I don't think you should be out late with this man."

"I am aware of his reputation, but I guess I succumbed to the wine-and-dine line. It has been a long time since I had some romance in my life, and it felt good. Too good. I will have to watch myself better."

"What did you two talk about?" Todd asked.

"We discussed hospitals, patients, and job-related stuff at first. Then he got more personal. He wanted to know about my divorce, and he told me that he and his wife are separated. Do you think this separation has anything to do with Gina's death?"

"It could, and then maybe the separation was the result of other marital problems. Mrs. Pace is very friendly with Mark Jacobs, for instance, but aside from the information you gathered, I really don't like you going out with this man. Does that sound possessive? I am worried about Allen Pace. We do not have enough evidence to bring him in, but I feel he is a loose cannon. I'm feeling guilty, too. I would like to take you out to dinner some evening. Would you go out with me?"

"Why, yes, Todd, what a nice thought." She was genuinely pleased and pleasantly surprised that he had asked.

"There is one other thing, and then I'll let you go. The funeral for Gina is going to be at 1:00 p.m. on Wednesday at Saint Francis Cathedral. Will you be able to come?"

"I am supposed to be at the cardiology clinic at that time, but I think some arrangement can be made. I'll talk to them tomorrow. Is it appropriate to ask if anyone there would like to attend?"

"Yes. I will be interested to see who does come. I've got to go. I'll talk to you tomorrow. Be careful, please," Todd said softly just before he hung up.

***

The shadowy figure of a man approached the darkened building. He used a master key to open the main door. Night-lights dimly illuminated the hallway. Quickly the man made his way to one of the offices. The key unlocked the door, and he slipped in.

Going to the metal desk, he sat in a worn chair and, with another key, unlocked one of the drawers. Inside were syringes, needles, vials of saline, and other drug paraphernalia.

He withdrew a vial from his pocket and drew some of the contents into a syringe. Then he rolled up a sleeve, placed a tourniquet on his arm, and made a fist. In the dim light from the window he could see the veins rise. He plunged the needle into the largest vein. The reaction was immediate, like a flash of light and color, with a mind-blowing orgasm of sensation. Ah, the relief!

"Oh God, how I needed that," he mumbled.

The room twisted and turned around him. A mist came up before his eyes, and Annette emerged in a shimmering gown. Her golden hair swirled around her face. Those sweet red lips came close to his face. He reached out for the illusion, but it escaped him. She was giggling as he reached and missed. Laughter echoed through his brain, scorching and terrifying.

The mist cleared, and she lay before him, silent like a corpse. He ran his hands over the breasts. Her flesh was hard and cold. Pernicious lesions sliced across the stomach and opened up those heaving breasts. She stirred. Her eyes opened, releasing a fire-like light. "G-Gina!" he screamed as he fell back in the chair.

The laughter was there again—ghostly, unearthly laughter, searing hot, shattering light and gnashing teeth. Above it all, Gina's eyes burned in torment. Gossamer hands reached out for him, enveloped him, and possessed him. Kisses of death and caresses of life mingled and intertwined in his chest. She tore at his organs. He wrested himself out of her control. Horror turned to lust with the fire of desire in his groin. He tried to mount her, and she turned and bit him with white gnashing teeth. On and on they fought, neither getting the upper hand. The aurora borealis of the mind pulsed with energy like an engine driven by passion.

Hours passed. The hunk of human flesh stopped writhing, and peace put out the soul fires. His mind shook off the mist, and he found himself covered in sweat and lying facedown on the floor. Rolling onto his back, he opened his eyes.

The lights were gone; the room was back to its usual self. With difficulty he picked himself up. Heavily he flopped into the chair. His clothes were rumpled, and his keys were on the floor. Leaning over to recover them, he found this little chore such a labor. The room was still vulnerable to spinning. Laying his head on the desk, he decided to sleep a bit more.

Several more hours passed. Eventually this shadow of a man picked himself up and shuffled to the door. Painfully, he made it down the hallway and out the main entrance. He was relieved to find nobody around. And so he headed home.

CHAPTER 10

Tuesday, November 29

A bell was chiming over and over again. Through the fog of her mind, the church's Gothic spires soared and then faded. Annette opened her eyes and rolled over. As she looked at her clock radio, it took a moment for what she saw to register.

"Holy moly, it's ten o'clock," she stammered out loud. The door chimed once more. "Oh, that must be Theresa. She is here to clean, and I am not awake, let alone up. What is happening to me?" she mumbled as she grabbed her robe off the chair and threw it over her nude body.

Annette felt a little dizzy, so she didn't run down the stairs. The chimes kept up their racket until she got to the door and opened it.

"Mrs. Pace, I was worried when you didn't answer your door right away," said a large brown woman in a blue uniform with an old brown coat half open. "Are you okay?" The cleaning woman, Theresa had never seen Mrs. Pace so disheveled.

"Yes. Come in, Theresa. I just overslept."

"I'll just get busy, never you mind. You go back to bed, and I'll bring you some breakfast." Theresa, as always, was so thoughtful.

"No thank you, just the usual. I'll get dressed and get out of your way," Annette said as she walked toward the staircase. "By the way, is this really Tuesday?" she called out, but Theresa was already running the vacuum and couldn't hear.

***

SFPD was bustling with activity. Todd passed Jim in the hallway and stopped him. "How is the Williams case going?"

"I'm on my way to a meeting with the crew. By the way, I have a report from an insurance company that verifies that Gary Williams took out two thousand dollars in life insurance on the victim six months before her death! I had him pulled in for questioning. He was very belligerent. I'm going to have him watched," Jim informed Todd.

"Very interesting. I was suspicious of him from the start, and you know the husband has the highest probability of being the killer, especially when there is money involved. I'll come to the meeting with you."

They continued down the hall together, discussing other cases and various strategies. When they came to the meeting room, Jim entered first.

"Good morning. As you know, this is day seven of this case, and we need to work harder to bring it to a close," Jim Collins began. He stood before a room filled with uniformed and plainclothes officers. A chalkboard behind him had various names and locations written on it.

Jim continued, "As you can see, we are having some problems. Here we have a list of suspects, one witness, and a very few pieces of evidence. We need more conclusive evidence. Today Maria Fuentes and Martin Sykes are going out to the university to search for evidence there. John and Roger are going to Amador County to interview the one witness again. Did you call and make those arrangements, John?"

"Aye aye. Roger called a Mrs. Stevens yesterday. She is expecting us around two this afternoon," John Marsh answered.

Turning to the chalkboard with a pointer, Jim discussed establishing motives. "All four have flimsy alibis. I think we need to clarify those and put pressure on them to talk. You each have your assignments, and I expect a daily report on the progress. The fellows from Drug Division couldn't meet with us today, but they are looking into those problems. Most of these suspects are possibly using drugs or have a history of drug use. Dr. Pace is one of them. I want you to have that info on your suspects ASAP. So make that your first priority. Are there any questions?"

Maria Fuentes raised her hand. By nodding his head in her direction, Jim acknowledged her. "I understand that the victim's funeral is tomorrow. Is it acceptable that some of us attend? I think many of our suspects will be there, and we can observe their behavior."

"I think Maria has a good point. However, it has been my experience that people are on their best behavior at such occasions and rarely do you observe anything useful. Todd and I will both be there simply because he is a relative and I am a friend of the family. If you have a day off and want to go, that is fine, but Todd and I will be the only ones on official business. The funeral is being held at Saint Francis Cathedral, so there is room for lots of people. I would like to meet before that, however. I've scheduled a meeting here at 10:00 a.m., and I need to hear from everyone. But you can come in person or by phone or send a memo. Just communicate some progress tomorrow."

***

At the university, Elly was taking another test. Scanning the test one more time, Elinor decided she had given it her best. Looking up from the pages in front of her, she realized that she was one of the first to have finished. She wasn't sure if that was a positive sign. A reappraisal of the test made her more confident. It hadn't been that difficult. Gathering up her backpack with books, she rose to take the test to the front of the room.

"How does it look? Do you think you did well?" Dr. Jacobs whispered to Elly as she laid the completed test before him.

She smiled enigmatically. "It was okay. I wondered if you knew that the funeral for Gina is tomorrow at 1:00 p.m. It will be held at Saint Francis Cathedral," she whispered so that she would not disturb the other students who were still taking their tests.

"Thank you. I didn't know that. I will try to go and show my respects. She was a fine student, and I'm sure you all miss her very much."

"I'll see you tomorrow, maybe. I have another test to study for, so I must go," Elly answered as she moved toward the door.

After opening the door to exit the classroom, Elly entered the hallway, where she met two people. Elly thought she recognized the woman, and the woman certainly recognized Elly. "Hi. It is Elly, isn't it? I am Sergeant Fuentes, and this is Sergeant Sykes. I met you at your apartment. I came with Lieutenant Markam last Saturday."

"Oh yes, that is where I met you. I take it that you are here on business. Am I right?"

"You are right. We need some orientation. Can you direct us to the mycology lab and Dr. Jacobs's office?" Maria asked.

"Well, you will find Dr. Jacobs just inside this door I just came out of. It is a lecture room. He is conducting a test. The lab is just down this hall; it is the third door on your left. You probably will find the lab assistant in the supply room, which is just across the hall from the lab. You can't miss it as the receiving and dispersal window is quite large. His name is Bob something. I can't remember his last name at the moment, but he will help you. Dr. Jacobs's office is in the wing of this building that is parallel to this wing. There is an atrium in between, and his office number is 250 or something. His name is on the door, so it is easy to find."

"Gee, we were lucky to run into you, Elly. Thanks for the info," Maria Fuentes acknowledged.

"I need to go, or else I would take you to meet Bob. But I think you will be okay," Elly explained as she started down the hall in the opposite direction.

The two sergeants walked briskly up the hall until they came to the supply room. They knocked on the door next to the supply room window.

A tall fellow who had glasses with thick lenses and a shaggy mop of brown hair answered the door. "Yaw, what I can do for you?" Bob the lab assistant asked.

Both officers produced their badges, and Maria introduced them. Then she explained the purpose of their visit: "We need to see the lab and ask you some questions. We are investigating the murder of one of the mycology students, and the information you give us will assist us in bringing in her murderer."

"Gosh, I didn't know we had a murder here. By the way, I'm Bob Huntley, the lab assistant."

"The murder didn't take place on the campus, but the poison that killed the victim might have come from this lab," Sergeant Martin Sykes clarified.

"We keep all the specimens here preserved or under refrigeration. The students extract chemicals from the fungi all the time for various research projects. All the chemicals and related supplies are here. Over in the lab you will find the hardware of mycological research, such as microscopes, incubators, and other growing equipment."

"Do you mean you can grow these mushrooms right here?" Maria asked.

"Yaw. In fact, you can grow many species in your kitchen or basement at home. Let me show you," Bob said as he directed them to the lab across the hall.

The lab assistant unlocked the door and let them in. The room smelled slightly of newly plowed earth. Row upon row of counter space stretched across the room. Each counter was equipped with sinks and stools. On the back wall there were cabinets with glass doors displaying many microscopes. The side walls were shelved with numerous terrariums, each with a lighting system and heat source.

Referring to his notes, Officer Sykes asked, "Do you grow *Amanita* mushrooms here?"

"Let me look. Which species of *Amanita* are you considering?"

"*Amanita ocreata* and *Amanita phalloides*," Martin answered.

Bob took the register where all the terrarium systems were logged and scanned it. "No. They grow quite prolifically in the wooded areas around here at this time of the year, and the students have completed that portion of their study, so we don't have any you can see here, but I have several pounds of them in the supply room fridge."

"Do students extract the poisons from these poisonous mushrooms in their studies?" Maria asked.

"Dr. Jacobs is of the opinion that because these specimens are so poisonous, he tends to give information about them in the beginning of the semester to protect the student out in the field from accidentally poisoning himself or herself," Bob informed them.

"Maybe we should go back to the supply room and look it over," Maria suggested while she looked at Martin to make sure he agreed.

Bob watched both of them to make sure that he was certain of their agenda. When he was assured of the plan, he moved on. As he led them toward the supply room, he rambled on about fungi. "*Amanita* species are responsible for 90 percent of mushroom-induced fatalities. Everyone should learn about them before they touch any wild fungi."

Maria and Martin were looking at each other in wonder. Neither could imagine picking toadstools in the woods, let alone eating one.

Again Bob opened the supply room door, but this time he was letting the police officers in. "This is where we have our sterilization equipment. It is referred to as the oven. Actually, it is like an overgrown pressure cooker. We keep other large pieces of equipment here too, like the trays over on the right and the stands, heaters, and lights, which are hanging on the wall in front of us. Then on your left we have the glass equipment. It's all in those drawers and on the shelves."

The room was neat and well organized. There was a desk in the room and file units that Bob did not need to explain.

"This way, please," Bob instructed as he led them through the door at the back of the room. They entered a room filled with terrariums on one wall and a bank of large refrigeration units on the other.

"This is where we keep most of the extracted chemicals, some of which are poisonous, and the specimens found in the field and harvested from our terrariums," he said, pointing to the refrigeration system. "Would you like to look inside?"

"Yes, if you have the poisonous chemicals from the *Amanita* in there," Martin asserted.

"We do. They are called phallotoxins, and they are found here," Bob instructed them as he opened the refrigerator door on the right. Inside were many shelves with numerous boxes on each shelf. Bob selected one and removed it for them to see. "There isn't much to see," Bob said as he opened the box, displaying rows of neatly stored vials of clear tan liquid. Maria whipped out a camera and took pictures.

"Do you have a supply of syringes and needles here too?" Maria asked.

"Those are back in the main supply room we just came from, in the glass department."

"Is it possible to take a sample vial and some syringes with needles with us?" she inquired.

"Well, I think so, but I have to log it in the book."

"Do we need a court order to get one of these boxes of vials?" Maria asked.

"Gosh, you have to ask Dr. Jacobs that question. These are very dangerous chemicals, and he is really cautious about who touches them," Bob informed them. His hand was shaking. He carefully lifted out one vial, put it in an empty box, and labeled the vial and the box. Then they proceeded to the main supply room, and Bob showed them the syringes and needles. Then he took out a logbook and entered the vial, syringe, and needle.

Maria and Martin watched this intently. "May we look at that log when you are done?" Martin requested.

"Yes, this is where we log the chemicals with date and time. Then there is another log for technical data, like temperature and humidity."

Bob laid out the first log for the officers to look at. Maria asked, "I want to see the entries for the last couple of weeks and specifically the week before Thanksgiving, please."

"Here they are." Bob showed her the page.

"I am taking a picture of that. Does Dr. Jacobs always check out that much at a time?" Martin asked.

"Sure, for the students in the lab and their experiments. They are searching for an antidote to the poison."

"Do students have access to these chemicals stored here?" Martin probed.

"Not usually. Sometimes a grad student does, but he or she has to complete all sorts of paperwork first. We don't have any student entries for November at all. Normally the students never get past that window in front."

"Tell us how these chemicals are controlled in the lab," Martin questioned.

"We are really careful—I help in the lab all the time. Each vial has a serial number on it. That's what I was logging in the logbook. We assign one vial for two students. This way the students monitor each other. They check their vial in and out, and then they log how much of the vial they used. It is a good system. We know what happens to each drop."

"Is it possible to get a copy of that page of the logbook for November, and a student roster for those classes?" Maria inquired.

"I can give you a copy of the logbook, but the roster you have to get from Dr. Jacobs."

"Bob, you have been very helpful. We may be calling you for a deposition," Martin advised.

"Gosh, I've never heard of a deposition. What is it?"

"A deposition is just a statement that the district attorney's office takes. They ask questions, like we did today, but it is recorded for the court. It saves time and money because it often takes the place of you being called as a witness," Maria explained.

Soon Maria and Martin were once again in the hallway, but this time they were walking toward Dr. Jacobs's office. When they reached the door, it was locked. The sign on the door, exhibiting the office hours, indicated that he was due any minute. They passed the time telling jokes and discussing their children's latest foibles.

"He would be late when we are waiting here," Maria said in a quiet voice.

"Hush, I hear someone coming," Martin whispered.

A man of medium height with dark brown hair and light complexion appeared, purposely walking toward them. He was neatly dressed in light brown slacks and a brown tweed sport coat over a moss-green silk turtleneck pullover.

"Are you waiting for me?" he asked nonchalantly.

"We are waiting for Professor Jacobs. Are you he?" Martin asked politely without showing his badge.

"Yes, what can I do for you?" Mark replied as he unlocked the door to his office.

The three stepped into the office, and then the officers introduced themselves. "I am Sergeant Martin Sykes, and this is Sergeant Maria Fuentes. We have a few questions to ask." This time they showed their badges as they nudged the door shut.

"I really have a very busy schedule today, so if you could be brief, I would appreciate it," Mark announced with a scowl.

Martin Sykes explained the case that they were investigating and the reason that they needed more information. Then he launched into the first question: "We have been talking to your lab assistant, Bob Huntley, and it seems you have some logs relating to how the students are assigned their chemicals in the lab. Could we see those for November?"

"I don't know why you are wasting your time and mine with this lab. It seems obvious to me that Gina Williams just picked and ate the wrong mushrooms. A fatal error, you might say. But if you must see those logs, I will get them for you," Mark Jacobs said as he went to the file drawer to look for the data.

It took some time to locate the pertinent entries in the log. Finally, they found the entries for the week before Thanksgiving, which showed that on Wednesday, November 17, a vial of phallotoxins was issued to Gina Williams and Elinor DeMartini. Then at Maria's suggestion they counted the total number of vials issued that week and compared them to the total checked out of the supply room.

"These numbers do not match," Maria announced.

Scanning the entries, Mark said in a controlled voice, "These chemicals aren't like narcotics that have to be carefully controlled. Sometimes the lab techs or I just slip up once in a while, and the numbers get a little off. We are human, and there is just a margin of error. I wouldn't get excited about it. This is a classroom situation."

"Where do you log the return of vials from the students?" Martin asked.

"They each write out a release slip as they receive the vials and when they turn them in. We do not have any other paperwork on the subject. Now I have to get to my next class. I am late as is." Mark was raising his voice.

"We would like copies of these files, and then you may go," Martin announced.

Mark glared at Martin intently and then in exasperation said, "Let me call Bob. He can copy them for you." He went to the phone and dialed. "Bob, I need you right now! ... Yes, in my office."

A few minutes later, Bob arrived. "What can I do for you?" he asked.

"Copy whatever these officers want, and lock my office after they leave. I have an exam to give," Mark said as he handed the log to Bob with a shaking hand. Without any pleasantries, he stormed out the door.

***

The cardiology clinic seemed like a refreshing change from the pressure of her exam schedule. Elly liked the idea of applying her knowledge instead of regurgitating what she had learned on a cold, impersonal paper.

As she sat with Kat McKinney, pouring out her love of working with patients, she said, "I really enjoy getting them to tell me their stories. Many patients have lived such exciting lives."

"On the busy days, however, you will have little or no time to hear their stories. You will be doing well to get the procedure done and move on to the next one," Kat warned. Starry eyes never held much value in her book. "This is the procedure manual. I want you to sit here and take fifteen minutes to read and memorize the EKG procedure. Then I want you to meet me in exam room six. It is a female patient. I will help you do the test correctly."

Kat was skilled at teaching Elly the technique of doing a simple EKG. Elly did it well, but she was slow since it was her first time.

"You are a little inefficient, but you will get faster with time," Kat told her as they walked out of the exam room together. "When Dr. Pace comes in, he will want to instruct you in the theory of all those squiggles."

The time passed quickly as Elly observed various tests and read procedures. Later, Dr. Pace came into the office and asked for his new employee. He found Elly reviewing charts with Kat.

"Here you are. How is the new member of our team doing?" he asked Kat.

"I think she will turn out just fine. By the way, Doctor, Elly tells me that Gina's funeral is tomorrow at 1:00 p.m. Doctors Minix and Carpenter think we should close down the clinic for two hours tomorrow so everyone can attend. Is that agreeable with you?"

"Certainly. Are we sending flowers too?"

"Yes, Doctor, that is all arranged," Kat replied with a smile.

He reached out to Elly and said, "Come into my office. I want to teach you about EKGs today," as he winked at Elly.

When Elly saw the wink, she looked at Kat to see if she reacted. Kat's face was a mask. Elly didn't know how to read it.

Elly followed Allen Pace into his office. He closed the door behind them. "Just pull your chair around here, Elly, so we can look at this together," he said genially. Elly complied cheerfully, but she was on guard.

"Have they all been treating you well? I want you to get plenty of experience."

"Kat has been most helpful, and the others have been very nice. I am learning loads," Elly said, displaying a glorious smile.

"You are beautiful when you smile like that. My patients will be lucky to work with you."

"That is very kind of you to say, Dr. Pace."

"Now, Elly, I asked you to call me Allen, and I meant it," he said as he slipped his left arm around her shoulders. "Mm, you smell so good!"

Elly struggled to get his arm off her shoulders. "Please, Allen, I want to learn about the EKGs!"

"I just want you to know you are appreciated." Turning back to the EKG tracing, he said, "This is a QRS segment, and this is called a *T*." For several minutes he continued to explain his technique of analyzing the test.

He really was very good at teaching, and he gloried in it. Gradually Elly grew more at ease with him. She found she liked his manliness, and being so close to him was not a problem. When he suggested that they have dinner together again, she was not ready to say no.

"I really am very lonely, and I would be so pleased if I could treat you. Look at it as a celebration of your new job," he said, looking at her with soulful eyes.

Elly remembered her conversation with Todd the evening before, and she felt a pang of guilt as she accepted the invitation. "I do have to get home early, and I am not dressed for a fancy restaurant like we went to last night," she replied.

Allen took delight in brazenly looking Elly over. "I think you look great, but we can find an informal restaurant that will treat us right, if that makes you feel more comfortable," he said with a twinkle in his eyes. They walked together to Pace's car and drove across the city to an intimate restaurant.

The restaurant Allen chose was close to Elly's apartment. It was a tiny bistro with a very active bar. The seating arrangement was different this time. They sat opposite at a very small table, and no matter how Elly sat, her knees touched Allen's.

This is too cozy, she thought to herself. She was feeling vulnerable again, so to get his attention back on food, she said, "What do you recommend on the menu?"

His eyes said he wanted to devour her, but he managed to put his sexual longings aside and recommended several dishes on the menu.

The waiter took their order, and the wine steward helped them choose a wine. Dinner arrived, and they began to eat, but Allen could not keep his eyes off Elly. She began to wonder if he was capable of hypnotism as she felt very drawn to him.

"I am really very lonely," he started, observing her every move. "Would you consider coming home to my apartment with me tonight? I'm not on call. We won't be disturbed."

"I'm sorry you are lonely, but I can't go to your apartment. I … I don't know you well enough," she stammered. "I'm just an employee, not a-a plaything."

"I promise not to touch you. I just like talking to you and knowing you are near me."

Sure, you won't touch me! Elly thought to herself. "I really think it is out of the question," she managed to say with more conviction. "I can take a taxi home if you won't—"

He took her hand in his and spoke in a honey-smooth voice, "I'll do anything you want, my pet."

"I want this relationship on a professional basis. You have been generous with taking me out to dinner, but that doesn't mean I am obligated to go home with you." Elly did everything she could to keep her voice from trembling. She slipped her hands away from his grasp.

"I understand perfectly. You must realize you are very important to me. I don't take just anyone out to dinner. I took you because there is no one else I would rather be with, and I must admit I got too needy. Please accept my apologies," Allen spoke earnestly.

He reached for her hand again, but she retracted both her hands and pretended that this was the most natural thing to do. He liked her spirit and vivaciousness.

"Do you like to travel?" he probed.

"What little I've been exposed to has been delightful. I am looking forward to graduation from the nursing program. I want to go to Hawaii in the worst way, especially this time of the year." Elly had a way of becoming very animated when she was discussing something near to her heart. She felt comforted and secure that the atmosphere was no longer so threatening.

They discussed areas of mutual interest. As Allen whetted her interest with adventure, describing exotic places in flourishing detail, he watched her reaction carefully. "Islands in the Pacific and the Caribbean. Lonely beaches with sand so pristine that no human footprints mar the view. Ah, it is so wonderful to lie on those beaches with the sun warming your body deliciously."

She listened to him as he described fragrant flowers and raindrops dancing on a secluded cabin roof by the sea. "I love the sound and the rhythm of the rain on the roof. It brings out the best in people. Sensuously hypnotizing, relaxing," he said, describing every feature down to the last pleasantness with feeling.

He was a master at telling her what a woman most wanted to hear. Every sublime expression on her face was a carrot dangling in his face, urging him on, until it became quite late. "I'm so sorry you are going to be short on sleep. I do want you to go home and dream of someplace wonderful and imagine being there with me."

Then Todd silently slipped into Elly's thoughts. She needed to justify having dinner with this philanderer. *I should be gathering information, not listening to a seductive song-and-dance routine.*

"Speaking of dreaming, I should get going. I must get a good night's sleep before my classes tomorrow. By the way, did you seduce

Gina with these stories?" Elly asked in a low, steady voice. She watched as the words cut through Allen like a sharp scalpel.

"I don't understand what you are asking. Gina was only an employee to me. I treated her to dinner every now and then, but she didn't have your class or intelligence. She did not mean to me as much as you do," he said with embarrassment.

Elly could feel her cheeks flush hot with anger. "She didn't mean much to *you*?! She was pregnant with your baby! How can you be so crass?" she hissed.

Abruptly, she slammed down her fork, stood up, and announced, "Don't bother to move. I'm taking a taxi home. I'll see you tomorrow." Without another word, she walked briskly to the door and was gone.

Allen dejectedly watched Elly leave. A wave of impotence crashed into him. The loss changed to anger, and he whispered hoarsely to the empty chair, "You just wait, my fine cunt. You are going to get the fuck of your life!"

CHAPTER 11

Wednesday, November 30

Most of San Francisco was fast asleep; however, Pace tossed fitfully with longing in his sweaty, rumpled sheets. The harvest moon had decayed to a silver orb shining on the horizon. Its luminescence was a faint issue in the predawn hours. The apartment was a borrowed one, and Allen wasn't so comfortable in it. When he got up in the dark, he stumbled over furniture on his way to the bathroom. "Damn chair! What is it doing in the middle of the room?"

He would give anything at this moment to be home in Sea Cliff, cuddled up with Annette. She would accept him from the rear, and she wouldn't even wake up. He could get his rocks off and go back to sleep. What if he got dressed and drove over there? Would she mind if her teddy bear let himself in and crawled into her bed? Surely by now she had forgiven him. She might be happy to see him.

Quickly, he dressed and walked down to his car. The streets were dark and lonely. A patrol car passed him. An old drunk lay on the sidewalk on one corner, his travails arrested by vino. The drive to Sea Cliff took a quarter hour. The cold car numbed Allen's sexual drive. He just wanted a warm, receptive body to cuddle up to so he could go back to sleep.

He almost drove past his house. The driveway had a strange car in it. No, not a strange car, it was Mark's car. "That rotten bugger. How dare he be in my driveway?" he mumbled out loud.

Suddenly the thought came to him: *Mark could be plugging my wife!* A cold chill electrified his spine. *Dam him! I'll strangle him if he lays a hand on her. My first impulse is to use my car to ram the screws and bolts out of Mark's car, reducing it to dust.* Clutching the steering wheel fervently, it was all he could do to control himself. *What holds me back is that it would total my beautiful Alfa Romeo. Instead, I'll park across the street and turn off the engine. I feel miserably alone.*

It is like my childhood. They would hold parties in those fancy houses, and I was never invited. I wasn't accepted by them. I would sit outside and imagine the girls with their tantalizing twats. Someday they would take notice. Someday I would make them want me, seek me out even, but now I feel alone again and left out in the predawn chill. His fist crashed down on the steering wheel and barely missed the horn. *I must get ahold of myself. Making a scene would not help. A good plan is in order.*

I have never suspected Annette of having an extramarital affair in the past. Why would she be doing it now? Maybe there is another explanation. Mark's car broke down and he had to take a taxi back to Tiburon. Or he could be sleeping in the guest bedroom because Annette is afraid to be alone. I would love to see his face when he sees me stroll in for breakfast. Wouldn't that give that drag queen a drop in his drawers?

Finally he felt brave enough to open the car door and walk up that familiar walkway to his house. He stood at the door for a minute or two, wondering if Annette had changed the locks and imagining what he would encounter inside.

Ever so silently, he opened the door and tiptoed inside. The hallway and staircase were dark, but Allen could find his way blindfolded. The door to their bedroom was part way open. It just took a nudge to open it farther. In the dim light he could see that the bed was occupied, but was there one or two?

Allen crept into the dressing room and quietly stripped off his clothes. Then once again he approached the bed. This time he slipped in beneath the covers.

The perfume was hers. Moving closer to the shape beside him, he could feel the delicious warmth. He could feel his passion rise. As he reached out for that cherished body beside him, his manhood urged him onward as he ran his fingers over the shape, which moaned in return. Moving into an intimate position, he could feel those sweet buns. He cuddled up to them with furor. Allen ran his hand over the thigh and down between the trembling legs to stroke the clitoris, but to his surprise he found a cock and balls!

Instantly he grabbed them in his hand and twisted them with all his might!

"Argh!" Mark screamed.

But Allen was on top of him, pounding him with his fists. "What the fuck is this cocksucking fag doing in *my* bed? Get out, you lousy turd!" Allen yelled as loud as he could. He shoved Mark out of the bed and onto the floor. Allen stood on the bed in all his manly glory, shouting obscenities at Mark.

The lights abruptly went on. Annette screamed, "Get out of my house!" to no one in particular or perhaps to both men. "Allen, what are you doing here? Why are you standing on the bed, and what did you do to Mark? Where is he?" she demanded.

"He's right here groveling on the floor. He will live long enough to get his clothes on and scuttle out the door," Allen growled in a deep voice as he sat down on the bed.

Mark slowly, painfully picked himself up and put on his clothes. Annette paced back and forth, raving about how Allen had no right to come into *her* house and cause such an uproar in the middle of the night. Allen jumped off the bed and lunged at her. Spinning her around, he slapped her over and over again, throwing her on the bed as a final measure.

"Shut up!" he growled at her. Whirling around and confronting Mark, he yelled, "Get out of this house *now!*"

Mark could not look at either of them. Still pulling on his pants and stumbling in his untied shoes, he made his way to the door. Noisily, he found his way down the stairs and out the front door.

There was silence as they listened to the car drive away. Then Allen said in a menacing voice, "And now, my fallen angel, you are going to feel the thrust of a real rod!"

***

The moon had set. Venus rose in the east to welcome the dawn. Annette, dressed in a warm robe, sat at the kitchen table, phone in hand. "Mark, oh Mark, how are you?"

"I still feel a bit shaken, but I'll live. Did Allen leave?" Mark responded.

"Yes, finally. The hospital called with an emergency. I'm going to have the locks changed today, and I've been thinking about some additional protection. I don't like guns, but maybe mace or something would be helpful. I also was thinking of asking for police protection. What do you think of that?"

"I'm not sure why you didn't change the locks earlier."

"I thought we were going to make up and act like decent married people again," she said in a small voice.

"Okay. Are you still interested in going to Gina's funeral with me?"

"I was so worried that your face was all beat up and you would not want to be seen. I am presentable because my bruises are in places nobody will see. And if Allen is there, I want to show some solidarity or something. I don't want him to think that he can just push us around," Annette said with hope.

"My wounds are front and center. I have a black eye and a cut lip, but I can say a terrarium fell on me or something. I think you are right; we need to make an appearance. I like your spirit, Annie, and I do love you. Thank you for the beautiful part of last night. It was second to none."

"It was nice," she said dreamily.

***

Hovering over the typewriter, Maria Fuentes was busy at work. At her side was Martin Sykes, who was giving his side of the report she was typing. They had both come to work extra early to get their narrative done on time.

"I'm disturbed that Mark Jacobs thinks it was an accidental poisoning. If Gina was at that cabin with someone, then that other person would have been poisoned too," Maria postulated as she paused in her typing.

"Maybe there is a body we haven't found. If another body exists, it could be anywhere. Let's check missing persons," Martin offered.

"That is a good idea. I wonder if Jim or Todd thought of that one. Help me with this part I'm writing. I am trying to describe how Mark Jacobs changed as soon as he knew we were officers. Do you remember that?" Maria asked.

Skimming over what she had written, he proposed, "You can say his deportment *appeared* to change. That will make it more objective. Also, I would like your opinion on something. Do you think Mark Jacobs would be a valid expert witness? He seems to be too involved to me."

Maria stopped typing and turned to Martin. "Right on! I think we need to talk to Jim and Todd about that. They have to talk to the DA about it too. Now, could you get me a cup of coffee? I need a burst of energy to get this done by ten."

***

Elly arrived at Saint Francis Cathedral early. She wasn't sure how long the trip by bus would take, and she didn't want to be late. Coming late would mean she might not be able to sit in front with Todd, or she would have to walk up the long aisle alone, in full view, and she wasn't into bringing obvious attention to herself.

The mortician was orchestrating the flower arrangements and other funerary embellishments. The organist was warming up the pipes. Elinor was impressed by all the activity, and she was glad that Gina was going to have a very beautiful memorial.

Walking up to the casket, she felt slightly apprehensive. It was a pale gray with silver trim, and across the closed portion of the casket was an immense floral spray of pink roses and a mass of white orchids. Gina looked like she was only sleeping. The rose-colored dress that Elinor had so lovingly chosen for her looked wonderful. Gina had always seemed fresh and joyous in that dress. It was really a summer dress, but then spring and summer were Gina's favorite seasons. As she lay in the casket, that mass of strawberry blonde hair had never looked so disciplined. In her hands she held a single white rose.

"She really looks like the picture of beauty, doesn't she?" said a soft male voice.

Turning toward the voice, Elly felt a chill. She said, "Hello, Dr. Pace. It is so nice you could make it." Then she returned to staring blankly at the casket. She could feel the hair on her head stand erect as he came closer.

He slipped his hand around her waist, but she recoiled and aggressively whirled around and confronted him in a low hissing voice. She said, "Please keep your hands off me!" Out of the corner of her eye she could see Todd coming down the aisle. She turned and walked toward him. "Am I glad to see *you.*" She greeted him with a generous grin.

"You weren't home last night. Did you have dinner with *him* again?" Todd said in a low whisper.

Elly wrinkled her nose and shot back, "Yes. He was simply awful!"

Todd was aware of her anger, but he wasn't sure if part of it was her reaction to his prying. "Would you have dinner with me tonight?" he said, trying to make amends.

"That sounds heavenly," she said and her eyes sparkled. "I have so much to talk to you about. And I'm very sorry I missed your call last night. You have to realize, I can be of help to your investigation by talking to this womanizer."

Todd rolled his eyes and chuckled. "You scare me, the way you walk into the lion's mouth!"

Elly looked around the gathering crowd to see if there was anyone she knew. She looked for Gary but didn't see him. She recognized many of her school friends and staff from the cardiology clinic. Everyone was talking softly, and then the room became silent. With soft lyrical notes, the pipe organ struck the cords of the requiem.

The service lasted slightly more than an hour. Every eulogy was impressive. So many wonderful hours of Gina's life were revisited. She had so many friends and loved ones who shared their stories. Elly could not help thinking that Gina would have enjoyed the event. She wondered if "the love of her life" was enjoying this celebration and if he was the murderer.

The processional slowly followed the pallbearers with the casket out the church's doors and into the sunlight. Elly watched the assembly pour out onto the sweeping stairway leading to the street.

"I haven't seen Gary. I thought he wouldn't miss Gina's memorial," Elinor said as she scanned the crowd.

In the crowd Elly recognized Dr. Jacobs. "Todd, Dr. Jacobs looks like he has been in a fight. And who is that stunning blonde with him? She looks familiar."

"That woman is Annette Pace, Dr. Pace's wife. We think Mark Jacobs had a run-in with Allen Pace early this morning from what our stakeout tells us. It is interesting that he showed up today," Todd said dryly.

"I think I'll go over and have Dr. Jacobs introduce me to Mrs. Pace," Elinor said as she looked up at Todd.

"Don't look at me. I'm not going to stop you. Go ahead, but don't count me in," Todd said as he shrugged his shoulders.

Walking toward Dr. Jacobs, Elly noticed Allen was watching her. "Hello, Dr. Jacobs. It was so nice of you to come. Gina had a very beautiful memorial service. Wouldn't you agree?"

"It is nice to see you too, Elinor," Mark acknowledged, and then he turned to Annette. He said, "This is Elinor DeMartini, a student of mine. She has recently started working at the cardiology clinic."

"Elinor, I would like to introduce you to my friend Annette Pace."

Annette and Elinor shook hands. Elly noticed that Annette's hand felt lifeless like a dishrag. Annette smiled in an obligatory fashion and abruptly turned to talk to another woman close by. Elly felt let down. She recognized Annette from her past, and now she was being rejected. Even Dr. Jacobs smiled and followed Annette's lead.

Elly wandered back to Todd. "Was that fun?" he asked, trying to cheer her up.

"I know her from my childhood, but they sure are snobbish, aren't they?"

"Don't take it personally. They are in a club of their own, and they follow its standards," he said to soothe her.

Elly was not the only one upset by the encounter. Annette whispered to Mark when they were alone, "That woman you introduced to me, Elinor, I know her from somewhere. A déjà vu experience, but I can't recall the name or the whole story. It really unnerved me."

"You could have seen her on one of our mushroom trips with my students. I should think that is the most logical explanation. By the way, I see Clair over by that pillar. Didn't you want to talk to her?" Mark said casually.

"I still feel strangely about that encounter, but maybe talking to Clair will get my mind off the subject," Annette suggested.

Clair was dressed in a fashionable black and white checked suit with a large black hat and accessories. She was one person who could look spectacular in black. Her face was set as in a mask, but she smiled wanly as Annette and Mark approached. "It is so nice to see someone I really want to talk to," Clair said in welcome. "Personally, I find funerals depressing. How are you holding up?"

"I will live through it. I wanted to talk to you about meeting with Allen. I want to insist that he agrees to your employment. I made an appointment to meet with him on Friday about five. Can you fit that into your schedule?" Annette said assertively.

Cocking her head to the side, Clair scrutinized Annette. "Is he interested in meeting with us?"

"Yes, I talked to him this morning," Annette said crisply.

Taking a deep breath, Clair responded, "I'll be there."

The hearse was pulling away from the curb for its slow drive to the cemetery for interment. Mark, Annette, and Clair watched the procession solemnly.

Darrel was suddenly at Clair's side. "Clair, the car is waiting. Don't you want to go to the cemetery with us?"

"Us? Who is coming with us?" Clair asked, barely hiding her surprise.

"My secretary Tish and Kat McKinney," he said, avoiding Clair's eyes.

Clair wrinkled up her nose and shook her head no, but she said, "Okay. Let's go."

***

"That was one of the nicest funerals I've been to in a long time," Kat announced as she used her key to open the clinic.

"I haven't been to that many, but it was rather pretty. Just the sort of funeral Gina would have preferred," Tish said to make conversation. "I have loads of work to finish before five, and I had better get going."

One by one they dribbled in. Allen looked exhausted and cranky. Everyone in the office gave him a wide berth. Elly had just finished a report and needed to present it to Allen. She dreaded going into his office, but there was no way to get around it. Wasting time wasn't really her style of working; she had to plan a way to minimize his anger. Carefully she scanned the report for any errors. She couldn't find any. Next, she took pains to look her best; she combed her hair and applied lipstick. Finally, there was nothing else to do but just do it.

Allen's door was closed. Elly knocked. "Just a minute," she heard him say. There was a long pause. "Come in," he said.

The room was dark; Allen sat in his chair with his back to the desk. "I'm wiped out, and I was trying to take a nap. What do you need?"

"I'm sorry I appeared rude to you at the memorial. I guess I have been under a lot of stress. And I think you have been too. I just came to deliver this report and offer an apology," Elly offered.

His chair swiveled around, and Allen confronted her. He looked rumpled. Elly had never seen him that way. It concerned her.

"Thank you, Elly. You are always very appropriate. Let me see the report."

She handed him the report and sat in one of the chairs to wait for his review. After looking it over, he said, "It looks good, but I would like you to use single spacing. Your spelling is excellent, and so is the quality of your work." He passed it back to her.

When she rose to leave, he motioned her to sit down. "I need to talk to someone about Gina. Since you were her friend, I thought you would be the best one," he said with a great deal of sadness in his voice.

"I find it hard to express how much I miss Gina. We were very close. I didn't know she was pregnant until after she died. I don't even know if she knew," he lied. "I would like you to forgive me for misrepresenting the relationship that I had with Gina, God bless her soul. I'm sorry."

Elly once more felt herself drawn to this complex and intriguing man. "I feel very honored that you would share this with me," she said with heartfelt compassion.

The phone rang, shattering their mood. "Allen Pace here ... Yes, she is here. Put the call through."

"When the phone rings, it is an outside call for you, Elly," he said.

Again the phone rang. This time Elly answered it. "This is Elly speaking ... Oh yes, we need to make arrangements for dinner ... Yes, you can pick me up at the clinic at six. ... I too have a lot to do, so I have to work late ... I'll see you then." She hung up.

Allen had watched her intently throughout her conversation. Elly felt slightly embarrassed to have made dating arrangements right under his nose.

"Well, I need to go. Dr. Carpenter has a cardiac stress test he is conducting, and he asked me to help him. Is there anything else you want to talk about?" she said as she rose to leave.

"Go ahead. I'm going to catch a few z's, and I'll also do some teaching with you later. I'll come and get you," he said as he stifled a yawn.

The afternoon flew by. Elly was enjoying working with the patients. Heart disease affected the whole person's life, professionally, socially, and in terms of lifestyle, for example, eating, sleeping, and exercise. The wife of one of the patients complained she had difficulty getting her husband to cut out salt and butter. She needed lots of reassurance, and Elly was good at providing that.

Four thirty rolled around, and Elly was finishing a report she was typing. Allen walked up to the desk. He looked rested. His hair was combed, and he had put his tie back on. "I'm feeling much better now. As soon as you are finished with that report, could you come into the echo room?" he said with a smile.

Elly nodded her head in agreement and completed the report. Dr. Carpenter was in his office, and she delivered it to him. "Very nice. You certainly have a good rate of turnaround time. Are you feeling more comfortable working today?" he asked.

"Yes, thank you. I still don't feel I could assist you or the other doctors completely on my own, but I can do a few tasks well."

"The patients enjoy you. One remarked just this afternoon that she benefited from talking to you. I think you helped her feel much more relaxed, and the test went better for it. Keep up the good work," Dr. Carpenter said. His philosophy was to work with the staff as a team, and the best way to encourage excellence was to acknowledge strengths.

It was almost five by the time Elly got to the echo room. Allen was seated at the console in the semi darkened room. "Hi, Elly. Just come and sit by me. I'll run through some of these films."

"Gee, it is awfully dark in here," she said as she sat down.

"It has to be this way to see the screen accurately. The echocardiogram uses ultrasound waves to help me see into the heart and vessels. Watch this. Do you see the fluctuating motion here?" He was pointing to the image in the center of the screen. "This is an atrial valve that is malfunctioning."

It was like a TV image, but the pictures here were black and white. The heart's contractions could be viewed in action. Allen showed her patient after patient and explained in detail each decrease in function that the images exposed. Elly was so interested in watching every abnormality that she didn't hear the office staff leave until Kat came to the door.

Kat announced, "I'm going to lock up and turn off all the lights, okay?"

"Lock the front door and leave the lights on, thank you. Good night," Pace said to her.

The lessons in echocardiogram technology went on for several minutes. Then Allen switched to how the test was administered. "This is the device that picks up the signal from the heart. See, it is like a ball that rotates. I put some of this lubricant on it and run it over the patient's chest, like this." He applied it over her hand. Then in a soothing voice he said, "Would you like to practice?"

Looking at Allen, Elly was wary of what he had in mind. His face looked innocent and didn't indicate that his intentions were anything but professional. "Okay," she agreed in a tiny voice.

Stripping off his tie and shirt, he exposed his muscular chest. Elly felt a shock of electricity run through her. She wasn't used to a man she only knew professionally nonchalantly ripping off his clothes in front of her. She jumped back in dread. Allen was aware of Elly's reaction, but he laid down on the bed on his back and acted as if it was nothing unusual. He assuredly informed Elly of how to apply the device to his chest to get the echocardiogram. Doing what she was told, she rotated the device over his chest and watched the monitor. "Oh, this is great. Your heart is beautiful," she said, unaware of the double meaning.

But Allen wasn't missing a heartbeat. He was sensuously conscious of Elinor's excitement and, most of all, the closeness of her body. Reaching for her hand, he guided it over his chest. "This is the aorta, and this is the vena cava." Then he ran the device over his abdomen. "This is the ascending vena cava." Without disturbing Elly, he loosened his trousers and ran the device over his groin. "This is the femoral vein and the femoral artery."

The image on the screen was fuzzy. Elly turned to see Allen with his penis in his hand, stroking it. "You're *gross!*" she exclaimed, dropping everything and trying to escape. But Allen was faster. Grabbing her arm, he forced her down on top of him. Elly struggled to free herself, but he was stronger. Rolling on top of her, he sat on her legs and used his rear to immobilize her. He pinned her shoulders down with one arm and ripped at her blouse with the other, kissing her as he worked.

"No, no, nooo!" she screamed as loud as she could while she beat him with her fists with all her strength and tried hopelessly to bite him. Panting, she could hardly breathe with his weight on her. His head and one arm bore down on her chest and throat as he pulled and tore at her underwear and skirt. She could feel him force her legs open and plunge his cock into her.

"You are quite a wildcat, aren't you? Well, I like my women with some spunk!"

She felt herself slipping. Memories flashed before her of the little girl being ravaged by her stepfather. The paralysis of fear held her mute witness. Choking and in pain, Elly made a last futile attempt to shake off her rapist, but she was too weak to be effective.

"That's it. Relax. You will enjoy it more."

Outside the clinic's main doors, Todd had arrived and was futilely pounding on the glass double doors. Examining the situation, he could see the lights were still on, and he was sure that Elinor was inside.

The din of Todd pounding on the door went unnoticed by Allen and Elly, who were deep in a struggle to overcome one another. Allen roughly maneuvered Elinor by flipping her over so that he could enter her from the rear, even if she resisted. He held her with his weight pressing down on her. Sobbing, she relented to get it over faster as she felt defeated. Gritting her teeth against the pain each thrust brought, she was unaware of the noise behind her.

Suddenly the lights came on. A strong hand grabbed Allen and forced him off of Elly. "You damn fuckin' rapist!" Todd screamed. They grappled together until Todd handcuffed Allen with his hands behind his back. "Don't move, or I'll charge you with everything in the book!"

A pair of gentle hands threw a blanket over Elly. Todd helped her up and took her out of the small room. "You are safe now," his kind voice said.

Elly's eyes were clamped shut. She bowed her head in shame and sobbed uncontrollably. The compassionate man helped her to the restroom. She had trouble walking on her own, and he supported her with an arm securely placed around her waist. Just as they reached the restroom, three officers walked in the door. "Maria, will you take care of Elly? And you men come with me," Todd directed.

Allen was slumped on the floor, hobbled by his trousers and with his hands secured behind his back. His face was contorted with frustrated rage, and he glared furiously at the officers as they approached him. "I want my attorney!" he shouted vehemently. "I'll get you for entering without a warrant, false arrest, and-and everything I can."

"I am arresting you for criminal assault and rape," Jim advised just before reading him his rights.

"It was consensual sex. You've got it all wrong—and you are trespassing!" Pace screamed.

After Pace was removed, the crime investigation team took over. The room and its contents were photographed and cataloged in

Sergeant Martin Sykes's book. The rumpled, bloody bed sheet and the torn and shredded clothing were bagged for evidence.

The ambulance arrived. Sergeant Maria Fuentes helped Elly who was wrapped in a blanket into a wheelchair and out to the ambulance.

Todd emerged from the clinic to see them off. "They will take good care of you, and I will come to the hospital to pick you up as soon as we finish with Allen Pace," Todd reassured Elly.

She nodded her head in return as the attendants closed the ambulance doors.

Maria rode in the back of the ambulance and held Elly's hand. "They will do a pelvic examination on you when we get to the hospital. Don't let it frighten you," Maria explained. "They will take lots of pictures also—not the kind you would keep in any family album, but they will be important when we get to court."

Elinor continued to keep her eyes clamped shut and nodded her head in affirmation. Her mind reeled from fury to guilt and self-pity.

"I should have known better, I keep thinking. He is the sort of man who always gets what he wants no matter what. And I should have known that."

"No man has the right to treat a woman this way, Elly. You should not be hard on yourself."

The ambulance lurched right and then left and came to a halt. Elly could hear voices outside the van, so she assumed they had arrived at the hospital. She was aware of flashes as if the media were there to photograph her torment. She pulled the blanket over her head. The EMTs gently but efficiently transferred her to a gurney. Maria was yelling at someone to step aside. The gurney moved, and the lights and odors changed. Elly knew she was in the hospital, but she kept the blanket over her head because she was afraid someone would recognize her.

Unexpectedly, the gurney came to a stop. She could hear the curtains being pulled around her. Peeking out from under the blanket, Elly looked around her. "Ms. DeMartini, you are safely in the hospital," said a middle-aged woman in white scrubs. She took vital signs and then went on to explain the procedure and how important it was to document her ordeal. Another woman came and asked for insurance, but Elly didn't have her purse.

Maria sat by her side, holding her hand to comfort her while they waited for the doctor. Dr. Korbin arrived with a nurse. "Hello, Elinor DeMartini. I am Dr. Debra Korbin. I need to examine you for injuries," she said in a professional way. Elly nodded her head in reply. Running her fingers lightly over Elly's throat, the doctor asked, "Is there some pain here?"

"Yes," Elly responded in a hoarse voice.

"Is it difficult to speak?" Dr. Korbin asked.

Elly nodded in reply.

"Take some photos of this area, Karen," Dr. Korbin instructed the nurse.

"Did you experience your assailant hitting you?" the doctor inquired.

"I think he slapped me. He had his arm across my neck, and he leaned on it. I might have passed out, I think," Elly answered with a trembling voice.

The examination continued with each bruise and abrasion noted and photographed. The process took at least an hour. Elinor was impressed by the thoroughness of it. However, it was a relief to have it out of the way when they were finally finished. Elly turned to Maria and said, "What am I wearing home?"

"Is there anyone at your apartment we can call to bring you some clothes?"

"No," Elly said sadly.

"Let me make a phone call, and I will be right back," Maria said with a twinkle in her eye.

Todd arrived hours later. With him came the district attorney Bud Thompson. "This is Bud, Elly. He is going to be handling this case. Also, I brought something for you to wear," he said, shyly presenting her with a bulging paper bag. Elly perked up and took delight looking in the bag. It was an expensive exercise suit. "I got you something that didn't need an exact fit because, I'm sorry, I'm not good at guessing women's sizes."

"It's perfect!" she said with a weak smile that lit up Todd. He wanted her to start the healing process, and this was a beginning.

CHAPTER 12

The Following Day

He sat by a filthy window, gazing out at the rain crookedly streaming down the pane in little rivulets. The room was unlit even though it was still dark. The power had been shut off after months of unpaid bills. A camp stove was set up in the kitchenette, and a kettle of water whistled the siren warning of boiling water. Gary lethargically shuffled over to the stove and extinguished the flame to save on fuel. Listlessly he poured himself a cup of instant coffee and then returned to his vigil at the window.

This was not a day that held any hope of starting a job. Because of the rain, construction was at a standstill all over the Bay Area. The life insurance on Gina was held up by the investigation into her death. If Gary had the money to buy gas, then he could pick up Gina's things and try to sell them. It was the old problem that it took money to get money.

The shipment of dope was due any day. That was one ray of hope. He had to collect from his customers, of course, and that was never easy. Those stinking rich guys held onto their money tighter than the poor ones. They didn't flinch at his entreaties, and not even his treats had done much good. He had to think of something to impress them with the reality of the situation. Gary lifted a grimy forefinger to scratch his two-day beard. He needed power to shave.

A plan was what he needed, but he was not good at creating plans. He liked to watch movies to see how the characters solved their problems. He needed to watch TV, but his was not working. Maybe he could move in with someone with a working TV? There was a guy in the apartment below him who had a tube. Maybe? No, he'd gotten busted a couple of weeks ago. The place was swarming with cops. Gary would like to avoid the cops as much as possible. There must be someone else.

The rain and the rivulets consumed him again. His dearest wish was to get out of the city and into the woods. He could last a long time on very little by camping. Out there, the rain could be a little inconvenient, but it never stopped him. He could live off the land, one step ahead of the game warden. Smiling to himself, he remembered the times of getting a deer out of season, and they never caught him. Gina never approved of his stories. She had the nerve to tell him once that if she heard of him poaching, she would turn him in. No loyalty at all, the stupid bitch!

There was a noise outside the door, and then someone was knocking. Gary opened the door a crack and said, "Whaddya want?"

An old man from down the hall was standing there. "We got two papers this morning, and the missus and I thought you would like one for the want ads." He didn't wait for an answer and scuttled off after shoving the paper into Gary's hands.

Throwing the paper on the table, Gary sat down to make a peanut butter sandwich out of the stale crusts he had. As he was spreading the peanut butter, he glanced at the paper, and something caught his eye.

The headline read, "Prominent Cardiologist Accused of Rape." Gary read on. Yes, it was Dr. Allen Pace they were talking about. And the bugger was out of jail on bail. Maybe he would be a good source of funds.

***

Annette had been up since the first light of dawn. She had experienced disturbing dreams about her childhood all night involving a dark-haired girl who was a playmate and a heroine from the past.

Still dressed in her robe and slippers, she made her way to the door off the kitchen, which led to the basement. Opening the door, she paused before going down the stairs. Did she really want to dig up the past? Yes, or else it would haunt her too much. She paused at the bottom of the stairs to orient herself. She decided the trunk that was filled with history was in a corner. It was an old trunk that had been in the family for several generations, and she hadn't seen it for years. The corner she chose had many shelves on the wall, and tucked under the last shelf was a curtain that hid more shelves. When Annette drew back the curtain, a notebook fell off one of the shelves and onto the floor.

As Annette bent down to pick up the foreign object, the title of the notebook caught her attention. It was written in beautiful calligraphy: "Gina's Diary." Annette almost dropped the book in her fright. What was it doing here? Had Allen hidden it here? Or had Mark? They both came down to the wine cupboard on occasion.

Staring at the diary, Annette felt that it had a life of its own. She desperately wanted to ask someone what she should do, but whom could she confide in?

The old leather trunk brought her back to her original plan. Carefully she put the diary back on the shelf, but in a more secure place, and in doing this she put it out of her thoughts for now. Then she turned her efforts to the historic trunk.

The trunk was over two hundred years old. When the lid was opened, it emitted odors from the past. It was a musty but comforting smell, like old perfume and lace. The top shelf contained ancient linens, ancient handmade lace, and pieces of bygone fashions. The shelf divider was fragile, so Annette took meticulous care in removing it. The second layer was what Annette was seeking. There in neat piles were old picture albums.

One by one she reviewed each album. After she'd reviewed several, suddenly a shiver of delight ran down her being, for in her hand lay the one picture she had been searching for.

⁂

Elly awoke feeling as if she hadn't slept at all. Every muscle made her aware of the scene from the previous night. The memories were excruciatingly demoralizing. Allen Pace—what had Gina seen in him?

Had he been such an animal with her too? Poor Gina had poor taste in men, or maybe she was masochistic.

Crawling out of bed, Elly hobbled into the bathroom. Scrupulously she avoided looking in the mirror. Denial would be her haven. Using it like a prism, she would depend on it to refract any painful thoughts she did not want to face. She felt a distinct aversion to taking on the world today. Luckily her last midterm was over. One sick day from school would be justified, and she would not miss much. With the decisions for the day taken care of, she went to bed and fell asleep.

Hours passed. The light in the room was brighter. The street noise was up, and again Elly awoke. Outside a light drizzle fell. The gray day depressed Elly even more. She decided to take a hot, soothing bath.

She needed to cleanse her body of a creepy clinging thing. It was as if his hands still clutched her. His odor was still in her nostrils, and his voice rang in her head. There was a need to escape, to find that inner peace so vital to one's being. Would another bath wash away the guilt and the pain? Elly had sat in the tub numbly last night too. But did the odor go or did she feel cleaner? No!

As the water gushed into the tub, she grabbed a box of bath salts and dumped some into the foaming water. This was followed by a bottle of bath oil. They were formerly Gina's salts and oils. There was something therapeutic about using them, as if Gina was helping Elly purge the pollution from her body.

The tub was full, and Elly dipped her hand in. It was very hot but tolerable. Inch by inch she lowered her sore body into the bubbles. Oh, it felt so good! If only she could spend the whole day in this warm liquid place. It was like going back to the womb. She took a sponge, filled it with the warm fragrant liquid, and squeezed it out over her head. It seemed to wash away the painful memories from the night before.

The water grew cold. Elly reluctantly crawled from the tub and wrapped herself in a large towel. Mesmerized, she watched the whirling water escape, leaving in its wake the rosy but mournful fragrance of a dear friend. Walking aimlessly out of the bathroom, she walked into Gina's room and flopped on the bed.

The bed still smelled faintly of Gina. Elly had not noticed this since Gina's illness and death. Reaching out, she gripped the pillows and brought them to her. She hugged them as a frightened child clings to its mother. "Oh, Gina, how could you love that man? How could you bear his child?" Elly wailed and broke into sobs. Tightly clasping the pillows with desperation, Elly felt overcome with the events of the past week.

***

Jim Collins sat at his desk that morning, working on some reports that had to be done that day. Suddenly Todd burst into the office. "Who let that fucker out on bail!" he blurted out.

His outburst startled Jim, who jumped up. "Come in, Todd, before you blow up entirely," Jim encouraged him, closing the door behind Todd. "Now, take a load off. Have my cup of coffee. I haven't touched it, and I can get another."

"We've got that Pace dead to rights, and he didn't deserve bail," Todd said in a voice louder than what was necessary. "Who's the friggin' judge?"

"It was Klineman as usual. He didn't think Pace was going to leave town, and maybe he is a patient of Pace's. I've heard he has a pacemaker or some sort of heart problem. Pace's attorney came up with the bail."

"What did they set the bail at?" Todd asked in a calmer voice.

"One hundred thousand dollars. Sounds like the big bucks to me, but maybe it is chicken feed to Pace."

"Did his wife come up with it?" Todd asked, not really expecting Jim to know. He just wanted to get that idea out for speculation.

Jim just shrugged his shoulders. "All I know is the attorney is on record for the bail." Jim changed the subject. "How is Elinor?"

"She is bottling it all up inside her. She didn't want to talk about it last night. She was very silent as if talking was going to bring back the pain," Todd said. "I took her home from the hospital last night. I picked up some Chinese food on the way home. She ate very little, and I got the feeling she wanted to be alone, so I left. I felt really bummed out."

"Surely you're not blaming yourself for this one? You are the star witness; you bagged him in the act. Bud Thompson doesn't think he has a leg to stand on with that breaking and entering charge that Pace wants to pin on you. And the medical reports show that he tried to strangle Elinor. In addition, he will never get a jury to believe that it was consensual sex instead of rape."

"It will be her word against his. And I bet he has friends in high places. Maybe I am jaded because of all the cases of rape I've seen that went south because the defense had an in with the judge or someone and the perp went free. I've seen too many of them," Todd said sadly.

"I think it has something to do with how you feel about Elinor, too. Have you called her this morning?" Jim asked wisely.

Todd left Jim's office feeling slightly more positive. He had found he had a problem keeping his anger in check. Was this profession getting to him, or was his behavior normal? He was so deep in thought, he hardly noticed people as he passed them in the hallway.

With relief he entered the sanctuary of his office and closed the door behind him. The more he thought, the more he realized he had never experienced the comforting of someone close to him who had been brutally raped. He would have to put some thought into anything he would say to Elly. *Yes, there is some guilt there too. I could have prevented it from happening if I had arrived earlier. Why did she go out to dinner with that man? Doesn't she understand that a man like Pace gives only to get? How will the jury look at this? They might think she was leading him on, but that doesn't justify him being so rough with her. I know my thoughts are confused, and I am in turmoil. I must be careful in talking to Elly. I must never imply that I am blaming her.*

Finally he felt he was ready to call Elly and truly support her. The phone rang over ten times before she answered. He spoke before she could say anything: "I was beginning to worry. You don't have your answering machine on!"

"Hello, Todd. I don't know why I turned off the answering machine. I'm doing all sorts of erratic things today."

"I want to be part of your healing process. Can I take you out to dinner tonight?" Todd said hopefully.

"That sounds nice, but my wardrobe is really limited since my best blouse and skirt were destroyed last night. Does it make sense that he should pay for the clothing he has ruined?"

"If you wait to have the judge decide on it, you will starve to death waiting for the money," he said, trying to be funny.

She didn't laugh but changed the subject. "I got a very strange phone call from Mrs. Pace. She wants to take me to lunch downtown and talk to me about her husband. She sounded very nice and not vindictive, so I agreed. What do you make of that?"

"After the way she treated you at the funeral, you want to see more of her?"

"She apologized for that. She said she was so overwhelmed—that's her word—when she met me, and she was so embarrassed that she had to turn away. She really did impress me as being rather congenial. Not charitable, but authentically friendly."

"When is this lunch happening?"

"In a couple of hours. Also, I think this rape and Allen's violent behavior makes him even more of a suspect for Gina's murder. What do you think?" She didn't wait for his answer. "His behavior is erratic like he is under the influence of something like drugs."

"The judge has said that all the evidence so far has been only circumstantial. I understand Allen was released from jail this morning on bail, paid by his attorney. I wanted a drug screen done on him, but the judge overruled it. Elly, I'm not very happy when I see people in high places getting off because they have money and the law allows this to happen."

"I don't understand!" Elly said in frustration.

"We didn't charge Pace with possession of drugs because we had no evidence, but the judge is making it difficult to get that evidence. If Allen was a street person, it would not have been a problem. But he isn't. I'm sorry. I'm not myself today. Forgive me if I am not very positive."

"I sort of know where you are coming from. It must be frustrating for you."

"Thank you. Now I'll pick you up for dinner about six, okay? Also, we have a concert date for tomorrow. You still want to do that?"

"Yes to both. I think I'll get something to wear for the concert today. Thank you for reminding me. I'm playing sick, but shopping is good therapy for me."

"I'm so glad you aren't going to work today."

"I called them this morning. I just said I was ill. I didn't say any more."

"That was a good idea. What are you going to do tomorrow when it comes time to go to work?"

"We can talk about it later. I want to give it more thought."

＊

The rain had run its course, and by late morning it had stopped. Elly, dressed in jeans and a sweater, wanted to visit her favorite used clothing stores where fashionable women sold last year's haute couture on consignment. There she could find beautiful garments for a fraction of the original value, and they usually looked nearly new. Her favorite store was Pennies from Heaven, located on a side street off Clement Street. It was the sort of store that was open only by reservation, so Elly had called ahead.

Ringing the doorbell produced a female-like person with a Mohawk haircut, long fake eyelashes, and large beaded earrings. Her face was tattooed with butterflies on the right cheek and a rose the size of a dime on the left side of her chin.

"I was told to ask for Rainbow Sky. Are you she?" Elly asked quietly.

"You've got that right, lady. Come right in, dearie," Rainbow gushed in a musical falsetto.

The transvestite led Elly down a hallway and into a large room lit by three large skylights in the ceiling. The area was filled with many racks of dresses, suits, and blouses. Hats of all shapes, colors, and sizes decorated the walls, along with gloves, artificial flowers, and belts for accents.

"You wanted something in a dress, lovey?" Rainbow inquired.

"Size eight, I think, and something romantic," Elly shyly requested.

"Why, darling, we specialize in romance here," Rainbow said as she held up a lovely cherry-red-colored silk dress with a flowing skirt and a simple jewel neckline. "How about this number? The neckline is lovely, and the skirt flares nicely. Do you like it?"

"Ooh, it is lovely. May I try it on?" Elly said as she felt the filmy, silky fabric.

"I've picked out several for you to model, and then we will decide which works the best," Rainbow said as he ushered Elly toward a dressing room.

"Elly, is that you?" said a contralto feminine voice floating out from the end of the large room.

"Yes, it's me, Nell. I'm trying on these beautiful garments that Rainbow selected," Elly called out.

The strikingly tall middle-aged woman was Penelope Charlov, who was the owner, manager, and buyer and the confidant of the patrons of Pennies from Heaven. Nell, rolling her eyes, approached Rainbow with the stride of an army general. Turning with arms akimbo to the closed curtain of the dressing area, she addressed the curtain: "How do you like my new assistant? I think she gives the place a feminine touch! By the way, did you bring that tender morsel Gina with you?"

The words cut through Elly like a knife. "No, no," she stammered. Then she blurted out, "She is dead!"

"Grace be Jesus! I am so sorry, I didn't know," Nell apologized in a softer voice. "What happened, an accident?"

The curtain parted slowly, and Elly stood pale-faced, with tears spoiling her mascara, in a lovely red silk dress that hung limply on her body, accentuating her grief.

"Mercy me, we aren't going to have any luck with this dress or any other until we work on *you*, lovely," Nell said as she took Elly's hand and led her toward her office. Calling over her shoulder, she gave orders to Rainbow: "Bring that Chinese robe, and go out and get some pastries—you know, my favorite ones with lots of gooey goo."

Nell held the door open to her office. The room fascinated and distracted Elly. On one wall was a hand-painted mural that looked like an English garden. The table and furniture were Victorian, white metal, and lacelike. A large umbrella and potted plants completed the effect.

"Do you like it? This is where I come to get away from it all," Nell announced as she ushered Elly to the chaise lounge. "We are going to make you very comfortable, and you are going to tell Mother Pennel-ope all!" she gently commanded.

There was a tapping at the door. Rainbow opened the door a crack, thrusting her hand through with the Chinese robe. "I'll be back in a flash with the pastries," she gaily announced.

"Thanks!" Nell called out as she took the robe. Turning to Elinor, she said, "Let's get you out of that dress and into this robe. You will be so much more comfortable."

Silently Elly followed Nell's instructions. The dress slipped off easily, and the robe was comforting. When she was wrapped in the robe, she sat down carefully on one of the chairs at the table. A cup of tea was offered. Wanly, she accepted the offering as if it were a medicinal potion.

"I know how you felt about Gina. You need to talk to someone, a real woman who can understand," Nell advised as she placed a box of tissues in front of Elly.

"I was raped last night!" Elly exclaimed as she burst into tears.

Reflexively, Nell pushed the tissues closer to Elly and dryly asked, "A man?"

Covering her face with one of the tissues, Elly weakly nodded in affirmation.

"I didn't know 'they' had any other way of doing *it*."

"No, you don't understand. This was real, forceful *rape*. It came out of a professional setting. I am so sore that I can't sit comfortably. And he tried to choke me!" Elly looked searchingly at Nell's face and then continued. "What he committed was a crime! Even men in the community would call it that, and I think the man who raped me killed Gina!"

"I'm sorry, I misinterpreted what you said. Let me get this straight: Gina was murdered, and you were criminally raped. I always thought of you as an all-American type, you know, worry-free. I am amazed. What did Gina die of?"

"I think she was poisoned!" Elly hung her head and softly sobbed.

"Have you talked to the police? Why would this man want to kill Gina? She was such a sweet young thing."

Angrily, Elly responded in a deep, tortured voice, "He was her lover and knocked her up!"

There was a pause. Finally Nell said, "When you were here with Gina in the good ol' days, the way you two acted, I would have sworn you were lovers!"

"We were very close, but then she met this man and got into drugs. One thing after another happened. He is married, and I think he wanted her to have an abortion. It was agonizing."

"I bet it was painful. You loved her, didn't you? I mean physically loved her as well as emotionally. I know, I am gay too, and I know a woman who loves women when I see one." Nell looked intently into Elly's eyes. Elly gave not a glimmer of a rebuttal.

**

The table by the window seemed awfully conspicuous, but Annette didn't want to miss Elly. The time seemed to drag by. The longer Annette waited, the more she wished her curiosity had not gotten the best of her. In her mind she carefully reviewed her conversation with Elinor. Elinor really had sounded interested. Furtively, Annette glanced at her watch for the tenth time. *She is a half hour late; I think I will order lunch.*

The salad arrived, and Annette sadly ate alone. Then the server approached and asked, "Madam, are you Mrs. Pace?"

When her identity was confirmed, he informed her that there was a call waiting in the manager's office.

"Mrs. Pace?" Elly began. "I've had an awful morning. I'm sorry I'm so late contacting you, but if I get a taxi, I can be there in maybe ten minutes. Will you wait for me?"

"Thank you for calling. I will wait another fifteen minutes. I'm having lunch right now, and I can take my coffee with you."

Within the allotted time, Elly walked through the door. She looked rather rumpled, and her eyes were red and swollen. Cautiously she sat in the chair the server offered.

One look at Elinor and Annette realized that Elinor possibly had been the target of the rape she had read about in the paper. Carefully, Annette chose her words. "There was a rather disturbing article in the paper this morning. Dr. Pace was arrested for rape. Do you know anything about this?"

"Is this the reason you wanted to have lunch with me? And, yes, I was the ... victim," Elly said in a hoarse whisper.

"I wanted to talk about quite another matter, but shall we say this terrible act takes center stage. I'm very sorry. He is capable of being a violent man. I'm feeling at a loss for words."

"Did you post his bail?" Elly asked, feeling a bit more in control.

"No, I didn't know a thing about it until I read the article in the paper this morning. That is not a nice way to find out about your husband's activities," she said, revealing some of her own frustration.

The sandwich arrived that Elly had ordered, and the two sat in silence as Elly ate and Annette drank her coffee.

"Is there any way I can help you recover from this dreadful assault? I feel responsible in some way. Allen and I are separated, as you probably know, and maybe that is why his behavior has been so uncivilized. If you have had some garments ... ruined in some way, we can replace them."

"My best and only skirt and blouse were torn, and my undergarments are ... beyond repair," Elly said haltingly. Her eyes filled with tears.

"At least those are easily replaced. I would love to take you shopping this afternoon. We will find some wonderful suits at a special shop I know. A nice blouse to go with the new suit would be nice—and accessories. Would you let me do that?"

A wave of relief flooded Elly. She almost had to pinch herself to know this was real. "That would be so appreciated, but I look so awful to be going into a nice store. I will feel out of place," she said as she looked at her untidy sweater and worn jeans."

"Don't let that bother you. I'm in jeans too. As soon as you are finished, we can get started."

***

The late afternoon light was fading as Elly reached to turn on the table light in her apartment. It had been a most bizarre day. She really was not enthusiastic about having dinner with Todd. However, the alternative plan of being alone was not inviting either. The point was that she must take care of what she had said she'd do tonight, even though putting up a front was getting tiresome.

In desperation she turned her thoughts to positive ones. The new outfit was more than she'd ever dreamed of owning. Caressing the soft rust-colored wool with her hand, she loved the nubby texture of the fine tweed. It was very special, and it reminded her of Annette and all the topics they had talked about.

If the world were perfect, she would be having dinner with Annette. Not that Annette had invited her. It wasn't even a choice, just a fantasy from the past.

The doorbell rang, shattering her daydreams.

Throwing open the door to give the most dramatic effect, Elly greeted Todd. "Surprise! Well, do you like it?"

"Wow, let me look you over. You look great," he said candidly. With affection, he presented her the bouquet he had hidden behind his back.

"Ooh, they're beautiful. I really love flowers." She hesitated and wondered if he wanted a kiss or a hug. The pause became awkward. Slowly she raised her arms, wrapped them around his neck, and reached up to kiss his cheek. In a spontaneous gesture, he put his arms around her waist and drew her closer to him. "I've been thinking about you all day," he whispered in her ear. "I want to help you forget last night, but I need for you to tell me what is best for you."

Gently she pushed him back so that she could look into his face. "You are very sweet. For now, let's just go and have dinner." His hard masculine body and shaving lotion odors overwhelmed her. Last night's memories were still full of those smells and feelings. The repulsion was hard to resist. It was not a romantic feeling.

***

The evening fog had rolled in and surrounded the houses at Sea Cliff. Annette had a roaring fire blazing in the fireplace. She had just placed an aperitif and glasses on a little table when the doorbell chimed.

She used the newfangled intercom to check out the visitor. It was part of her new security system, and she liked to use it after sundown especially. When the caller was identified, she answered the door. "Come in, Mark. It is nice to see you," she said as she opened the door for him.

Lunging toward her, he attempted to kiss her passionately, but she turned quickly so he awkwardly pecked her cheek. "I've wanted you in my arms all day, love, and now you turn away from me?" He pouted.

"You and I are going to have a very serious talk, and depending on the outcome of our talk, I will decide what to do about dinner."

Mark was taken aback. He meekly followed Annette into the living room. In a formal fashion, Annette primly placed herself in the more straight-backed of the two chairs by the fireplace and motioned for Mark to take the chair opposite her. The tray with the glasses and the aperitif sat between them, but Annette made no attempt to offer any to Mark.

"My accountant tells me you are already behind in your loan payment. I would like an explanation," Annette coolly announced.

"I can't be more than a few hours or one or two days late? It is hard for me to imagine why you would get upset over a trivial twenty-four to forty-eight hours," Mark casually remarked, but inside the red flag of worry arose.

"Can you guarantee that it is in the mail, or can you pay me in cash right now?" Annette said coolly in a determined voice.

"I'm short of cash right now. I don't usually carry that much money with me. It's dangerous to carry great wads of bills around. I could get mugged, robbed … Let's go out for dinner. I would like to take you somewhere very special—my treat." His voice trailed off. He had never seen Annette so controlled and angry.

"I don't think we can have dinner until this is settled. Why are you so strapped for money? Doesn't the university pay you? Lately you have taken most of your meals here, so what are your expenses aside from your house?"

"There were some debts from the past. I made some foolish investments, and I owe on my taxes."

"Haven't you left out the *biggie*?!" She let her voice rise, and her face was hard and cold.

"I don't know what you are talking about," Mark said as innocently as possible.

"I am referring to your drug habit!"

"I only take an occasional sleeping pill. I wouldn't call that a *drug habit*." Mark too raised his voice, and his face was flushed.

"I have proof that it is more serious than that. Down in my basement, someone had stashed a diary of Gina's, and in that diary is enough to say you have a very serious drug problem. You even take delight in addicting your students and lovers! Ah yes, the police would just love to read that diary!" Her face was crimson as she thrust herself forward to scream in his face. "Do you see the picture? I think you have been doping me, and I don't like it. You had better get me that money, fast!"

A wave of nausea swept over Mark. Glaring into the fire to avoid her eyes, he searched for something to say. It reminded him of his mother berating him for wearing his sister's clothes. Small and helpless, he couldn't explain himself. "Maybe I should go. I can't deal with this right now," he said, his courage dissipating with the seconds. He urgently needed a fix.

"Why do I always get mixed up with weak, stupid men?" she mused. "Yes, go like a slinking yellow dog! I want that payment on the loan by Sunday, or I'll call the loan," she shrieked.

They walked in silence to the door. In the doorway, Mark turned to Annette and wailed, "Gina didn't mean anything to me! I have only loved you."

She felt like an amazon cleansing the world of vulgar scum as she slammed the door in his face. The cold hard door comforted Annette as she leaned against it. The dead bolt was secure. Tonight she wanted to feel safe. It was not going to be easy with no one she could trust.

In the kitchen she prepared some soup and a small salad. In her mind was a longing need to talk to someone. It had been a nice day. *I felt like a big sister comforting Elinor, and it brought up memories of our childhood together. If I close my eyes, I can see that swing that we played on. In those days of innocence and curious adventures, we had been buddies, and to be with her once more was so sweet.*

The peaceful reverie was shattered by the phone. It rang several times before Annette could bring herself to answer it.

"This is Allen; I am returning your call." His speech was slurred.

"Are you drunk?" she snapped back.

"Angel, you don't sound hap-p-y tonight. Would you like me to come over and cuddle up with you?"

"It would be better to see you tomorrow, I think, when you are sober. I found something that will interest you. And I had lunch with Elinor today. We went shopping and replaced those garments you *tore* off her."

"You idiot, that will make me look guilty! What did you find that is so inviting? Does it have anything to do with Elly?"

"First of all, you *are* guilty, so face it like a man. No, nothing of Elinor's, but it belonged to Gina. I found the diary in our basement."

"You didn't tell Elinor about it, did you?" he asked in a panic.

"Yes!" she lied, but she couldn't resist persecuting him.

"You vindictive *bitch*! Don't you know she is friendly with the detective on Gina's case?" he roared. Then there was silence. When he spoke again, his voice was more in control. "Where is that damn diary *now*?"

Annette couldn't keep from smiling or telling another little fib. "Mark was here, and he took it with him for safekeeping!"

CHAPTER 13

Friday, December 2

"TGIF," Jim called out to whomever would listen to him as he applied the key to his office door. From down the hallway, he could hear someone gaily whistling a familiar tune. Jim could not resist sticking his head out to see who was so happy to be whistling Beethoven's Ninth. "I'll be a dawg burn, what makes you so giddy, Todd?"

"What the hell? I love my work! What else could it possibly be?" Todd's face was full of wide-eyed innocence and a grin from ear to ear.

Jim cocked his head to get a better look at his friend. It occurred to him that Todd had told him he had a date last night. "So, she's feeling better?"

"Yep. I don't want to give you the wrong impression. She let me hug her." His voice changed to seriousness, and he became thoughtful. "Elinor might need some counseling. I am going to call social services. They should have been on her case before this."

"Is she withdrawn?" Jim probed.

"Yeah. She looked great though, so I think her self-esteem is intact. It seems Annette Pace took her shopping yesterday and replaced the clothes that were damaged when Allen Pace raped her. Isn't that one for the books? Her impression of Annette was that she was very cooperative and generous. Elinor confided something else—she and Annette had played together as children."

Todd continued, "In your report two or three days ago, you were under the impression that Annette was withholding or would withhold information. Maybe we need to talk to her again?"

"Annette wasn't bribing Elly, was she?" Jim asked.

"Apparently she didn't give Elly that feeling. In fact, Elly was quite adamant about that. It was the only subject that she really got excited about."

"It might be defensiveness. The thought that Mrs. Pace, her childhood friend, would somehow try to harm her too may be so repugnant that she can't bear to even consider the idea," Jim carefully explained.

"You have a valid point there. Let's continue to keep a watch on Annette and get Fuentes over there to interview her again. Are there any other developments?" Todd asked.

"This will interest you. In my mail was this notice. It is a clarification from Economy Life that Gary Williams did take out a two-hundred-thousand-dollar life insurance policy on your sister approximately six months before she died!"

Todd could only shake his lowered head. When he looked up at Jim again, his eyes spoke of anger mixed with sadness. "I guess we need to ask that character a few more questions," he said between his clenched teeth. "Anything else?"

"The watch on the Pace residence reported last night that Mark Jacobs arrived there at 18:23 and exited at 19:08. Evidently he looked dejected and never returned."

"Sounds like they had a falling-out over something," Todd offered.

* * *

The crisp moist air felt refreshing; morning was Elly's favorite time of day. This morning was such an improvement over the day before that it couldn't be anything but great. She had awakened with a strategy for dealing with Allen. Todd's words had stuck: "If he tries to fire you, you can get him on sexual harassment charges!" It wasn't going to be fun going to work, but somehow Todd's pep talk would carry the day. Her nursing classes would keep her distracted, and she wouldn't have to face the torture squad until one in the afternoon.

The misty clouds were breaking as Elinor bounded down the stairs to the street. As she was adjusting her backpack of books, a truck abruptly drove up to the curb. The event meant nothing to Elinor as she turned to walk the half block to the bus stop.

"Hey," a gruff voice rang out. "Hey, you, with the backpack, *stop*!" he shouted again.

Elinor turned to see who was shouting and realized it was Gary! "Oh God," she mumbled as she started to walk faster. She heard the sound of feet pounding the sidewalk behind her, and she started to run. Silently she prayed the bus would arrive at this crucial moment.

"Damn bitch, stop when I call you!" Gary growled as he grabbed Elinor by the collar.

"Get your filthy hands off me," Elinor hissed back. "Leave me alone!"

"I need to collect Gina's things. They are mine, ya know," he said, his voice taut with anger.

"I can't help you now; I'm on my way to school. Here is my bus. You can call me on Saturday, and we will make some arrangements," she hurriedly said as she wriggled free and dove for the open door of the bus.

Gary could only stand on the sidewalk and watch as Elinor disappeared into the crowded bus. Shaking off the feeling of defeat, he turned and walked back to Elinor's apartment building.

Greedily he evaluated the windows of Elinor's apartment that faced the street. They all looked locked and painted shut. Warily, he climbed the stairs, watching for witnesses. Elinor's door was locked, and the dead bolt was thrown. Quietly he cursed to himself and tried to think of another plan.

***

The papers were strewn across the desk in disarray. Mark sat with his head in his hands, trying to straighten out the events of the night before. Why was she coming on so strong? Is she so greedy that she can't have compassion for him? Would she really inform the police of what was in that diary? He found that talking to her about the money issue was the most difficult. He couldn't even acknowledge that he needed to come up with $1,500 in the next couple of days. Money had always been the prickliest of subjects.

My last paycheck had arrived last Friday. How difficult it was to remember. It must be here or somewhere else. Did I pick it up? That brandy last night was the problem. Brandy always makes my mind thick and forgetful. I crave to go tripping off on crack, but I have a lecture to give in fifteen minutes. Ah, that is it! Yesterday the supply came in, and the paycheck was already spent. Why is it so hard to remember the exact figures? Surely I hadn't spent all of it. Lethargically, he rummaged in his pockets and drew out the contents. There was a set of keys, a wallet, some breath mints, and a few cents in change. The wallet produced five dollars, and a pair of tickets fell out, tickets to a concert. *I wonder if Annie will go with me.*

Sigh. He knew it was time to go to the lecture hall. What was it that he was going to talk about? Was the class on chapter 8, or was that last week? Chapters 8 and 9 were somehow linked, but his mind failed to tell him the connection. As a last resort he opened a book, but it wasn't the textbook for the ten o'clock class. A dizzy feeling accompanied by nausea came over him. Maybe he was too ill to go to class. Yes, that was it, he was too sick to lecture, sick enough to go home.

His mind was working now. Picking up the phone, he called the teaching assistant, whom he asked to carry on without him. Mark told him would not be available this Friday because he was ill.

***

"We are supposed to do *what*?" Todd could barely disguise his anger.

"I'm sorry, but we cannot tail Allen Pace anymore without just cause. His attorney sent a nasty letter to the boss, and he said to stop hounding him," Jim carefully explained. "Allen Pace feels he is being harassed."

"Allen has his nerve. Okay, okay, but I think the boss knuckled under again! Maria told me this morning after I left you that the budget will stretch no further, so we have to cut off surveillance of all the other suspects as well."

The news hit Todd hard. His body slumped in the chair as if the weight of the words were pushing him down.

"The chief is under the impression that we don't have a viable case, and he wants to put the manpower where there is merit. I am going to continue on the case; however, my resources are limited," Jim revealed soberly.

Todd looked up at his friend with gratitude.

Jim then said, "I think Gary is into drugs in a big way. He may be a pusher. A big shipment of cocaine came into Oakland last night, and a man of Gary's description was near the wharf. The cops missed a bust by three minutes. We know Gary was upset that Gina was pregnant, and he knew he wasn't the father. She was using heroin, and I think Gary deals in that too. To cap it off, Gary has this insurance policy that he took out on Gina just months before she was killed. In short, I think he is our man."

"If you are right, he would need an accomplice. I don't think he is capable of using a sophisticated poison like the one that destroyed Gina," Todd offered.

"Then is the helper a woman?" Jim probed.

A look of puzzlement crossed Todd's face. "It is hard for me to imagine that one of the known women in this case would team up with Gary!"

"Right on, but when we find one on drugs, we will be close." Jim was warming up to the discussion.

"You could be right. Drugs could be the driving force, but my gut feeling is that it is much more complex than that," Todd advised.

***

The phone seemed to always choose to ring when her mouth was full. It was one of those numerous inconveniences of working and eating lunch at the same time. Wagering on another bite of her sandwich, Kat McKinney tried again. *Ringgg,* the phone went again. It was Dr. Pace's private line. Just as Kat went to answer the phone, Dr. Pace picked it up himself, and the line light flashed in silence.

Down the hall in his office, Allen Pace whispered into the receiver that the party should hold while he closed his door for more privacy.

Cautiously, he went to the door, looked both directions, and then closed the door quietly.

"All clear?" the gruff voice of the pusher inquired.

"You can't come here. I'll meet you someplace, but not here!" Allen spoke quietly but vehemently.

"I've got news for you, something you would like to know," the pusher said, taunting Allen.

"Tell me. We don't have to play games. Maybe you do that with other customers, but I don't bother with trashy junk," Allen responded haughtily.

"The cops are off your tail, so now I can come to your office, at discrete times of course."

"How do you know? Maybe they are setting a trap."

"One of my customers clued me in—they ran out of money."

"The police department ran out of money?" Allen asked incredulously.

"Something about putting their people on other cases to save money. I think they are giving up. Now if you want what I have, then you will be at your office at seven tonight." The pusher hung up before Allen could answer.

Staring at the phone receiver as if it was something he had never seen before, he mumbled, "Shit! Now what will I do?"

Kat watched the line go dead. She was organizing the last of the reports for filing. Nervously, she watched the clock. Elinor would be here at any moment, and she was dreading her arrival.

In the back corridor, a door opened and closed. The footfalls were heavy, the type a man would make. Around the corner Dr. Carpenter appeared. He walked up to Kat's desk.

"Are you okay, Kat? You look so pale," he said offhandedly as he picked up the morning mail.

"I wasn't expecting you for a couple of hours, and I was afraid that it was Elinor," Kat explained.

"Allen called me and asked me to talk to Elinor if she gives you any trouble," he said quietly. "It isn't a nice job, and we need to share responsibility."

"I'm so relieved. I was afraid that Allen would have to talk to her, and that would mean fireworks."

George Carpenter winked at Kat and said, "I'll be in my office if you need me."

Feeling more relaxed, Kat returned to the files to complete her former job. Behind her, Kat heard the main door open. Someone came in, but Kat continued to work and waited.

"Hello, Kat, how are you today?" Elinor greeted her, trying to sound normal.

"Just a minute, Elinor. I want to complete this, and then I want to talk to you."

Elinor sat down at one of the desks and put her books and purse in the drawer. She was wearing her new stylish exercise outfit that Todd had gotten for her. She hoped it would give her confidence. Friday they did mostly stress tests, and the staff dressed more casually.

When the last file was taken care of, reluctantly Kat turned to Elinor. "Let's get a cup of coffee and sit in the kitchen instead of out here."

Elinor followed Kat's ample frame to the little room they called the kitchen. Silently they each poured a cup of coffee and sat down at the little table. Kat was obviously agitated.

"I'm sorry, but we had a reorganization meeting yesterday, and we are hiring an office manager who will free me of all of the office work, so I will have more time to spend working with the patients. Unfortunately, this means we won't need a part-time person anymore," Kat said hurriedly as she massaged her coffee cup.

"Right out of the blue you all decide to hire an office manager! Aren't you really just telling me I'm fired?" Elinor said as she felt her anger rising.

"We do not consider it as firing because you have been here only one short week. You were classed as temporary part-time help on probation anyway. We simply have no more work hours available," Kat carefully articulated as sweat beaded up on her forehead.

"You can't just shove me out the door. I will sue for compensation. You haven't even acknowledged that I was brutally raped by my employer, and that is sexual harassment at its worst," Elinor hissed in reply.

"Elinor, I don't want to inflict anymore pain on you. There has been a change in the office, and that is the issue, not your relationship to … Dr. Pace," Kat rationalized.

"I don't believe you!" Elinor snarled.

"Would you like to talk to Dr. Carpenter? He has generously made himself available to talk to you," Kat offered self-righteously.

"How nice of him. Yes, I will have a few words with him," Elinor defensively answered.

Elinor stood up brusquely, turned, and marched in the direction of Dr. Carpenter's office. Pausing a moment at his door to gather her thoughts, she knocked before she could lose her nerve.

The door opened almost immediately. In a slightly unkempt suit with a flowered-pattern tie, George Carpenter stood in the doorway. "Come in, Elinor. I think you will be most comfortable in this chair," he said as he directed her to the stuffed leather chair.

Perching herself on the edge of the chair as if at any moment she would run for the door, she blurted out, "I think I am being unjustly fired."

"Now, now, Elinor. You are a very skilled employee and we are going to miss you, but there is no position available anymore because we are getting an office manager. You are very compassionate with the patients, and you are going to be a fine nurse. We simply have been thinking for several weeks about how we can run this office more efficiently. The office manager has lots of very good ideas to make this clinic run efficiently, and she is starting on Monday. She was considered before you had your unfortunate incident. I'm sorry you were hired during this decision-making process."

Is he telling me that Pace hired me with sex on his mind and not for a business reason? Elinor thought. The ideas poured in like a torrent, churning like a tornado in her head. She took her time in answering him. "It may have been a mistake to hire me, but I was legally hired. Then I was sexually harassed and assaulted. Now you are telling me that hiring me was not part of the plan. My job doesn't exist anymore? You are forcing me into suing this office for compensation. Don't you see that my rights have been violated?"

"I don't think histrionics will get you what you want. If you sue, the attorneys will make loads, and you will feel all the more violated. Dr. Pace's attorney will explore your sexual history with a fine-toothed comb, and they will use any indiscretion against you. You will find it difficult to get a job in medicine again. I am trying to find a peaceful and sane way to resolve this problem so you will get the best outcome. I will recommend you to other offices. You will get the first opening available. I am making this my personal project. It causes me a great deal of pain to see you mauled by the system. This is the best way, believe me."

A solemn pall hung over Elinor. With sadness, she realized that this was not a problem she could solve with this otherwise kind man. *It would be better to agree on the surface and to resolve the problem another way.* "Okay, I will accept your help," she said, rising to leave.

"Thank you, Elinor. It has been a pleasure working with you. I will talk to Allen about giving you some compensation also. You will have enough to get you through school comfortably."

So, they are going to buy me off, she thought. Her face flushed with anger. Hurriedly she closed Carpenter's office door behind her. The ideas tumbled through her brain. Blinking back the tears, she ran and retrieved her backpack and purse. To exit, she had to walk through the waiting room that was now filled with patients. Guilt, anger, and shame filled her whole being, and walking past innocent patients made her feel the sting all the more.

It was such a relief to reach the street at last. Blinded by her roving thoughts, lost in the turmoil of her mind, she wandered along the street. She was oblivious to the large car that drove up beside her and startled her with the horn. Spontaneously, she started to run in fear that it was Gary again.

"Elinor, wait. It's me, Annette!"

"Thank God! I need to talk to someone."

The car's soft leather bucket seat engulfed Elinor as she sank into it. It didn't matter where they were going or what they were to talk about; her mind was too upset to handle any more.

"This isn't very polite to say, but, Elinor, you look like you've had an awful morning. If you have an open few hours, let's go to my house and have a nice talk," Annette said gently.

"Whatever. Yes, that sounds like the right thing to do. Where do you live?" Elinor said weakly.

"Just on the other side of the city. I think you will like something I have to show you," Annette said, trying to arouse some interest in Elinor.

Numbly, Elinor watched the scenery go by. It was starting to rain again. The warm, dry automobile felt sheltering and comforting. Gradually Elinor's mind began to function again. "What brought you so close to the cardiology clinic?"

"I was meeting with my accountant, whose office is very close by, and I just happened to come along as you came out of the clinic. What happened when you went to work today?"

"They fired me. I really need to talk to an attorney about this. It is getting rather complicated," Elinor blurted out.

"I don't understand," Annette said with a recently acquired innocent facade.

"Oh, they say they are hiring an office manager and they just don't need me, but I don't believe them."

"Actually, I've been trying to convince Allen that the business would run more efficiently with an office manager. It is possible that they started taking my advice. However, I think they should adequately compensate you for your pain and grief, but you don't need to hire an expensive lawyer to force the issue."

"But I feel I'm being bought off. Like, I'm being forced to take a bribe to shut up or being paid like a prostitute. Then I think about all the other women who are sexually harassed, and if somebody doesn't fight back, the system will never change."

"Elinor, you won't get anywhere by martyring yourself. Allen will hire the hottest lawyer in the business, and you won't have the money to hire anything more than a mediocre representative. You will get your reputation dragged through hell, and you will emerge an impoverished pariah whom no one will hire. Is that going to make you feel better?"

I can't think straight now, Elly thought. She said in a small voice, "Annette, I know where you are coming from, and your argument is logical. I just need time to think it through and digest it all."

To Elinor's relief, they turned into a driveway that led to a gorgeous Tudor-style house. Wonderful; she could change the subject. "Your house is very nice. I'm glad you brought me here."

"It isn't at its best this time of the year, but it is warm and dry. I think you will like it."

The door yawned wide open into a grand entranceway. Elinor felt she had shrunk in size suddenly. The high-vaulted ceilings intensified the overwhelming effect. "This house reminds me of the castles I used to read about in fairy tales," Elinor exclaimed.

"Yes, this entryway sold the house the first time I saw it. I want to show you something in the kitchen, and then I'll give you a tour of the house."

With unabashed awe, Elinor's eyes scanned all the beauty she saw. When she and Annette entered the large kitchen, she could not contain herself anymore. "Wow, a stove with six burners and a barbeque!"

"We used to give big parties, and I will again. I used to be a professional chef." Annette was reveling in Elinor's joy.

On the dinette table lay a large old album. "This is what I wanted to show you." Carefully Annette turned the pages and then stopped. "Look. This is when you were about three."

"It is astonishing that we should meet after all these years," Elinor said, her voice filled with respect.

Page after page was filled with photos of two little girls, one with dark hair and one a blonde.

"I worshipped you then. You were my heroine. These were taken at my, or rather our, grandfather's summer home one magical year," Annette said dreamily to Elinor.

"Was that the only summer? I thought there were others."

"Oh, there were, but not many pictures survive. Our other encounters were briefer. Unfortunately, my mother, who was a tyrant, did not want you around. Our grandfather Longacre was more compassionate. He knew your mother and liked her better than Grace, who was my mother. I think he engineered secret meetings for you and me. Then when you were five, your mother married and you all moved away."

"Annette, I had even forgotten your name. It was so good of you to remember me and then recognize me when we have both have changed so much. Do you have any other brothers or sisters?" Elinor asked.

"No, do you?"

Elinor shook her head no and, with a great feeling of need, reached out for Annette's hand. "Thank you for sharing all this with me. Your timing was perfect."

"Don't worry about Allen. Justice will be served, and we will work together. Do you have someone in your life?" Annette inquired.

"Well, it is a long story, but I have a very close friend with the San Francisco Police Department."

"Anyone I've encountered? What is his name?" Annette persisted.

"Todd Markam. He is a detective. Why do you ask?"

"Well, the thought occurred to me that you could come and share this huge empty house with me and we would both be better off, but if you have a lover, that might be difficult."

"That is an interesting suggestion. Todd and I are not lovers. We are just good friends." Elinor was feeling uneasy.

Annette was sensitive to Elinor's discomfort and decided to try another topic. "Let me take you on a house tour."

***

Several hours later, Elly was panting as she frantically ran up the hill, feeling the strain in her legs and the heaving of her chest, aching to rest. It was raining harder, and although her exercise suit shed streams of water, her feet were soaking. Each step squished musically. Running was a great way to clear the mind and think logically, and she needed that right now. There were so many difficulties to process, and they could change her life one way or the other. *The rape and loss of employment suit gnaws like a beast at my soul. I have a palpable hatred of Allen Pace. Is Todd offering me romance, and if so, can I handle it? I have a need to depend on someone and a nagging feeling of distrust of Annette that makes me insecure.*

The sun had set hours before Elinor had started her run. The streets took on the magical glow of the Christmas season with a spectrum of lights reflected in the puddles. Rain seemed to flow like sheets of glass as the streetlights caught the liquid panels of a rainbow of glittering fabric. Elinor loved the city lights at this time of the year.

Carefully, she crossed Van Ness Avenue and continued up Sacramento Street. The tree-lined street offered a different feeling. The lights were dimmer and spookier. Lafayette Park loomed up in the rain like a jungle full of danger, and she hurried past it. It made Elinor kick harder and drive her feet home.

It was almost seven by the time Elinor reached her apartment. Panting, she retrieved her key and opened the door. To her relief, everything was safe. All day there had been a scolding fear that Gary would break in. She should have called Todd and told him about the unwelcome meeting with Gary this morning, but she didn't want to be a pest by always calling with problems.

Todd would be picking her up in a half hour. She should have allowed more time. Quickly she showered and carefully made up her face. The new dress shimmered in its delicate simplicity. She critically surveyed her image in the mirror. The colorful garment lit up her face in a romantic way, and this cheered her up. She was ready by the time the doorbell rang.

***

It was as if the rain had washed people and cars off the street. A lone truck drove into the parking lot of the cardiology clinic. A burly form without rain gear plunged from the truck to the protective cover of the awning at the clinic. A few lights were on inside. Gary looked up and down the street. There wasn't even a stray dog in sight.

He banged on the door of the clinic several times with no response. "Damn, that fucker better not bug out on me!" Gary growled at the door. Working on the lock, he couldn't see a way to open it. "Shit," he exclaimed. Mulling over his options, he decided to leave.

Suddenly a security car pulled into the parking lot and shined a spotlight on Gary. To defend himself, he drew his jacket over his face and stood still. Blaring through the rain, an amplified voice called out, "State your business."

"I had an appointment with Dr. Pace, but he doesn't seem to be here. I'm going home now," Gary yelled out. Carefully he edged out into the rain and then ran to his truck.

The security vehicle lowered its lights while Gary was opening his truck door. Then it focused the beam on the door to see if there was any damage visible. None was evident.

Gary slowly got into his truck and started the engine. The security car waited until Gary had driven out of the parking lot and down the street before it continued on its rounds.

***

In the concert hall, a roar of applause rang through the building as the lights came up. Todd and Elinor stood up and clapped as hard and as enthusiastically as possible to show their appreciation, as did many of the other concertgoers.

"Didn't that last movement send you to heaven?" Elinor exclaimed as the applause died down and the attendees started to file out for the intermission.

Todd gently nuzzled Elinor's neck as they slowly edged their way down the narrow aisle of seats. "It sure did, especially because I am here with you," he whispered in her ear.

Elinor turned to smile at him. "Let's get something to drink. I'm awfully thirsty. They generally have refreshments in the lobby," she suggested.

While they inched their way through the throng, Elly idly scanned the crowd to see if there was anyone she knew. Quite by accident, a familiar form caught her eye.

"Todd, look! Over in the far right aisle. There is someone who is tall in a green dress, and she has a head of hair like Gina's!"

Carefully he followed Elinor's gaze. "You must be thinking of the description that woman in Amador County gave us." Todd took time to watch the movements of the suspect. "Let's go and introduce ourselves to this mysterious woman," he whispered conspiratorially to Elly.

Her smile blazed up at him as she nodded her consent.

Packed into the large lobby, people were everywhere. Elinor worked her way around the periphery, trying to keep the mass of strawberry blonde hair in view. Todd, who was larger, was having more difficulty politely maneuvering through the clutches of concertgoers. He was trying to keep both Elinor and the questionable person in view.

The first to get close to the person in the green dress was Elinor. The strange individual had her back to Elinor. First Elly turned to see how close Todd was, and when she realized he was near, she reached up and tapped the woman on the shoulder, saying, "Excuse me, don't I know you?"

Reeling around, the person gasped loudly when she saw Elinor, and she plunged through the assembly in an effort to escape. Elinor was in close pursuit. "Stop!" Elly called. All the faces turned to Elinor and then made room for her to pass.

Struggling with the high heels, Mark was terror-stricken. He made it to the stairs. Leaning on a baluster, he removed the shoes and dropped them. Swinging down the staircase, taking three steps at a time, he almost got to the street before Todd was halfway down the stairs and commanded him to stop. Mark could not look up as he dove through the exit door to the street and ran as if the dogs of hell were at his heels.

When Todd reached the street, the woman in green had vanished. Elinor was close behind him, holding the discarded shoes. "I'm positive that was Mark Jacobs," she said, offering the shoes to Todd.

"You're right. Those shoes look too big for the average woman. Let's find the manager's office, and I'll call to have him picked up."

***

In a panic, Mark ran in circles, trying to find where he had parked his car. Taking cover in a doorway, he surveyed the environment for pursuers, but no one seemed to be following him. With his panic subsiding, his mind was clearing, but he seemed not to remember on which block he had left the car. Then he saw a red neon sign. Vaguely he recalled the car was near a sign like that one. Parking in the rain had disoriented him, and now that the weather was better, Mark had lost his way. The car was patiently waiting on a dark street. He scrambled to get into the safety of his car, lock it, and think through all that was on his mind. "That malicious, snoopy Elinor! She spoiled a good concert. I was enjoying it," he mumbled to himself. "Possibly she didn't recognize me. I should have just ignored her." He sighed. "Someone was bound to recognize me someday. I just didn't need it tonight."

Cautiously he moved his car out onto the street and headed for the Golden Gate. All was going well until he turned west on Lombard. Unexpectedly, flashing red and white lights glared in his rearview mirror. He managed to pull over before the siren started.

"What seems to be the problem, Officer?" he asked in his normal voice.

The young officer shined his flashlight into Mark's pale face and announced, "I need to see your driver's license and car registration."

*

"Well, I must say that was the best concert I've ever been to. Thank you for the exciting evening," Todd said merrily as he backed his car out of the tight parking spot.

"I'm so glad you liked the concert. It was perfect, and it was exciting seeing Mark all dressed up like that. Are you going to confiscate his clothes for evidence when they bring him in for questioning?"

"Yes. They probably have him singing right now. This puts a whole new light on Gina's case. I'm going to get the ball rolling early tomorrow. We need to show Mark's picture to Mrs. Stevens. My mind is mush tonight. It must be the beautiful music or the lovely company. I think it is the latter. Where would my gorgeous companion like to go for a very late dinner?"

"I have some nice salad fixings and cold cuts from the deli at my apartment. Would you like to dine at Chez Elinor?

"Hmm, it sounds delicious. And I know the way."

The traffic was reasonable after they got away from the civic center. Shortly, they were pulling up at Elinor's apartment.

"I'm so glad you are with me. After my run-in with Gary this morning, I find I am constantly looking over my shoulder. He really worries me."

As they ascended the stairs to Elinor's apartment, Todd advised her, "Don't open your door until you are sure it is someone you can safely let in. And call me as soon as you hear from him tomorrow. Don't you have plans for a visit with your boys this weekend?"

As they entered the apartment, Elinor told him of her plans. "I'm glad the weather is clearing. I think we will go hiking around the Presidio and have lunch at Fisherman's Wharf. My boys like the sea lions that like to sunbathe there."

Choosing an apron to protect her precious dress, Elinor's domestic image was not lost on Todd. "Can I help you with anything?" he offered.

"Just make yourself comfortable, and I'll serve the food out there, where we can sit on the couch," she advised as she gathered up the ingredients for sandwiches and salads from the refrigerator.

"Would you be available to come with the boys and me tomorrow? They really seemed to like you, and I would certainly appreciate your company too," she suggested as the late night supper was served.

His smile was generous. "You know I would love to come with you and your kids, but duty calls. The boss took everyone off Gina's case except Jim and me, so the responsibility is really on our backs. I am truly sorry."

"Will you go up to Amador County with the picture of Mark in strawberry blonde curls?" she inquired.

"Yes." He sighed. "Someone has to do it, but I'll weasel out of it. Fax machines are wonderful, you know."

They finished eating and talked on. Todd moved closer to Elinor and put his arm around her. The closeness of her warm body and the sweet smell of her hair were intoxicating. He turned her smoothly to face him. In slow motion he kissed her ever so lightly on her lips. He felt her shiver and instinctively draw her closer to him while he nuzzled and kissed her neck. "Would you let me make love to you sometime?" he whispered as he nibbled on her ear.

She relaxed in his embrace and didn't answer immediately. "Just hold me and kiss me. It feels so wonderful. I feel so safe in your arms. I don't want you to let me go."

The beeper in his pocket suddenly sprang to life. "This beeper has the worst timing," he apologized as he removed it so he could read it. "I need to call in."

Slowly he got up as if his heart wasn't in it. Dialing the number, he waited for the response. "This is Markam ... What time did they find him? ... I see. Have you called Jim Collins? ... Sure, I will be there in about fifteen minutes ... You're welcome."

Wearily, he quietly placed the receiver back on the cradle. He walked back to the couch and sat down heavily. "I would love to go on holding you all night long, but unfortunately someone found a body, and they need me."

CHAPTER 14

G arishly lit by police floodlights, the cardiology clinic looked menacing in the early hours. Todd pulled into the parking lot crowded with official vehicles. It was 00:32 as he glanced at his watch and wearily he extricated himself from his car.

Scanning the building to take in the whole picture, he approached the front door. Inside, the waiting room was filled with equipment and police staff busily working at gathering evidence and securing the area with yellow tape. Slumped in a chair was a middle-aged, gray-haired, brown-skinned man holding his baseball cap in his hands. A staff policeman was interviewing him. Todd stopped and was introduced to Mr. Lopez. The officer explained that he was the person who had called 9-1-1 when he found the body. After he had properly acknowledged the man, Todd continued down the hall toward the action.

The once elegant office was smeared with blood. "We seem to be coming to this office too often," Todd announced as he nodded his head to Jim Collins.

Jim looked up and smiled grimly. "I hope this is the last time. By the way, did you meet the janitor who found the body?"

"Yeah. I said the usual and came directly here."

At his feet lay the gray-faced corpse of Allen Pace. He was half on his side, his face in a pool of blood. As Todd walked around him, he saw that the legs were tangled in the chair legs in an awkward way. Todd sighed. "Is the coroner on his way?"

"Edwards is coming. He should be here within the hour."

Quietly the two compared notes and discussed strategies. They waited to turn the body as the coroner liked to have the body untouched.

"We contacted the security people who handle this office, and there is an interesting entry. It seems someone of Gary Williams's description was here around 19:00. He was observed banging on the door at that time. It will be interesting to see what Tim Edwards comes up with for a time of death," Jim offered.

"Well, well, what do we have here?" said a deep voice at the door.

Jim and Todd both exchanged pleasantries with Tim Edwards, the affable coroner. He was clothed in a black suit that looked like it barely fit him. Edwards shuffled his ample body through the doorway and looked officiously at the body.

Quietly, he went about his duties. Carefully the gloved hands rolled the corpse over so that the blank, glazed eyes stared up at them. "Hmm, I would say this fellow got a nasty blow to the right side of his head here first," he said, pointing to a red and blue gash on the right side of Allen's forehead. "He might have been stunned by that assault, enough to make him fall out of the chair. What really killed him, however, was this slash on his neck," he announced. Then he opened his bag and brought out his forceps to help him investigate the wound better. "This is interesting. The wound was probably executed with a very sharp instrument like a scalpel. And then when in position, the assailant twisted the sharp point, causing all this laceration and bleeding."

"That laceration on his neck is also on the right side, so wouldn't he have to have been still upright when it happened?" Todd asserted.

"I think you have a point there. It seems quite obvious now that you mention it, but when I open up this wound fully, I see it started on the left and was brought around to the right. The assailant was right-handed or at least held the weapon in his or her right hand. It is a powerful gash, but within the abilities of a woman," Tim said as he looked at the floor around the body. "Here are tufts of his hair. The victim's head was pulled back by his hair, and his neck was sliced open while he was in a seated position."

"Do you think the murderer pushed him over then?" Jim asked.

"That is possible. Maybe this person went through his pockets," Tim added as he looked over the clothes on the body. "This pocket has some blood on it."

Jim and Todd looked at each other quizzically. They watched attentively as the coroner inspected the pocket in question. Tim Edwards cleaned out the pockets. There were keys and a wallet that contained $600. "Well, it is my guess we can rule out robbery," Tim announced.

A large solid bronze statue of a horse was lying on the floor behind the body, and it also had tufts of hair on it. It was taken as evidence.

"Let's have the place searched for the weapon and also any used gloves. Looking at the smear marks, I think the killer covered the trail. Carefully inspect the sinks too. It is my guess our visitor washed up. I want an inventory of everything in this room." Todd reeled off his orders mechanically. "Don't forget fingerprints."

With care, Todd stooped and inspected the carpet. He added, "Take as many blood samples as possible. Maybe our murderer cut himself accidentally while he worked."

Jim collected Todd's notes and added a few of his own. Together they emerged from the death scene, both deep in thought. The time had flown by. The janitor had been released, and most of the outer office rooms had been thoroughly mapped and photographed with the evidence gathered.

As the detectives entered the foyer, some officers were wheeling in a gurney to remove the body. Outside, the signs were in place. The cardiology clinic would not open its doors today.

***

Mendocino County is on the Pacific coast and is a favorite weekend retreat for San Francisco professionals looking for a place to relax and forget their troubles. It was the middle of the night, at one of the cabins. Snuggled in bed, most people were asleep.

Galloping hooves gamboled through a meadow with sheer excitement on a warm and misty summer day. In her slumber, Clair clung to her mount with all her strength, but she could feel herself slipping. The dream image was shattered by an earth tremor. In a flash the horses turned back into overworked pillows, and Clair realized the vibration source.

"Hon-ney, wake up. Your beeper is going crazy!" she said, barely disguising her annoyance.

There was a scramble for the light. "Wha-at? Where is the damned thing?" Darrell exclaimed.

In the blue light shining through the skylight, he turned to see Clair sitting up beside him and holding something in her hand.

"Sweetie, you're disoriented. Here it is. It must have fallen into the bed when it went off. It's the hospital's number," she said, reading the numbers that glowed in the dark.

Wearily, Darrell turned on the light and dialed the number. Several minutes passed as the exchange routed the call. Clair snuggled down in the covers to listen to the raindrops galloping across the roof.

"George Carpenter." The voice came through the phone like the whine of a distressed dog.

"What's up?"

"Oh God, I'm sorry to disturb you in the middle of the night ... He's dead! Allen is dead!" George blurted out in a half-whispered growl. Before Darrell could respond, George rambled on about the police and how they wanted to interrogate everyone. "We must protect Annette! Isn't she up there in Mendocino with you?"

"Yes, and we will do our best," Darrel mumbled when he had a chance. He finally signed off.

He hung up the phone with a heavy hand and flipped off the light. The chilling, numbing cold crept over him, forcing him back under the covers. In the dark with his eyes wide open, he was staring at the void.

Clair awoke several hours later and was surprised to find her husband still beside her. "I thought my knight in shining armor was needed back at the hospital," she said with a yawn. "What was that call about?"

"That, my dear, was opportunity calling!" Darrell said with a satisfied look on his face. "The king is dead!"

Curiosity drew Clair over to Darrell's side of the king-sized bed. With her face filled with an impish grin, she said, "Whatever do you mean, you old tease? You look so strange."

"Allen is dead, and that means I am top dog in cardiology. I am certainly going to make the most of it."

Clair could not hide her surprise. "You can't mean it. Allen Pace, dead?"

"Murdered in his office at the clinic with some sharp instrument," Darrell said in a lifeless monotone.

Grimacing in distaste, Clair turned from him as if he held the body in his lap. "And I get stuck with telling Annette," she said in a deep howl.

"We can't let her withdraw her support from the clinic. The cops want to question her. Protection is what she needs. The press will hound her, and we need to see to it that they don't cause her too much pain and grief," he pleaded.

"Okay, what do you want me to do?"

He was having trouble suppressing his ambitiousness, so he wanted to keep it simple. "I need you to break the news to her and sympathize with her. You are far better at that than I am."

***

Elly couldn't sleep. She sat upright in her bed reading up on her legal problems when she should have been studying. She noticed that it was getting later in the morning.

"Between 40 percent and 65 percent of female workers claim to have experienced sexual harassment on the job, and less than 5 percent file complaints," Elly read. She had a book from the library she had borrowed to read about litigation. "In addition, it can take years and hundreds of dollars in legal fees."

"I am beginning to realize Dr. Carpenter has a good plan if he can get Allen to agree," she said out loud. "I should be compensated for losing my job on top of being raped," she announced to the wallpaper as she threw the book aside. "It is ironic that there is more protection for dogs and cats than for women!" she grumbled to herself.

Anger and remorse had given her a fitful night's sleep, and this book was not dispelling her feelings. *Aren't doctors supposed to be compassionate? How can they be so unfeeling and cruel?*

Depressed and frustrated, Elly once again tried to direct her energies toward studying. Several textbooks were scattered over the rumpled bed. Listlessly she turned the pages, but the turmoil of the last several days was not going to let the knowledge flow.

"I can't keep dwelling on this mess. It is going to drive me crazy!" she said out loud. "I wish Todd was here. I am so lonely." With this thought in mind, she recalled the night before and worried that she had not given Todd enough loving support. "I didn't tell him how much I want him to make love to me," she sobbed.

As if on cue, the phone rang. Elly rushed to pick up the receiver and caught it on the second ring. "Oh, I'm so glad you called."

"Mom? Are you okay?"

"David, you are really up early." There was a hint of disappointment in her voice.

"We have a movie we want to see. Could we go to a matinee?" David pleaded.

Elly was happy to hear from her son, and it was a reality check on what was really important in her life. She spoke without enthusiasm, "I had plans to go for a hike, and you saw a movie last time, but if you would rather see a sci-fi movie again, let's do it."

The emptiness that came crashing in when she lowered the receiver was palpable. Suddenly, she realized that what was really important was being grateful to have the opportunity to see her kids, even if she had to see another sci-fi movie. She was sorry that she hadn't expressed much interest when she was on the phone.

***

That same morning across town at the police station, the morning review of cases was in progress.

"Is there a connection between Gina Williams's death and Allen Pace's murder?" asked a young officer at the morning conference.

Todd couldn't help smiling at the officer's question. "That is a very valid assumption to make. I want you all to take photos of Mark

Jacobs with and without drag as you make your rounds today. We also have a warrant out for Gary Williams's arrest."

The lines of exhaustion creased his brow as Todd continued to brief the morning staff assigned to the Pace murder. A wave of relief washed over him as Jim brought the meeting to a close with some inspirational remarks.

Walking back to his office to collect his jacket, he glanced at his watch to see if it was late enough to call Elly. Jim walked silently beside him.

"When we have Elinor come in for questioning, I think that Maria and I should interrogate her," Jim advised.

The words cut through Todd like fire, but he didn't want Jim to know he was uncomfortable with the whole business of Elly being subjected to an investigation. "Fine. I want to see what Edwards comes up with for a time of death, and I want to see more justification for your questions first."

Jim eyed his friend and gently patted Todd's shoulder. "I will respect your feelings, but you know she has the best motive we know of, and we cannot justify ignoring her as a suspect."

"I'm going to call her now. I'll tell her you will be in touch," Todd said with a sigh as he reached for the office door. "And then I'm going to get some much-deserved sleep."

***

Annette and Clair walked along the cliffs of Mendocino. Annette was pensive and remote as if she were mesmerized by the ocean pounding the coast. The gray-blue waves rose up with the fury to conquer, their flags of foam flying in the wind. Then down they came, curling their foam under while crashing on the boulders. The storm had lost its will to continue, and only the sea was clinging to the memory of the night's deluge and persisted in pounding the coast.

Annette's eyes caught every wave. She was mesmerized by the power of the never-ending assault on the rocks. "You know, there is something very reassuring about the ocean. Its ebb and flow seems eternal. It is one thing in my life that has never failed to entertain me. I think it symbolizes God for me. Never ending, never changing, yet always different. Strong enough to destroy, but when you run it through your fingers, it is soft and difficult to hold.

"It sucks out my emotions. I always feel cleansed by watching the waves. They are like me this morning, angry and a little sad. The gulls say it so well when they dip and swoon and screech their obscenities at each other."

Clair let Annette ramble on. She only spoke when asked a question, and that wasn't often. An hour had slipped by as they walked the cliffs of Mendocino. Weathered by many storms, the two-story house they had left behind seemed to melt into the scenery.

"I can't seem to see it," Annette was saying.

"I'm sorry. I must've not heard you right. Do you mean the house? It's over there shrouded by cypress trees," Clair offered.

"No, I don't mean the house! My future is what I can't see. Where am I to go from here?" Annette pleaded.

"You could travel. Go back to Paris in the spring. Haven't you told me that your life was the most idyllic when you lived near the Sorbonne?"

"Travel, alone?" Annette retorted.

"There must be lots of people who would love to go with you. I wouldn't worry about that now. Just look at all the opportunities. Let's go back to the house and have some breakfast and talk with Darrel. He always has lots of wonderful ideas," Clair said in her best cheerleader style.

Bright streaks of sunlight were just beginning to challenge the clouds. The freshly washed soil released puffs of vapor as the warm sunlight touched the hillside.

"It's really amazing how beautiful it is today. Terrible human tragedies have taken place, and yet the world doesn't miss a beat. I guess I saw too many movies when I was young. In a movie when there was drama and mayhem, the sky would break with thunder and lightning. How different this peaceful scene is by comparison. Speaking of reality, what do you think Darrel and George want to do with the cardiology clinic now that Allen is out of the picture?" Annette asked.

This abrupt change of conversation startled Clair out of her own reverie. "Gosh, I would think they would vote to continue business as is. Allen's death certainly leaves a gap that needs to be filled. I have heard that there are several young cardiologists who would be willing to buy into the clinic," Clair answered.

"You realize that in order to keep my investment in the clinic, I need to see real assurances that I am, in fact, going to receive a competitive return on my money. Otherwise I will take my investment elsewhere."

They were nearing the house. Clair welcomed the opportunity to get Darrel involved in this conversation. Annette was no longer the grieving widow. She was ready to plunge ahead into the future.

As they neared the cabin, Clair realized that one more topic needed to be discussed. Handling the police was the ugliest of subjects to address. Time and stories would have to be matched to make them believable. The last thing any of them wanted was to arouse suspicions within their small group, as well as among the larger menace of the authorities. Clair racked her brain trying to think of a plan, but to her surprise, Annette broached the subject on her own.

"I suppose the police will want to burden us with questions," Annette mused out loud.

Clair turned to Annette and stopped her in her path. "Darrel and I want to spare you any unwanted intrusion. We can tell them that you are too distraught to talk to them or that Darrel is keeping you sedated or something," Clair said hurriedly.

"It is all right, Clair. I can handle it. At this point it doesn't seem very real to me. The fact that he is dead, I mean. The police can be difficult, but I don't think they will be unreasonable."

Shrugging her shoulders, Clair unlatched the lock on the cabin door. She could smell the freshly brewed coffee. Maybe Darrel could change Annette's mind.

***

In Tiburon at Mark's house, Mark was returning after a long night in a jail cell in San Francisco. He came home exhausted to find an unexpected guest.

Awaking with a start, Gary rolled over to see a very disheveled figure glowering down on him.

"How stupid of you to come here and take over my house!" Mark said in a fury.

"Don't give me your bucket of shit! Where have you been? I waited for you to show up all night," Gary retorted. His body ached from spending the night on Mark's lumpy sofa, which didn't help his disposition.

Mark swiftly turned and stomped into another part of the house while yelling, "I spent the night in a filthy jail, and I am in no mood to deal with you."

Growling with an unintelligible reply, Gary sat up, trying to clear his head and sort out the developments. In an almost reflexive act, he grabbed the remote control wand of the TV and turned it on. As he flipped through the channels, something caught his eye.

The news program blared forth, "Police are searching for witnesses to come forward who saw someone leaving the L&P Cardiology Clinic last evening." Blah, blah, blah, they went on.

Gary felt like kicking the TV into telling him more information. As if to irritate Gary, the anchors went on and on with trivia without exposing the guts of the case under investigation.

"Hey, Mark, did they put you in the slammer for this murder at the cardiology clinic?"

His question fell flat. Mark was showering and couldn't hear him. In his frustration, Gary paced the floor in front of the TV, trying to sort out his uneasy feelings.

In the main bathroom, Mark ran the shower at full tilt to drown out any noise and his persistent worries. He could not remember a time when he felt less in control of his life. Gary had never just barged into his house without an invitation. He had no money for him and needed a way to stall the inevitable confrontation that would arise over this mess. Besides, Gary could have murdered Allen, and he must be handled with care. On top of these problems, Annette would be expecting some show of solvency with a loan payment by tomorrow. Impossible. How could life be so full of strife? Spending the night in jail had enhanced Mark's anxiety and repugnance for the future.

The hot water turned cool and then cold, jarring Mark out of his fearful fantasies.

Listlessly, Mark scanned his wardrobe and settled for jeans and a blue work shirt. He wanted to wear something simple. The last impression he wanted to make on Gary was one of substance.

When Mark finally emerged from the back of the house, he held two cans of beer in his hands and offered one to Gary, who was stretched out on the sofa. Mark pulled up the only other piece of furniture, a hassock, and sat down to share a beer with his unwanted guest.

"That's right considerate of you, Mark. I was thirsty," Gary said as he watched Mark's every move. Seeing nothing extraordinary in Mark, Gary turned his attention back to the TV, but its lack of information did not respond to his immediate wishes.

"What do you know about this murder at the cardiology clinic?" Gary eventually asked.

"They held me all night because of that and asked me endless questions. I'm not very eager to talk about it," Mark replied, trying to arouse some sympathy.

"That isn't what I mean. *Who* died?"

"Oh, I am sorry, I thought you knew. It was Allen Pace."

They sipped their beers in silence, each lost in his own thoughts. Gary switched channels and sat staring at an old movie. He was mesmerized by the scenes on the tube as if it were the greatest show on earth. When a commercial came on, Gary took the initiative and asked, "Did you do it?"

"Do what? Why should I kill Allen?" Mark shouted in surprise. "What makes you think it was me?" he said in a calmer voice.

"Weren't you plugging Pace's old lady?" Gary taunted.

"We are or were lovers, but I was Allen's friend, too. Who have you been talking to?"

Gary ignored the question. Seeing he had Mark in a vulnerable position, he said with an evil smile, "I'm here to collect some money. Shall we change the subject to that?"

Mark got up to pace the floor and gaze out the window. Somehow he had to get Gary out of the house. The empty street beyond his driveway made Mark curious. "I don't see your truck out there. Where did you park it?"

"I had a friend drop me off. Don't you have some food in this dump? I'm hungry," Gary replied.

"The cops are probably looking for you, Gary, and they are most likely watching this place now."

"You can't scare me, you nerd," Gary sneered as he rose to go to the kitchen. "I'm not leaving here without my money!"

***

Later that evening, Todd called on Elly to take her out to dinner. An intimate restaurant was chosen. Todd felt awkward. The events of the night before hung on him like a cobweb, light in weight but irritating. Dating a suspect was unwelcome and was compromising him professionally, and he knew it. But, he had feelings for her that he could not resist.

Elly also felt the strain. She had promised herself that she was going to be romantic, flirtatious, and very feminine. Needing him had become paramount, and yet she knew he would show distance.

They were quiet through most of the dinner until the dessert arrived. The candle flame that decorated the table had shortened. Todd sat on one side, and Elly sat on the other side of the table. Their only conversation had been small talk all evening, and the specter of the dead Allen hung between them like an approaching hurricane.

Finally it was Elly who broached the forbidden subject. "Do you think a man or a woman is responsible for Allen's death?"

"It's too soon to say. Did they call you today for questioning?"

"Yes. My appointment is tomorrow at two. It frightens me. Will you be there?"

"I won't see you at all. I think that is best. Detective Collins is handling your interview. He will do all he can to make you comfortable. Just tell him every little fact and even your hunches. Did you write down everything that happened yesterday? You need to account for every minute after four until I picked you up at seven forty. When you were out running, did you see anyone you know, or visit an ATM, or buy something?"

She shook her head sadly and concentrated on her sorbet. Then she raised her head and looked at Todd in the face, peering into his large brown eyes. She searched for a look of suspicion, but he had a kind and trusting face—or was it her imagination?

There was a period of silence, broken only by the clink of silver on china. Elly restored her courage and tried again. "After your phone call this morning, I gave myself a big Dutch uncle talk. I came to the conclusion that with Allen dead, there wasn't any basis for my sexual harassment case, and psychologically I have to let that one go. It was a hollow victory without compensation, but I feel that if I continue to let that eat at me, I will be consumed by it."

Todd watched Elly with fascination. "You may still be able to sue his estate. Maybe you need to ask a lawyer about that. I'm willing to support you with that just as I was before." His voice was as soft and warm as hot mulled wine.

Elly's smile was radiant. Todd forgot his uneasiness and took her hand in his. "Last night at this time, I wanted so much to hold you all night. Could we pick up again where we left off?"

She couldn't help not squeezing his hand. "Yes. When you had to leave last night, I was terribly lonely." Her voice trailed off to silence.

Todd cupped her hand in his right hand. With his left hand, he stroked her hand to soothe her.

Elly searched for the right words and then just plunged in. "I want desperately to throw off the pain of that night with Allen. It is hard to be brave. Yet the fact that I can talk to you this way and that you listen says so much. Yes, I can and will trust you. Let's go back to my place," she proposed softly.

He welcomed the change in feelings and paid the bill.

CHAPTER 15

Sunday, December 4

I t was early morning in Elly's apartment, where she and Todd spent the night. Todd got up early and dressed for another day at work.

"Honey!" Todd tenderly whispered close to Elly's ear. Fully dressed, he crouched by the bed. "I have to go, beautiful." Her eyelids fluttered as he continued. "You look so peaceful. I'm sorry to arouse you, but I didn't want to sneak out without saying goodbye," he cooed while kissing her lips lightly.

A smile creased Elly's face. She reached up, wrapped her arms around his neck, and drew him closer. Her warmth and softness made him reconsider his exit, but he was already dressed.

"What time is it?" she sleepily asked.

"It's a little after five, and I've got a murder to solve."

Elly stiffened in his arms and drew away from him. "I'm so nervous about going down to the station today. Could you please have lunch with me and get me to my appointment on time?"

Gently he ruffled her hair and then kissed her open, welcoming mouth passionately. "I'll call you. We'll work something out." He felt his cock responding. "Thank you for a very nice night." He fought back his desire. "You make it so hard to leave."

"You are welcome to come back, you know." She was more awake now. "I'll walk you to the door," she said as she pushed him away and wriggled to swing her legs out of the bed.

He gave her space and helped her up into his arms, but he gave an audible sigh as Elly stretched her naked form fully against him. Folding his arms around her, he held her for several minutes and then whispered, "I would kiss you, but then I wouldn't leave at all."

Pressing her breasts closer to his chest and then withdrawing from him with a coquettish giggle, she teased, "You had better get out of here quick, before I drag you back into bed."

"You are going to catch pneumonia if you stand here like this. Tell me where your robe is, and I'll get it for you."

"It's on the hook," she said as she gracefully moved across the room. He could not take his eyes off her strong, lithe body. "You are so beautiful," he purred, and he dashed to head her off and help her with her robe. As he wrapped the garment around her, he again showered her with kisses on her neck and shoulders. "I'm wild about you."

Playfully she took his hand and caressed her breast with it. Her nipples were standing at attention. Then she took his head in her hands and kissed him, running her tongue over his lips and plunging it into his mouth. "Um, you taste so good." Then she slipped from his grasp and jogged from the room toward the front door.

Todd spontaneously chased after her, snatching at the slippery robe to restrain her, but the robe came off in his hands as Elly squealed with pleasure, wriggling to free herself.

The cool light from the windows fell across the soft shape of her body and excited him beyond his control. Embracing her, he suddenly scooped her up and carried her back to the bed.

She tore at his clothes as he covered her with passionate kisses. "I can't let you go just yet." She sighed as she encircled his primed body with her legs, drawing him to her in an erotic clasp.

"Don't worry, my pet. This is one murder that will have to wait," he cooed as he pulled the covers over them and snuggled down inside her.

***

In a house in Mendocino, Darrell and Clair were replacing the phone that they had removed to prevent unwanted calls.

Click! The wall phone slid back into place. Darrell stared at the object as if he thought it would come alive, but it was silent.

"Thank you for replacing the phone. I don't like playing games with the police. It could backfire so easily. Besides, why are we hiding from them?" Clair asked.

Darrell glared at Clair. "I'm just protecting Annette. There is no harm in not answering the phone for one day," he said, defending his actions. Then he took a lighter position. "I think it is a real luxury to get away from a nagging phone."

"So, what are you going to tell them when they do call?"

"I don't think that it is inappropriate to tell them that it is my professional opinion that Mrs. Pace needed some sedation and some peace and quiet to recover from her great shock. I can state that she was too fragile to have the phones ringing all the time, so I unplugged them."

Clair looked at him and said, "In my professional opinion, if we all have to lie, it will create an opportunity to make us come off sounding like we are trying to hide something. I just don't like it." Clair's eyes sparkled with indignation.

"Look, when they call, I will explain everything, and when we all have to face them on Monday, they will see a recovered Annette and they won't know the difference. As a result, they won't ask you or me or Annette any embarrassing questions about our weekend."

"Tell me something. Are you trying to make excuses for Annette because she isn't weeping and being hysterical over Allen's death? It sounds like a very Victorian concept to be protecting her from something she doesn't seem to think is very dreadful. I just don't think you are thinking straight."

Darrell looked at Clair quizzically and shrugged his shoulders. Then he walked into another room. Calling back to her, he said, "Let's all go out for breakfast this morning. Call me when Annette is ready."

***

"The only news I want to hear is that the Pace murderer is behind bars!" Todd teased Jim as he greeted him.

The seriousness went out of Jim Collins's face. "Wow, you are a changed man. I've never seen you so chipper. I hope the news I have for you won't alter your spirits too much."

"Sorry, I missed the briefing this morning. Is the case moving along okay?"

"You didn't miss much. I can catch you up on the important points in a few minutes, but you aren't going to necessarily like the direction of things."

Todd, lost in his own thoughts, hadn't heard him.

"Let me guess. You were out with Elinor last night, right?"

Todd tried to disguise the light in his eyes and to dampen the compulsion to burst into and ear-to-ear grin. He took his time answering, but the fact that he felt ten years younger was hard to hide. "I have never met a woman who set me so aflame. Finally, my dear dead wife can rest in peace." Todd shook his head as if trying to clear his thoughts. "It is hard to keep the perspective going. I know she is a suspect, and she has a motive, but I'm not going to let my feelings for her cloud my professionalism," he said in a quiet, controlled voice.

Jim felt the weight of the reports in front of him. He wanted to celebrate his friend's good fortune, but he needed to tell Todd some news about Elinor that he would find hard to be objective about. "Come on, let's get this over with. Pull up a chair and let's get started."

Todd drew up a chair and braced himself.

"First of all, the officers went up to Jackson to interview Mrs. Stevens. It was a Saturday, and we thought that was a good time to talk to her. They took up ten mug shots of individuals as per regulations. However, Pat, who does the artwork downstairs, made a set of photos that showed each of the individuals in drag to look like Gina. They also included a set of mug shots of Allen Pace and Mark Jacobs. It was interesting that with all these choices, Mrs. Stevens identified over and over again the face of Allen Pace!"

"Damn, that's a winner. A positive ID, huh?" Todd interjected.

"Yes, but what does that mean? Did Pace poison Gina and then someone decided to get rid of him?" Jim let that one sink in and then posed another conclusion. "Or did one murderer kill both of them? Think about those possibilities." Jim paused to shuffle through his papers.

"Did they find Gary Williams?" Todd asked.

"No. He seems to have dropped out of sight. When the officers went to his apartment, the neighbors said he hadn't been home for the last forty-eight hours."

"Let's check the list of carjackings that happened during the last two nights. Maybe Gary in a desperate state of mind junked his truck somewhere and stole another vehicle," Todd suggested.

"I'll take note of that. It's a good idea." Jim waited to see if Todd had any other thoughts on the matter before he continued. "Another person we haven't successfully spoken to is Mrs. Pace. It appears that she went up to Mendocino sometime on Friday with Dr. Minix and his wife, Clair. The Mendocino phone number was given to us by Dr. Carpenter, but they didn't answer the phone until a few minutes ago when I called. Dr. Minix was contacted. I got a song and dance about Mrs. Pace's grief and how Dr. Minix sedated her and unplugged the phone so she wouldn't be disturbed to give her a good rest. In his opinion, she won't be able to discuss anything with us until tomorrow. He also said that they were planning to return to San Francisco this afternoon sometime."

An hour passed as Todd and Jim discussed the various witnesses and forensics reports. "I've thought a lot about this particular report," Jim said. "I'm just going to let you read it and then get your judgment," he said as he pushed the papers toward Todd.

Todd read the report in silence. Jim watched his partner's expression turn from interest to anger. When he had finished reading it, he slammed it down on the desk, spitting out, "Who is this turkey anyway?"

"His name is there—he is Elinor's ex-husband, and he is willing to give us a deposition!"

***

Elly waited anxiously in her apartment. She was frantic with worry about the upcoming interview at the police station.

Studying pharmacology had lost its glamour, and physiology was no longer exciting either. The textbooks and notebooks were carelessly scattered about. Elly dreamily satby the window, waiting for Todd.

Why had he sounded so strange on the phone? She couldn't help but wonder if his police work was getting him down. Or was it something she had said? As the scenes of the last twenty-four hours flitted through her mind, her going over every moment, nothing seemed out of place. She had given as much as she had received, and Todd was very loving.

The tasty lunch had taken most of the morning to prepare. She had made an extra effort to please him. When thinking of him, her whole body warmed with the visions. Sweet Todd, he appreciated everything she did for him—a thrilling man to satisfy.

It was sheer delight to see him coming down the street. Breathlessly, Elly ran to the door in anticipation. "Oh, Todd, I missed you so," she burbled as she threw her arms around his neck and kissed him.

There was a definite change in him, he was stiff and it put Elly's response in an awkward position. He did not embrace her or kiss her back, and it made her feel clumsy. She asked, "What's wrong, sweetheart?"

Taking her firmly by the hand, he led her to the sofa. "I need to get something clear with you." His voice was hard as steel, and it cut her to the bone.

"I read a report about you this morning that was so repugnant and nauseating that I find it hard to tell you about it." Todd looked at her as if his eyes were dissecting her piece by piece, searching for something he had not seen before. "I had to call the person myself who gave the information. That person was your ex-husband!"

Elly was shattered. "He hates me," she retorted defiantly.

"He claims that you are a lesbian! He says that you left him for another woman!"

"Todd, do you believe that?! After spending the night with me, something we both enjoyed? I don't understand your anger." She cried.

"You could be manipulating me because you are afraid," he said as he grabbed Elinor by the shoulders and raised his voice. "Were you in love with my sister?"

Shaking with fury and sadness, Elly blurted out, "Yes!" She turned away from him, unable to bear his reaction. "But I was not ever trying to use you or control you," she said in a smaller voice.

Todd sat in grim silence, watching her every move. "Did you murder or assist in murdering Gina?" he said in a voice so low and ugly, Elly could scarcely believe her ears.

"No and *no*! How can you think of such a thing?" Her voice was fuming.

Shaking his head, he said, "I don't know what to think. Maybe you should tell me about this affair that your former husband was talking about." His voice was cold and distant.

"Well, thank you for finally wanting to hear my side." She huffed with indignation. "My dear former husband, the infamous Professor De Martini, was a physically abusive alcoholic, and for years he was having affairs with his students. He would bring them home to have me cook for them like I was the servant. I struggled to do the best for my sons, so I tried to keep the marriage going without love. Then I met an older woman whose name was Charlene. She was very kind to me, and we became good friends. Without her unconditional love, I would have been crazy. She urged me to be independent and strong, to follow my own star and to shine on my own. That is when I got interested in nursing.

"Charlene taught me thing about my body I never knew before. The beauty of our lovemaking was awesome, beyond comparison to anyone but *you*. It pains me to think that is repugnant to you! Charlene died of cancer over a year ago. She is a part of me, and I miss her spirit every day.

"My relationship with Gina was different. It had no sexual side to it. It was like the roles were reversed. I took Charlene's part and was attempting to teach Gina about life to help her heal with her experiences concerning Gary. The problem is, I failed. I blame myself for her death only in that I wanted to save her from drugs and those horrible men she fell for. I screwed up." Her voice petered out.

They sat on the sofa, each of them lost in their private thoughts. Then Todd turned to Elly and spoke. "Would you call yourself a bisexual then?" He sounded very sterile and legal.

"Why must you package and label me?" She was the angry one now. "How can you play with my heart and soul in the morning and by noon be cold and cunning? You certainly had me fooled. I thought there was something special about our relationship. Now what can I think? You and your macho friends think women are just for one thing, and after you have had your fun, you trash them with terrible name-calling."

She took a deep breath. Tears came to her eyes with sobs. "I look for love wherever I can find it. But the love I am looking for is sincere and loyal, someone I can … trust." Her lip was quivering, and her eyes spilled over with tears. "I'm sorry you are biased against something you don't think society approves of. I am who I am, and that is that. You can reject or accept me as I am." She covered her face to hide her weeping.

Todd could not stay still another moment. He got up to pace the room and look out the window. Then he turned toward Elly and said, "Look, I don't want to hurt you. I just need time to think this through. I've never met anyone quite like you. I won't be able to date you while we solve this case anyway. That comes from the rules I work under, not from me."

The words fell like cold stones on her heart. "Will you talk to me if I call you?" she asked sadly.

"Yes, of course. And I am sorry I am so conventional that I don't handle all this well. It is just that I don't want to lead you on when I'm not sure of myself." His voice softened to a whisper. He was amazed at his own confession.

His greatest urge was to hold Elly one more time, but he resisted and changed the subject. "What do you want to do about lunch? I need to get back to work."

"I've fixed lunch for us. You are still welcome, if you can stand to spend a few more minutes with me!" she blurted out with the hurt in her voice undisguised.

The food was delicious, but neither Todd nor Elinor did anything but pick at their food. Elly felt nauseated, but she related to the interrogation that she had to face soon.

They rode down to the precinct office together in silence. Todd let Elly off at the main entrance and drove alone to the parking area.

Passing through the foyer of the main building, Elly felt very alone in an alien environment. The cold brass chilled her at the door, when she read the sign that said Investigations. It made Elly feel helpless as she turned the knob slowly and walked in. At the desk, she mumbled her name and had to repeat it to have it understood. The clerk's mechanical manner did nothing to help relax her as she directed Elly to take a seat and wait to be called.

Sergeant Maria Fuentes approached Elly with an extended hand. "Thank you for being on time. Come with me, and I will find a quieter place for you to wait."

Following humbly a few paces behind, Elly was led to the interrogation area and was left in a small waiting room, alone with several magazines to keep her company. The minutes dragged like hours. The chair got hard and uncomfortable. None of the magazine articles caught her imagination or interest. When Maria finally returned, Elly was so bored that she was actually happy to see her.

After walking down a short hall, they entered another room that gave Elly a chill. It was sparsely decorated. A small table and a few straight-backed wooden chairs were the only objects in the sterile-looking room. Maria offered Elly one of the chairs and something to drink. Elly only wanted water. Maria left, and once again Elly was alone. Scanning the room, she noticed that there seemed to be a one-way mirror facing her. She guessed its purpose.

There were voices at the door. Maria and Detective Jim Collins entered. Maria offered Elinor a glass of water and asked, "Do you remember Detective Collins?"

Their chatting about banalities was supposed to relax her, but instead Elly felt they were being inane, and it made her a little hostile. She wished they would get to the point.

"To begin with, I would like to hear about the circumstances that led to your employment at the cardiology clinic."

"I don't know why you are asking me about that. Todd and I discussed that at length before I applied. I needed a job, and I wanted to know more about Allen Pace," Elly said in a quiet, controlled voice.

"Didn't you think that Pace was involved with Gina, and isn't that why you wanted to know him better?" Jim asked.

"Yes, I thought he killed her," Elly softly said, not daring to look Jim in the face.

"And did you get to know him? Did you like him?"

"He was a very knowledgeable as a doctor, but he treated women badly."

"After your rape, didn't you really hate him and want revenge?"

"I wanted justice. I had been wronged, and he was trying to make it look like it was my fault. All I wanted to do was ... I wanted compensation, and freedom from sexual harassment." Elly suddenly felt claustrophobic and short of breath.

"Tell us about your activities on Friday, December third, Elinor. The people at the cardiology clinic tell us you arrived about 12:15 that afternoon and talked to Dr. Carpenter."

"Yes, he basically told me I was fired and I would be a fool to sue them over my rape and loss of employment."

In the interrogation room, Jim continued to ask Elly uncomfortable questions. "I want to hear about all your activities that Friday. Tell me more."

"You ask me the same questions over and over. I don't have anything more to say. I have had a terrible day, and I have lots of studying to get done," Elly pleaded.

Jim sat back and looked at Elly carefully. Then on impulse he pushed a report toward her. "I would like you to read this and give me your side of it."

"I can't remember *more*," Elly wailed. "There isn't anything I can tell you. Please, I want to go home."

"It says here that someone saw a person with an umbrella leaving the cardiology clinic at 17:20."

"I don't know anything about it," she answered weakly. "I told you before that I was running up Geary Street at that time. I didn't have an umbrella that night. It is impossible to run with an open umbrella, and I don't know what more you want."

Rising up like a charging grizzly, Jim paused and caught himself. He straightened up and walked toward the door. "I'll be back!" he called over his shoulder.

Todd had been watching Jim. He rushed out to meet him in the hallway. "What do you make of her, Jim? She is acting very strangely."

"It's obvious she is either guilty or hiding something. I don't know which, and I don't know the right approach to get it out of her. It could have been that your prior conversation has got her defenses up," Jim confided.

"She is certainly a reluctant witness. Let's let her go and have her followed. I haven't cut off all contact with her. Maybe I can gain back her trust, but let me think about it first," Todd offered.

Maria came out of the room and joined in on the conference. "May I offer some observations?" The men gave her a lukewarm affirmative nod. "I think she is an intimidated and traumatized witness. We need to win her confidence again. Didn't she take a genuine interest in our investigation of Gina's death? She identified Mark Jacobs in drag and pursued him. And, gentlemen, may I remind you that she has lost a close friend and has been raped? And, Todd ... ah, er, I don't know what has been going on between you two, but there is something. And we won't get anywhere badgering her! Maybe we should ask for her help and see how she responds," Maria offered.

Straightening his body to his full height, Todd looked scornfully at Jim, and then with his guilt clothed in indignation, he addressed Maria. "I think you should talk to her, Maria. Use a buddy approach and offer to give her a lift home." With that he turned and walked briskly toward his office.

Jim admonished Maria with, "I don't think I was badgering her, Maria. Todd is right. You should take over. I want a typed report in the morning."

Before Maria returned to the room where Elly waited, she gathered up some folders at the main desk.

When she again saw Elly, she was prepared. "Detective Collins doesn't have any more questions this afternoon for you, Elly, so now you are free to go. By the way, I was wondering if you had been given any information on support groups for women who have been abused and raped. If not, I have some information here."

"You are very helpful, thank you. I need to talk to someone who understands and isn't judgmental. It's surprising how many people do not want to grasp the truly nasty events that occur in life, but I can't really blame them. Everyone has problems of one sort or another." Elly was rambling on incoherently.

Maria smiled warmly and sat down. "I would be happy to listen if you need to talk it out, but this setting is rather oppressive. May I suggest that I give you a ride home and we can talk along the way?"

On the way to Elly's apartment, most of the questions were asked by Elly, like, "Do you enjoy working with Todd?" and "What is he really like?" These questions amazed Maria.

"Jim and Todd coach little league games in their spare time. At Christmas, they gather toys for disadvantaged children. They are likable guys, and Jim is a family man with two daughters. They are edgy right now. The chief has put them under a lot of pressure to solve this crime quickly because of its high visibility. We need your help too because you know all the people involved," Maria responded.

Maria asked Elly, "You seem to be in wonderful physical shape. Is that because of your running?"

"I run to handle stress. If I study too long, it really tightens up my body, but if I get out to run every day or two, it loosens me up and I function better."

"Do you run the same course?"

"Not always. Variety is nice, but there is a comfort in familiar surroundings."

"Is Geary Street considered variety or familiar surroundings?"

"It isn't my favorite street to run on because of the heavy traffic," Elly said in a small voice.

"Then why were you out there on a rainy night?" Maria asked.

"It was a matter of convenience. I was downtown Christmas shopping."

"Surely you didn't plan to run while carrying packages, did you?"

"No, I was looking for something for Todd, and if I had found it, I would have taken a taxi, but I didn't, so I jogged back to my apartment."

"Well, we are here; it was nice talking to you. I hope you can get back to your studying without problems. May I suggest something?"

"Sure," Elly said as she opened the car door.

"Give Todd some time. He will come around."

***

Sea Cliff, nestled in a cove, seemed to be a place of refuge for Annette, who was coming home at last. The weekend had exhausted her, and she longed for a quiet night at home.

Her wish was not to be granted. While she was upstairs changing into a comfortable silk dressing gown, the doorbell rang. Annette took her time answering the door with the hope that the intruder would get discouraged and leave.

Mark stood in the doorway looking sheepish. "I tried my best to get those funds for you by today." He had a speech prepared to give in his defense, but the phone rang and interrupted him.

Annette intended to close the door on him, but he stuck his foot in the doorway and followed her into the kitchen. "While I am on the phone, you can start a fire. One match will do it." Having dismissed him, she turned to answer the annoying phone.

"How are you? I was so worried when I couldn't get you yesterday. I heard the tragic news about Allen." Elly was trying to sound sympathetic.

Shrilly laughing on her end of the phone, Annette couldn't help being cynical. "Tragic? Don't you really think he got what he deserved, Elinor? Who do you think you are fooling?" Annette challenged. "Aren't you overdoing the Pollyanna act?"

"I didn't want to be too presumptuous. What I called about is to ask if you would still consider my company. I would like to talk about this soon," Elly suggested.

"You sound distressed, Elinor. Surely you aren't mourning Allen. What is bothering you?"

"This whole mess is getting to me. I am finding it hard to study. The questioning is driving me up the walls. Nothing is going right."

"Are you still seeing your detective friend?" Annette rolled her eyes at her guest, who had returned to her side.

"No, that is the worst of it. I am certain that he thinks I am the murderer. Having a judgmental person around gets old really quickly. I do not want to see him anymore."

"He sounds like a clod. Yes, I would like to talk to you. Come and have dinner here about seven. Just wear your jeans. I need to fly. Bye."

"I wasn't aware that you *knew* her that well," Mark commented as he admired how well Annette's voluptuous body was revealed by the clinging silk dressing gown.

Annette smiled mischievously. "There is a lot you don't know, Mark. Do you always listen to other people's conversations?" She didn't wait for his reply but gilded regally into the living area with an air of power. "Let's get back to your problem."

Like a cur with his tail between his legs, Mark followed Annette with his excuses. "The banks weren't open this weekend. It wasn't possible to make a transaction. Please give me a chance to take care of it on Monday."

Catlike, Annette stretched herself out on the love seat and smiled at her prey with a grimace that lacked any sincere compassion. "Monday then. By the way, what do you know about Elinor?"

"She is just one of my students," Mark meekly said as he sat down delicately in a chair by the fire. "She was a friend and lab partner to Gina. Allen supposedly raped Elinor. All I know is from the newspapers."

"It was in all the papers, but they didn't designate the victim!" Annette shot back. "Did you date her?"

"No, she isn't my type. I only have eyes for you, sweetie."

"Incredulous! What about Gina and all the others? Never mind. Do you think Elinor could have killed Allen?"

"Ah, you are so clever. Yes, of course, and she could have killed Gina too."

"Thank you for your opinion. Now I think you should go."

CHAPTER 16

Monday, December 5

Few places made Todd feel uncomfortable. The morgue was one of them. Waiting patiently in the office for Tim Edwards, the coroner, Todd shuffled through the available periodicals, looking for one that was interesting. A hunting magazine caught his eye. Checking the time and seeing that it was plenty early, he sat down to read. Opening the cover, he encountered an advertisement. The lovely dark-haired model was selling something of no importance, but the woman reminded him of Elly. Instantly memories of her flooded his mind. He was so absorbed that he didn't hear Tim come in.

"That must be quite an article to have your rapt attention," Tim said.

Todd, blushing, jumped up, holding the magazine like a boy caught reading porn. "Yeah, it's a good magazine. It is nice of you to agree to meet at this hour. I was having trouble sleeping, and finally I just gave it up and decided to work."

Tim unlocked the door to the cold storage area, and they entered. "We have Dr. Pace right here," Tim announced as he opened a door and slid out a gurney with a body shrouded in a bag.

"What I'm interested in is the wound Pace received on his head that you said happened before the throat was slit."

"Yes, let me show you this again." As he spoke, he peeled back the plastic bag, opening it enough to show the head area. "Look here, it is about two inches long and about half an inch wide."

"How did you know it was done first?"

"It's obvious: it bled a lot. Wounds made while the heart is still beating will bleed like that. Also, you can see with an eye loupe that the blood was coagulating and forming a scab at the edges."

"Can you tell me how long before death this wound was inflicted?"

"You will have the full report on your desk today, but basically I determined that this wound was inflicted fifteen to twenty minutes before this individual died."

"So, it could have been inflicted by someone other than the murderer?" Todd mused to the body. "Thank you, Tim. And what time did you estimate as the time of death?"

"Between 17:00 and 20:00, I would estimate. Sorry I can't be more specific," Tim apologized.

"That's not a problem. One other subject interests me. Have you gotten the blood tests back on the samples we collected at the scene?"

"I think I can manage that. The information should be filed. I'll just put away the body. And if you would like to come to my office, I have the files there."

With almost loving care, Tim closed up the body bag and tucked the body back into the refrigerated drawer. Todd followed his rotund comrade into the place he affectionately called his office. In the basement there were no windows, and *small* was too big a term for this closet-sized area with floor-to-ceiling and wall-to-wall files and a shelf with a chair that served as the desk. Scientific cartoons littered every open space on the walls and even some of the file drawers. Exposed pipes ran in various directions across the ceiling. Tim retrieved a stepladder to get to one of the upper files and, after some maneuvering, produced the requested report.

"The victim's blood type was O-positive. Most of the samples were of that type. However, there was one that came up A-negative. The second blood type is not the most prevalent in our population. I ordered some extra tests on the sample that was A-negative. It will take at least a week to get that one back. So, don't jump the gun on arresting anyone."

"I'll see to it that we get blood samples from every suspect. In fact, we will get them on everyone associated with the cardiology clinic. Thanks again for coming in so early, Tim. I really appreciate it."

Todd was so excited about the information he now possessed that he climbed the stairs two at a time. He longed to share the information with someone, but it was far too early for anyone else to be at work.

In the solitude of his office, Todd reviewed his notes. *Could Elly have seen something so frightening that she has suppressed the information, or is she being evasive to cover herself? Am I in a position to gently get the information from her? Should I bring her in to interrogate her, or should I win her over and ask her questions in a less intimidating environment? I would find it hard to be so divisive as to woo her without really being sincere and honest with her.* Finally, after much deliberation, he decided to call her when he thought she would be awake and before she left for school.

***

The classroom was emptying, but Elinor was nowhere in sight. Todd stood impatiently, waiting. He had been expecting to talk to her all morning. When he couldn't get an answer after dialing her number, it puzzled him, but as the morning wore on, his mind thought anxiously about things that could have happened to her—and that was how he had come to be standing outside her classroom.

The university's administration office was at first reticent to give him her schedule of classes. He had to produce his badge, which was something he hadn't wanted to do. Was he really here on business, or was he here just because he loved her? The ambivalence made him uneasy. Denial of his personal needs and desires made him focus on business until it came to showing his badge. It was at that point he knew there was something more sensitive than usual about his search.

All the students were in white uniforms. Was it possible she had slipped by and he hadn't recognized her? Then he spotted her. She was in the middle of a clutch of those women in white who reminded him of fluttering doves, chirping to each other, chattering and laughing as if a murder had not happened. She saw him too, but at first she glanced away quickly as if he were a painful sight. It seemed like an eternity before she broke free from her friends and approached him.

"Hello. Are you following me?" She was serious.

He ignored the question and instead asked, "I was wondering if I could buy you lunch?"

"Let me talk to my friends, and I'll get back to you."

The chorus of nursing students became silent, turning to look him over as Elinor discussed his proposition with them. Without much argument, they let her go, and she again approached him with a solemn face.

She said officiously, "I've got an hour, but if possible, I would like some of that time for studying. We can catch a quick bite in the cafeteria. It is the closest eatery on campus. Okay?"

"Sure," he said, slightly bemused at her laying down of the rules.

Silently they approached the cafeteria and got their food. Todd picked a table near the back, where he thought they would have the most privacy.

They started with small talk about Elly's classes and the weather. When Elly didn't volunteer why she wasn't answering her phone, he had to broach the subject himself.

"I was worried about you when I couldn't get ahold of you by phone. My only option was to come looking for you," he said as he watched for her reaction.

She smiled an enigmatic grin. "I spent the night somewhere else, and I'm going to move."

"Wait a minute, when did you come up with this plan, and where are you going to live?" he said with genuine concern in his voice.

"Wait nothing! Why are you calling me?"

"Okay, that seems fair. I wanted to talk to you and tell you that I missed you. How can I tell you how sorry I am that … our disagreement yesterday ever happened?" He paused and then said, "I need your trust, and I need your help in catching a murderer."

Head down, busily concentrating on each bite of food, she wanted to tell him their time was up and she needed to run. But rebellion lost and logic won out, so instead she proposed, "Give me some reason to trust you."

He thought for a moment and then said, "I had a dream last night that you and I were running and playing on a tropical beach. It is my ambition to make that dream come true, if you will work with me and that person whom we catch is behind bars. I won't wait for the trial; I'll take you to Hawaii and resume the vacation I had to give up."

Elinor looked at him with awe. "Are you for real?"

"I'm willing to swear to it," he said as he gazed into her eyes.

"Okay," she said haltingly, "it's a deal. And I want you to know why I am agreeing. For the first time since this sordid thing started, I feel that you think I am innocent. But I don't want you calling me. I'll call you."

"What are you pulling? If there is an emergency and I need to get to you in a hurry, I can't follow you around the university campus all day hoping to find you. What are you up to?"

Shaking her head, she said, "I'm moving in with Annette. One of the conditions I had to agree to is that you would not be hanging around or dating me. I don't want her getting suspicious."

Furrowing his brow, he sat back in his chair. "Did she offer you this deal?"

"She doesn't want me suing the cardiology clinic, and she has offered to pay for my education and to support me if I comply."

"And in exchange you will be celibate. Is that realistic? Do you know what I think about that?"

"Shush, be quiet. You will have everyone staring at us. I have my reservations too," she whispered. "She is being very kind, but somehow her actions are phony to me, and I am not sure I can trust her. There is a lot of anger and hostility raging inside that woman. She gives me the creeps sometimes. I went to the library and got out some books on grieving. Some of her attitudes are appropriate, and others would take a shrink to understand."

The pain of imagining Elly cloistered away with a madwoman brought out the protective instincts in Todd. He suddenly realized he wasn't there on police business. Gently he reached over and took her hand. "We have to have a way to communicate, if only for your safety."

She paused a moment and said, "I think the best plan is this: I will call you each day, and if you don't get my call, come looking for me. Also, I'm keeping my apartment, and I'll put on the answering machine. I'll check it each day. Leave a message if something comes up." She smiled one of her earth moving smiles. Then she said, "I've got to go. Sorry, time's up."

Wistfully, he watched her go and felt a longing he hadn't experienced since he was eighteen.

***

"We found a carjacking incident that has possibilities. A Nissan truck was taken at gunpoint from a fellow on this corner." Jim reviewed his notes as he pointed to the wharf area on the map. "We searched the streets in that area, and sure enough we found Gary's truck on a backstreet less than a half mile from the carjacking incident. We have a warrant out for his arrest on the charge of armed robbery and grand theft. The new license number is here also."

Todd strained to read the map. "When did the carjacking take place?"

"Friday night about 21:00," Jim responded.

"Excellent!" Todd exclaimed, and then he glanced at his watch. "It's time to round up Maria and head out to Annette Pace's house."

***

Clair Minix and Annette were lounging on the matching love seats in Annette's sumptuous living room. They had kicked off their shoes and were enjoying telling each other of their various adventures abroad.

When the doorbell rang, Annette sprang up abruptly and adjusted her white skirt. "It must be them," she whispered.

"Yes, I will be with you when you open the door, and then I'll excuse myself and hang out in the library until they are gone. Unless they have some other plan," Clair said as she smoothed the wrinkles in her black suit.

Impatiently the doorbell rang again. Annette was looking for her other shoe. She laughed at the absurdity of the situation. "If they only knew."

When they were both straight and feeling confident, together the two marched to the door.

Three of them! Annette gasped to herself. The black man was the most imposing of the three. She had met him before and liked his beautiful hazel eyes. The blond one had handsome bone structure, but he had a penetrating gaze and a tough, rough look to his face. She caught his name, Todd. *Hmm, this is Elinor's former lover.* The short dumpy woman, she had also met before, but she couldn't remember her name. Annette graciously invited them all in.

"We are sorry to intrude into your life at such a difficult time, but we are intent on bringing your husband's killer to justice," Todd explained.

Annette perched herself on one of the love seats and let the three find their own places. Todd remained standing by the fireplace. Annette wanted to throw them off, so she said, "I can't imagine what you find so important here that you bring half the police force to my home. Why, who is back at the station catching all the real crooks? I fully intend on talking to the mayor about this."

"I want to assure you that we only have a few questions, and if we could begin, this will only take the minimum amount of time." Then Todd read her rights and warned her that they were taping the interview. He hurried on to the first question: "Now, as I understand it, you and Allen Pace were experiencing some marital difficulties, and in fact you had separated. Can you tell us about that?"

"We were talking of reconciling. I wanted him to go through some drug rehabilitation. You see, I loved my husband dearly. Being separated was very painful for me. You can consult my psychologist if you want. He will tell you how I feel."

"Is it true that Mark Jacobs and you are lovers?"

Annette squirmed in her seat, and the color rose in her cheeks. "He is an old family friend. He has never been my lover."

Todd nodded his head knowingly and plunged ahead. "How did you feel about your husband's liaisons with other women?"

"I'm not sure what you mean," she started. She took a deep breath and appeared to be willing herself to relax. "There were several, but most recently was Gina Williams. Then in the newspapers there were articles about a rape. But women were always accusing him of rape when they were the ones who had seduced him. He was very handsome, you know, and I feel my husband was the victim of his generosity. My half-sister, Elinor DeMartini, has been the recluse of our family for most of her life. Being always jealous of me and the rest of the family, I think she was seeking vengeance through my husband."

The words crashed down on Todd as if he were the puck suddenly thrown out onto the icy middle of a hockey rink. "You are saying that Ms. DeMartini is related to you?"

"I'm sorry, I thought I was being perfectly clear. She is my father's illegitimate daughter by his mistress. This happened months before my parents' marriage," Annette announced as if she were reeling off the pedigree of one of her horses.

"But Ms. DeMartini was brutally raped by Dr. Pace!" Maria Fuentes blurted out.

"There are always two sides to every story, *Officer*! I have asked my sister to come live with me in hopes that she will feel less alienated from the family and therefore less implacable," Annette shot back.

"If you don't mind, I would like to shift to a different subject," interrupted Jim. "I am interested in hearing about your activities on the afternoon of Friday, December third."

"I picked up Elinor about one o'clock outside the cardiology clinic, and we came back here. There was a lot to talk about, and it was almost five by the time I drove her back to the center of town. I let her off on my way to meet the Minixes as we were going to Mendocino together. I let Elinor off at the corner of Geary and Stockton Streets. The Minixes met me at the garage that is near that corner. We took my car to Mendocino."

"Are you willing to give us a deposition confirming that for us?" asked Jim.

"I shall have to consult my attorney first."

**

There were plenty of parking spaces available, but Elinor didn't see Annette's blue BMW anywhere. A cold wind was coming up, and the sun, partially blotted out by the fog, was setting. Elinor felt chilled and tired. The books and notes seemed pounds heavier on her back.

There was no shelter and no bench to sit on. She was just about to give up and phone Annette when she heard the screech of tires as someone drove into the lot.

"I'm terribly late. So sorry that I got held up," Annette said as Elinor gratefully slid into the passenger seat.

"I feel blue with cold! I wish there had been a protected space to wait. Your car is warm and feels heavenly toasty. I am just glad you arrived before dark."

Annette began to speak as they entered the traffic. "Let's do what we planned and go over to your apartment and get some of your personal things. Then when we get to my house, I have some delicious leftovers we can quickly make a meal out of, and you will be a new woman again."

The Christmas traffic was worse than Elly had remembered, and their little excursion took longer than they had anticipated. They didn't get back to Sea Cliff until almost seven in the evening.

Two suitcases of clothing and other incidentals were all that Elinor had time to pack. With great relief, Elinor dropped her load inside the guest room on the ground floor of the house. Annette had given her the choice of two rooms, the one upstairs or this one. Elinor liked the downstairs room because it was closer to the library on the ground floor, even though this bedroom was smaller than the alternative one. It was probably the maid's quarters at one time, thought Elinor, but it didn't matter.

Unpacking her suitcases, arranging her books, and changing out of her nursing uniform took more time than Elinor had wanted. Her stomach was churning, and she had a headache from low blood sugar. It was worth the wait, however, as Annette had time to prepare an elegant supper for them.

During the meal, Elly chatted about her classes and minor incidents involving classmates. The subject of Todd was never mentioned by her. Annette, on the other hand, itched for an opportunity to ask about him. When no opening occurred, she said, "I met your friend Todd today. He was here with some other officers to interview me. He seems to be a bit of a wimp, but certainly he is nice-looking."

"Todd a wimp? I would call him measured and powerful, but I have never seen him flinch from anything."

"Maybe you just don't know him well. He reacted strangely to some things I said today, and I just thought if he was tough, he would show a poker face."

"What were you talking about when you observed this behavior?" Elinor asked cautiously.

"Let's see, I think I was talking about how wonderful Allen was when he was a loving husband. I did discuss the drug thing, but I don't know much about it."

Puzzled by Annette's response, Elly asked, "Did you imply that a drug dealer might have murdered Allen?"

Annette was relieved to have a way out. She offered, "Not exactly, but I might have hinted at it. Would you like some brandy? I love to sit by the fire with some brandy. Will you join me?"

"You are too kind a hostess. I would love to, but I have to get some studying done this evening. May I have a cup of coffee instead?" Elly noted that Annette had changed the subject, and she wondered about her prior comments and what they meant.

Hours later, Elly sat on her new bed in this new room and decided to work on her studying. She found her mind clouded with visions of Todd, Allen, and most of all Annette. There were conflicts that she really didn't understand, and this bothered her.

I need to think about some choices in front of me. I don't feel comfortable in this house even though Annette has done a lot to make me feel at ease. She says too many statements out of the blue, which confuses me.

When she talked about Todd, it was all I could do to keep my mouth shut, I was so afraid of saying something revealing. It was as if I wanted to trust her and pour my heart out so much. But then I thought, did she bring up his name just to goad me?

Another thing: She seems to know more about Gina than I would have surmised. I can't remember Gina ever saying she had met Annette. Knowing Gina, she would have had a lot to say if she had ever met Annette. It could be that Allen talked about Gina to Annette, but that doesn't sound like something he would do. He was cruel in a different sort of way.

I am surprised that Annette said so much about Mark Jacobs, my mycology professor. She spoke of him as an old buddy.

Annette is so strange sometimes. I wonder if I should talk to a professional about her behavior. When she talked about her conversation with Todd, I wondered what really took place.

Allen affectionately called Annette an angel. I would add a critical *angel. The way she rips everyone apart so vehemently means she is no good friend to anyone. No one is spared from her teasing cynicism. She is very much like her mother.*

Todd, on the other hand, is another deep subject. He wants me to trust him, but if he doesn't accept me, how can he ask me to put much faith in him? I could care very much for him, but I'm too afraid of being hurt, and that immobilizes me.

***

Slumped in an overused stuffed chair, Mark gazed vacantly at the list in front of him with his ears ringing. He had called all those people, and the most interested party was an old college friend. This buddy had not been overly generous in the past, but he said he would put two grand in the mail the next day. That was the best offer Mark had gotten. Depressed, shaky, and overly sensitive to sound, he was showing signs of drug withdrawal. It suddenly occurred to him that he couldn't even call Allen for help. The topic of suicide had broached his pained mind, but he had never liked the sight of blood, and the medicine cabinet was empty.

There was another problem that was lurking in the far corner of his house. The sound of the TV from that area was like gibberish pounding in his head. Gary the pariah was crouching in the other part of the house with the tube running all the time. Every drop of alcohol was gone, most of it wasted on that creep.

"And if I call in sick and cancel my classes, I can't even have peace at home without stumbling over that no-good jerk," he mumbled out loud.

The thought had dawned on Mark that the police may be interested in Gary's hideout. His mind felt like it was stuffed with cotton, but slowly he was formulating a simple plan. The only problem was that he would have to come clean. No more coke or crack, maybe an occasional exotic or even a little MJ on special holidays. Could he really dress up in his finery and go out somewhere without the support of his relaxing drugs?

On the other hand, Annette might find him more desirable, and that would make it all worthwhile.

CHAPTER 17

Tuesday, December 6

Elly hurriedly ran to the phone booth down the hall from her classroom on campus. She had promised to call Todd, and she was late.

"Hi, it's me! This is my daily call-in. How are things?" Elly's voice was full of sunshine.

"God, I've been desperate to talk to you. We have got to meet and have a long talk." Todd's voice was filled with storm clouds, and it came over the receiver like a clap of thunder. He was deep in his world of crime solving and was in a humorless frame of mind.

"Oh, I was hoping you would be in a good mood. I just aced a test, and I'm flying high on the glory of it. You aren't planning to burst my balloon, are you?" Elly's voice reflected her joy of accomplishment as well as her fear of tumbling into despair.

Fighting to control his temper and not frighten her off, Todd paused before he answered her. "Congratulations on a successful test. I know you work hard at your studies, but there are other important details to take care of. Plus, I'm worried about your safety. So where can we meet, and when?"

Elly instinctively took the receiver from her ear and stared at it while she contemplated his abrupt change in manner. Her sigh of resignation was audible. "Do you want to have lunch together? It is almost one, but I haven't eaten and ..." The last thing she wanted to do was frustrate him, but she too had a schedule. "I have another final tomorrow, and ..."

He didn't let her go on. Interrupting her, he said, "I'll pick you up in fifteen minutes. We can meet at the loading zone outside the library, okay? That is presuming you are still on campus."

"All right, if you insist." Her voice was dull and bitterly expressionless.

"Better give me a half hour 'cause I'm picking up sandwiches on my way over," he said urgently.

"Okay, but don't take too long. It is hard to study on an empty stomach. That test tomorrow is incredibly important, so studying is my highest priority. Take that as a warning. I can't fritter away the afternoon, you know." Once more she attempted to assert her own agenda.

Todd slammed the receiver down too hard, and Jim, who happened to be in his office, gave him a bemused grin and said, "Is the lady playing with you, my friend?"

"I don't know if it is some sort of defense mechanism or stupidity, but yes, she is frustrating. By the way, what is that device you're inspecting? It doesn't look familiar."

"This is the reason for my coming to visit you today. I just got this little widget in the mail from that high-tech company down the peninsula, Mercal or something like that. Anyway, as you can see, it's not much bigger than a book. Its size is what makes it so valuable. If I were to put it in my pocket and leave your office, you could track my movements all over the city. In fact, you could track me anywhere within a hundred-mile radius of this point. All you have to do is call up this program that came with it and plug in the right call numbers, and bingo, up on the computer screen would come a map. You would know my exact location! Here, look at it yourself."

Cautiously Todd took the device from Jim's outstretched hand. "Hmm, it could be useful, but you say a metal-lined something would block the radio waves or whatever? Do you mean the average automobile? If so, its best use is for you to put it on your dog's collar, so you will never lose him! That is, unless he gets into somebody's car," Todd said with a smirk.

"Be serious! Think of the money we would save tracking someone. Or when we send someone to bait a trap, they could be safely followed. There is a handy button on the top that you can press to call for help."

"What is the bite for this gizmo?" Todd asked with an air of suspicion.

"That is the kicker: with the antenna and all the hookups, it's almost fifty g's."

Todd couldn't help laughing. "I'll submit it in the next budget, but for now I have a woman waiting for me," he said as he handed the device back to Jim.

Jim felt crushed. He had thought this new device had a lot of potential. In defense, he took offense. "May I ask if this trip is police business or personal?"

"I'm considering it business. She is hiding a lot of information, and I intend to wring it out of her," Todd said sheepishly.

Standing up his full height and pounding his chest like a gorilla, Jim succeeded in looking comical. "I can just see you trying to kiss her and wondering if it would be better to bust her!" He chuckled as he walked out the door, his laughter ringing out joyfully all the way down the hall.

***

In an office building in downtown San Francisco, two people were having an argumentative conversation.

"I can't do it!" Clair shook her head to emphasize her point.

"We can just say an earlier time or claim that you had your wires crossed or something. You are under a lot of stress and you got the time wrong. Or I can tell them I picked up Annette first and then picked you up at the actual time of six forty-five. Which would you like to choose?" Darrell retorted, obviously irritated.

"That's not going to work. Annette has already told them that you and I picked her up at five thirty. If we give them a conflicting story, they will go back to Annette and get her mad. You know what that will mean. She will take it out on us somehow. If I lie as you want me to, then the cops will ask my boss for the records, which will show when I left work. And he will tell them six forty-five. I'm really stuck with that scenario no matter how much you and Annette would like to change it."

"I think you are putting tiger stripes on a mouse, but have it your way. Just remember, you have my career in your hands. Don't do something you will regret."

"Great. Thank you for your loving support! Here I am twenty minutes from an interview with the police, and I don't know whom to shaft. Life is never simple, is it?!" Clair said, only slightly disguising her resentment.

A pregnant silence engulfed them. After several tense moments passed, Clair, as if on impulse, abruptly jumped up and briskly walked toward the door without saying another word.

***

A soft breeze ruffled her hair but did not cool her. Anxiously, Elly looked up and down the street, wondering where Todd could be. "I'll give him another five minutes, and then I'm leaving," Elly muttered to herself.

Slowly, the traffic moved by her. Every compact blue coupe magnetically drew her attention. After hopefully searching each one, her interest waned and was replaced by indignation. "I could—no, I should—be studying and not out here waiting for something that isn't going to happen. I wonder what was so important that he wanted to talk to me about. Maybe he changed his mind."

The honking horn didn't immediately draw her attention, but the yelling did. Across the street, Todd was double-parked, standing by his car, waving his arms, and calling her name. Elly saw him and waved back then jogged across the street when the traffic would let her. Secretly she was very happy to see him. "I was beginning to think you weren't coming."

"Sorry, I got tied up at the office, and then there was a long line for the lunch," Todd admitted as he held up the bag as a peace offering.

They drove west to the hills of the old Presidio. Parking near the World War II gun emplacements, they ate their lunch in the car to keep warm.

"That was very satisfying; it truly took care of my problem. I was famished after that test. It really drained me. Now, what is so important that you had to talk to me?"

"We had an interesting conversation with Annette Pace yesterday," he began, but before he could get much beyond an introduction, Elly nervously interrupted.

"Yes." She giggled uneasily. "Annette gave me a fascinating description of you and the other officers. She thought a lot of your questions were silly."

"Oh, tell me about it." He was deadly somber.

"Well, she didn't give me a blow-by-blow description of it, more like a few insights. Like, I guess you asked at one point who she thought killed Allen, and she said she supposed his drug-dealing friends did it. Then she described each of you in rather unflattering terms. For instance, she thought you were a wimp."

Visually agitated, Todd removed his sunglasses and rubbed his eyes. The effort did nothing to ease his mounting anger. In a sudden violent move, he reached over and physically pulled Elly toward him. "Will you please give me the goddamn truth for a change!" he roared.

"I-I did! W-what is wrong with you?" She gasped nervously.

"Me, I'm just a poor straight cop who doesn't like being strung along with a bunch of lies by a woman he at one time admired very much." His voice wandered off, and his grip on her relaxed. His composure returned, and he asked, "Are you Annette's half-sister?"

"Yes!" she said in a small and submissive voice, hanging her head.

"Are you the black sheep of the family, and do you hate Annette and her family—and that is why she thinks you might have killed Allen, for revenge?"

Elly recoiled at the words, which stung her. "Yes, I am the inconvenient relative, but I do not hate Annette, nor did I kill Allen for vengeance. My childhood is a long, boring story I don't like to tell," she said plaintively.

"Well, I think you had better start boring me quick, because your sweet ass is on the line."

His remark irritated her, but she understood his anger and felt his seriousness enough to comply. "Let me think. I'm not sure where to begin. My mother was a very sweet and loving person. She was the secretary to Ronald Longacre, who is Annette's father. Lida, my mother, and Ronald had an affair, but he couldn't marry her because they came from different sides of the tracks. I am the love child of that match. Ronald was forced to marry Annette's mother because she offered her family's wealth and prestige to Ronald's estate. I was awkwardly born after their wedding took place. It is said that Ronald was more attentive to Lida than to Grace, his wife. This is the seed of the conflict and the reason I am ostracized from their family functions. My mother lost her job, and she was devastated by her treatment by this family.

"One person took pity on her, my paternal grandfather, who is also Annette's grandfather. Because of my dear grandfather's influence, my mother got a generous allowance for my support. He really liked my mother more than he liked Annette's mother, and his preferences were very thinly disguised. He always said I looked more like a Longacre than Annette did.

"When I was a child, my grandfather would invite me to his estate to visit. And because Annette and I were only ten months apart, I was invited to play with Annette and entertain her. However, Annette's nanny had other ideas. She saw me as an added burden and complained to Annette's mother. Then things changed. There was friction between Annette and I. As time went on, Annette became more and more cruel and picked on me constantly. It got so bad that I would get sick whenever an invitation would arrive. My mother guessed at what was happening and canceled the visitations.

"The years went by. My mother entered a bad marriage and became an alcoholic. Other family arrangements became more important, and so the years passed by when I didn't see my father or his family. I didn't have news of them except what I read in the papers. I didn't go to the funeral of my grandfather or my father. Those are the only things I regret.

"*Hate* is not the right term for my feelings. Is it a crime not to like them? I didn't tell you about my family because it sounds like I am putting on airs or something, and I didn't think that was appropriate.

"At Gina's funeral was the first time I'd seen Annette in twenty-five years. I didn't even recognize her at first. It was only after she came to me and proved who she was that the knowledge came to me that Allen was my brother-in-law.

"I regret that I haven't explained all this to you sooner. I guess I was in a state of denial that this was real and important," she sobbed.

Tears streamed down her face. Todd offered her a tissue and then took her in his arms and held her.

"I can't tell you how good it makes me feel that you shared this with me. Do you realize the danger you are in?"

"Well, I feel rejected. And when Detective Collins questioned me, I had the distinct feeling he was very suspicious, as if I was considered guilty until proven innocent," she complained.

"You have the best motive of anyone. The knowledge and the opportunity were both available. On top of that, you have a flimsy alibi. Then when we interviewed Annette, she told us that she left you off in the neighborhood of the cardiology clinic that Friday about five because you had an appointment with Allen! That blows your alibi to hell!

"What really worries me is that Annette also expounded on your motive by describing how you hated her family. In a court of law, it's your word against hers. In case you don't know it, that woman has a lot of credibility in the community. She can destroy you!" He purposely paused to let his words sink in, waiting before he continued. "That is why I needed to talk with you today. I think you are in a very precarious position, and I can and I want to help. The problem is that when you withhold information from me, my hands are tied. It's frustrating and poisonous. I apologize for getting angry a few minutes ago, but it was my feeble way of caring. Now, please, I know you have more to tell me. Speak, and I will suck up every word."

"What do you want me to say?!" Elly wailed.

"We are going to sit here until you tell all, and you know what that is. So if you want to get back to your studies, baby, then start talking."

With glazed eyes, Elly stared blankly out the window in silence.

Todd watched her mute, trembling body and felt compassion tugging at his conscience. "Why don't you start with Friday? Talk to me. Tell me every moment of that day," he gently prompted.

In a shaky voice, Elly started, "Yes, Annette left me off a few blocks from the cardiology clinic. She talked me into going to see Allen and had made an appointment for me. I was going to talk to him about losing my job. It was about five when I knocked at the back door and he let me in." Elinor stopped to compose herself.

"We argued. Then at one point he grabbed me. I was so frightened. Because I was kicking and screaming, he finally set me free. I ran out the door. It was very wet that night, and I ran all the way home. I swear to you, he was alive when I left him."

"When you were struggling with him, didn't he start being too intimate and try to stop you from leaving? Didn't you hit him over the head during your fight? You grabbed something off the shelf. Do you remember that?" he probed.

"Yes, the bronze horse. I didn't mean to do so much harm. I was afraid of another rape, but he was alive when I ran out the door!" She was uncontrollably sobbing now.

Once more Todd reached for her, but this time he was gentle. She collapsed in his arms as if all the air had been released from a balloon. She marveled at the warmth of his body and the shelter she experienced.

"Please, please, tell me you believe me!" she whispered, her face buried in his chest.

"Yes, of course. Did you see anyone else there?" he softly asked as he ran his fingers through her hair.

"No, I saw no one, but I don't think the outside door was locked when I ran out."

He sat back, contemplating how the DA was going to look at Elly's testimony. The silence between them made the tension worse, so he said, "You are going to be fine. I think the district attorney will agree that it was self-defense, but we have to find the other party. Without that, your case is much weaker."

"I did not see a soul, but I was in such a panic to get away that I was not looking around. Someone could have been hiding in the shadows."

"That evening you were excited, but I didn't detect anything unusual. You were angry about being fired, but you didn't say anything about Annette or a second discussion with Allen. Why did you say absolutely nothing?" Todd said with tension in his voice.

"First, I was thrilled that we were together, and I didn't want to spoil that. Second, I was afraid I had done something illegal. It was an act that so horrified me that I couldn't believe that I was even capable of carrying it out. It was a mixture of guilt, anger, and fear. Also, I was afraid that I could not trust you."

"You felt guilty? Guilt about what?" he asked.

"That I was so gullible to have let myself be manipulated into setting Allen up. I could have just gone Christmas shopping like I said. I should have stayed away."

"Elly, the way I look at it, you are the victim. Victims often feel guilty and blame themselves. It is strange, but it is natural according to the shrinks. You need to let it go. I'm sure your intentions were valid and that what you did was within the law.

"By the way, it is getting late. Would you believe we have been talking for three hours? Let me take you somewhere to call Annette and tell her you are going to be late. Then you can come and have dinner with me."

Her smile lit up the car. "I thought we weren't going to date!"

"Do I have your permission to change my mind?"

"I accept your changed mind, mister, but I do have to study tonight, so it has to be a quick dinner and nothing more," she teased, her eyes glittering with mischief.

Snorting a short laugh, he pushed her playfully aside. "Then you had better stay on your side of the car!"

***

Annette was not worried about Elinor being late; she was too engrossed in a discussion with Mark. There was nothing like money to make Annette amiable. He had presented his loan payment with flair as if it were a gift. All afternoon, they had been talking about the past when times were fun and less painful. Annette was even planning to make Mark one of her best food creations.

She had forgotten Elinor entirely, so when Elinor called, Annette treated her message with indifference. To Annette, the call was more of an annoyance than a social gesture; however, it was a reminder of unfinished business.

"That party last summer was the best. Do you remember Darrel was mimicking George and we were all laughing so hard? I thought I was going to burst! It still makes me silly when I think of it. Thank you for coming over to cheer me up, Mark."

"You know it is my pleasure, Annette. I would do anything to make you happy," Mark purred as he took her hand in his.

"Really?" Her expression changed to one of seriousness. "Would you give up drugs, for instance?"

"Yes, anything. I happened to come up with that idea on my own. I'll have you know that I am clean. I haven't had anything in several days," he said quietly, but he couldn't look her in the eyes.

"Very good! This didn't have anything to do with Allen's death, did it?" She was acting holier-than-thou again in her cynicism.

"Why? No." Mark tried to look surprised. "I just decided that it was not ... making me happy."

"Oh, never mind all your rationalizations. The future will speak louder than your words. Let's eat. I think my soufflé must be just right."

***

Todd drove to North Beach and chose the Italian restaurant that was his favorite. The lighting in the room was low that it blinded him once he walked in off the street. The slender young man who greeted them looked too young to be out of high school. Todd requested a table in the back.

They spoke little. Elly was preoccupied with her test in the morning, but a growing worry kept creeping in. Todd was talking enthusiastically about Hawaii and the places he wanted to take her. It irritated him that Elinor was not giving him her full attention.

"You are on some other planet thought-wise again! Come on, out with it. Something is. . . bugging you," he said, changing the subject mid sentence.

"Annette concerns me. No matter what I think about, little anxious worries sneak in without any invitation. For instance, I have heard that people act strangely when they are grieving. Do you think Annette would honestly mourn Allen? Or could she resent me? She didn't have a loving mother, nor did she get much more love from our father than I did. He just never was around.

"The other night, she was really weird. She was talking about your sister, Gina. She knew so much about Gina's inner thoughts that I began to suspect that she had read Gina's diary. Do you think Annette has the missing half of the diary?"

"Whoa, let me catch up to you. First of all, Annette must have some feelings for Allen, so it is possible she could miss him. Now, before I answer the last two questions, more information is needed. I want you to do something for me," he said as he fished in his pocket for something. "Ah, here it is." In his palm was a small tape recorder. "I want you to tape your next conversations with Annette."

"You don't think she will hear it running and get suspicious?"

"Did you?!"

"Are you implying that you taped me?" She gasped.

There was a rather guilty look on Todd's face as he felt culpable. "Okay, I'm sorry I didn't tell you. It is the cop in me coming out. But the important thing is that you need to cover yourself. This will help, and on top of that you will have our conversations in your possession. I do want you to trust me."

After considering his plan, she said, "I agree. I guess it will help my credibility. Tell me how to work this thing."

**

Annette and Mark had just settled into their dessert when Elly used her key and opened the front door. Annette was offended that they had been rudely disturbed.

She knew that Mark jumped at the sound as it reminded him of Allen.

"Elinor," Annette said coldly, "ring the doorbell before you come in, please. Don't you have any manners?"

"Oh, I'm very sorry. I didn't know you had company. Hello, Dr. Jacobs."

Annette was aware that Mark was so surprised to see Elinor that he only nodded acknowledgment.

Elly also showed shock at the sight of Mark Jacobs.

When Annette heard Elinor's door shut, she turned to Mark. "My new roommate is a bit of a bother. Didn't you tell me you would do anything for me?" she asked, her eyes glittering with ill-disguised fury.

Cold beads of sweat popped out on Mark's forehead. Her question went unnoticed. "I can't believe you let that woman stay here. She's friendly with a detective or something." He shivered, and his dry throat made his voice crack. He longed to take a pill or two.

Ignoring Mark's discomfort, Annette plunged ahead. "I thought she was one of your students. She happens to be my … roommate at the moment, but it isn't working out well." Annette was going to reveal Elinor's sisterly ties but then thought better of it.

"Isn't that a coincidence? I have an unwelcome guest at my house too. He's driving me crazy with all his racket." Mark was too wrapped up in his own troubles to concentrate on what Annette was plotting.

"An unwanted guest. What are you going to do about it?" Annette was genuinely interested, but Mark had ignored her question earlier, so she repeated it: "You *will* do anything for me, Mark, won't you? I need help dealing with her. If you help me, I will return the favor," she spoke in a harsh whisper.

Confusion racked Mark's brain cells. He couldn't think straight. He badly needed a hit of something, the symptoms of withdrawal were distracting. "Yes, I'll do anything. I told you that before," he said to pacify her.

***

Elly sat on her bed, stunned about having found Mark with Annette and stunned by Annette's actions. *It's déjà vu. She sounds like our old nanny. Oh, how I hated that witch. And now I hear it from Annette! The nerve of her. I can't have Todd over, and yet she has Jacobs over and makes me feel like the unwanted stepchild,* she thought to herself.

I would love to hear their conversation right now, she mused. Carefully she got up and tiptoed to the door to listen. All she could hear was the stereo and some unintelligible speech.

The cold doorknob was hard in her hand. Slowly she turned it until she felt the latch release. With care, she prolonged the opening of the door, feeling out any creaks with the door or the floor that might occur. When the door was ajar, she stopped working on the door and just listened. The voices were conspiratorial and soft. Elly had trouble not letting her imagination get the better of her. She heard her name, yes, and it was spoken more than once. Nothing else was clear. The whole clandestine act of snooping was tiring. Elly gave up. She closed the door quietly and returned to the bed to try to study.

Gathering up her books around her, Elly concentrated on reading her notes. The words swirled around her head. It had been an exhausting day. There was too much tension, and she hadn't slept well in this new bed. Dozing off, she lay at peace with her notebook on her chest until a sharp sound shattered her nap.

She awoke with a start. She heard footsteps on the stairs going up, two sets of them, evidence that Annette was letting that creep spend the night! Elly held her breath, straining to hear what was going on above her.

Looking down at the notebook on her chest, her dream suddenly came back to her. It was about a book ... Gina's diary. *Could it be in this house? If it was here, where would Annette keep it? Her bedroom? No, that is too obvious. The library has good hiding places, or a linen closet, or maybe a drawer? That's it. She spends much of her time in the kitchen. It is her private domain. She told me never to cook or have anything to do in there without her supervision. Could it be that she wants to keep me out of there for reasons other than I might make a mess? Maybe she is hiding something.*

Again she tried to listen to hear sounds of any activities upstairs. She could hear water running, which could mean a bath. Once or twice she heard Annette's laughter. Something cautioned her to be patient. *I can't leave this room quite yet. I will, though, and I'm going to find that diary!*

CHAPTER 18

Wednesday, December 7

A small night-light glowed reassuringly from the clock on the desk. It dominated Elly's field of vision, but it couldn't have been what awakened her. Disoriented at first, she struggled to get her bearings straight. Something had aroused her, but that noise from something was now silent. Slowly the events of the prior evening drifted into focus. Mark Jacobs was the unexpected guest of the household, and Annette had turned her hostilities on Elly. Yes, the words still had their sting. "I have company, Elinor, and we want to be alone," she had said in her most caustic way.

Thump, scrape, thump. Someone was coming down the stairs! Elly's lungs seemed about to burst, when she realized she had been holding her breath. Gasping, she clutched the down comforter closer to her face and waited. The footfalls stopped at the bottom of the flight of stairs. Elly felt someone's eyes on her door, and a chill went down her spine. Hastily she grabbed her largest book and poised her body so as to defend herself.

Then the footsteps started again, moving toward the front of the house. Elly heard the front door open and shut. A sigh of relief only came when she heard the car drive away. Now, with eyes wide open, Elly turned up the light on the digital clock to see the time. It was four fifteen in the morning.

Quietly replacing the book, Elly lay back under the covers and tried to relax. Her mind had another agenda, however. Scenes from the day before swam dizzily through her head. *Todd is basically a nice guy. He does seem to care about me.* A vision of the tiny tape recorder popped up. *Where did I put it?* She searched her memory. *It must be in a pocket. The lumpy bed is getting annoying. My body itches to move. I could study at the desk. No, I'm not in the mood for that. What I really should do is sleep some more, but I can't seem to relax.* Elly rolled onto her back and tried to think of nothing, but to no avail.

When she was lost in thought, an idea leaped forward. The notion captivated her and took charge. *This is the perfect time to look for the lost diary. If it is in the house, there is no better time to look than when Annette is not underfoot.* Ellie's mind whirled with plans and strategies for the search. She ruled out the basement as it was too scary with only one way in and out.

Elly rose quietly out of bed and dressed in sweats to keep warm. She pinned the tape recorder to her bra but didn't turn it on. She decided to take a notebook and a textbook with her so she could fake studying if Annette found her. Cautiously, she tiptoed across the room to the door. Like the night before, she listened carefully before opening the door.

The hallway was unoccupied as Elly had guessed. No lights were on that she could see. Nervously she glanced up the stairs and stopped to listen with care before she proceeded. The hardwood floors were scattered with oriental rugs, so Elly gracefully maneuvered in such a way that her feet only touched the soft, padded areas. The library door was wide open, much to Elly's relief.

It was a large square-shaped room with a wall-to-wall credenza complete with bookshelves on one wall. Two large leather chairs flanked the large windows at the far end, and the other walls were covered with books, neatly spaced on the shelves. A billiard table dominated the center of the room. Elly scanned the shelves, wondering where to begin. By the light from the window, she crossed the room to place her books on one of the chairs, when some magazines caught her eye. "If I was going to hide a notebook, those magazines might be the perfect spot," she whispered to herself.

The innocent magazines were only what they appeared to be. Elly decided to look among the books. The most likely hiding spot was the collection of Allen's medical journals that filled one of the shelves.

Carefully, Elly handled each one as she went through the stacks, but nothing was there. Time was passing. Elly began to worry that her search was futile. Her window of time was running out. Annette would soon be up.

Elly gathered up her books and tiptoed out the door. With each step, she tested for squeaks in the floor, but it took time. It seemed a mile to the kitchen the way Elly was going.

The cabinets were a new territory that held promise. Annette had discouraged Elly from exploring or cooking in this, Annette's private lair. Possibly she might keep a diary with her cookbooks. After several trials of opening cabinets, Elly found the right one. There were three shelves with recipe books. Meticulously she took down each book and looked inside it, and then she checked behind all the books. On the second shelf, as she was removing one of the small spiral-bound books, a small notebook fell out. "Oh!" Elly gasped. The small book was Gina's lost diary.

The whole cupboard was put back into ship shape condition. As she turned off the light she noticed it was almost 7:00, and Annette was making sounds upstairs. Elly gathered up her books and was hastily retreating to her room when Annette called down from the top of the stairs for Elinor to wait.

"You're certainly up early," Annette said in a cold, hard voice.

"Yes, I was studying … in the library," Elly replied in as cheerful a fashion as she could muster.

"Hmm, When I looked down the stairs, I am sure I saw the light on in the kitchen."

Moving slowly toward her bedroom door, Elly maneuvered to make a graceful exit. However, Annette had another agenda.

"Don't go hiding yourself in that room again. Come out and sit in the kitchen and have a cup of coffee. I want to talk with you."

Instinctively Elly felt for the tape recorder and turned it on. Then she followed Annette as she led the way into her sanctum sanctorum. Dutifully sitting down at the table, Elly hugged her books to her chest.

"You are hanging onto those books as if they were a security blanket. Put them on the table so you will be more comfortable," Annette commanded as she prepared the coffee.

It is a creeping thing, this feeling called fear that undermines our self-confidence and turns us into slaves. Elly obediently put the books on the table and hoped Gina's diary wasn't obvious. When Annette approached the table with the coffee, Elly could hear her own heart pounding in her chest.

"You know, I told you not to use my kitchen. There is no reason for you to have to come in here without me. And why were you sneaking about the house last night?"

"I wouldn't call it sneaking. When I can't sleep, I always study. Sometimes it is a very effective way to put me back to sleep," Elly said, defending herself.

"Well, it isn't going to happen again. I don't like my privacy interfered with. Take last night, for instance. You totally embarrassed me. You looked at my friend as if he were a cockroach. He happens to be a very old and dear business partner."

"Business partner?" Elly gasped.

"Yes, but it is nothing I want to discuss with you."

A heavy silence engulfed them. The crash of china shattered Elinor's nerves. Annette had slammed her cup down on the saucer as she stared at Elly.

When she spoke, her voice was shrill. "You have always been jealous of me. Green with envy! Look at what you have become. Studying to be a nurse! Your great ambition is to empty bedpans and be a disgrace to the Longacre name.

"No one knows I'm a Longacre! I've never used that name. It isn't a part of me. All I want is distance from it. Jealous, oh no! That was your bag. You were the jealous one. I at least had a loving mother! You only had Grandpa, and you hated it when he gave me any attention. Do you remember when you locked me up one day? They looked and searched everywhere, and then your nanny found me locked in your room. You told her I made you lock me up so I could have all your toys to myself. It was a rotten lie, and I got punished. I never wanted anything you had. I was just a frightened little girl, and you loved taunting me."

Annette's face turned red as she spit out, "You have always wanted what I possessed, *even* my husband!"

"I didn't know he was your husband until you called me. We met at Gina's funeral, but I didn't really want to admit you were my sister. It had been over twenty years since I last saw you.

"I needed a better job, so I applied to take the position Gina had just left vacant with her death. Allen was kind at first. I never encouraged his advances. And then there was that awful day. Please, you do remember that he criminally raped *me*!" Elly pleaded desperately to express her innocence.

"There is no doubt in my mind that you flirted with him, enticing him to make love to you. It was a very effective way of hurting me!" Annette replied coolly.

Annette's gaze fell on the stack of books, and her expression changed to horror as if an eight-legged venomous creature were creeping toward her. "That notebook looks familiar. Give it to me. I want to look at it," she darkly commanded.

The chill in the air became frosty. Elly handed the diary across the table and wondered how effectively the tape recorder was working. Bravely, she thought she would give it something good to record. "How did Gina's diary happen to be in your kitchen, Annette?"

"You stupid bitch, stealing from me. This is mine, not Gina's!" she said with vehemence.

For one slender second, Elly thought her first hasty assessment was wrong, and then she remembered something. "I didn't know you were pregnant and going to nursing school," she taunted.

Annette's face flushed. "That slut deserved to die. I really meant to ..." She was fighting for composure. "I found that diary in my basement. I am sure Allen put it there."

"The police want that diary. Why didn't you give it to them?"

"I was using it as a weapon to get Allen to give up drugs," Annette said with cold self-control.

"You know I have to tell them about it. It won't look good, you know. Do you think Allen killed Gina?"

A crooked smile creased Annette's face as she studied Elinor like a bug under a glass. "He was too ... too much involved with her to do that willingly. Why? Do you think he was guilty?"

"He was there, I think. He didn't like her being pregnant, and she wouldn't get an abortion. She was on drugs. He seemed to have so many reasons. Also, he possessed the knowledge of how to inject her with the poison from the mushrooms," Elly said carefully, hanging on every word.

"How little you know! Knowledge of mushrooms? He knew less than a worm. He couldn't tell the difference between an *Amanita* and an *Agaricus*. Yes, he was a big talker; he sounded like he knew a great deal. But what he didn't divulge was that I was the source of his meager understanding of fungi."

"You? It seems obvious now that you mention it. You are a friend and lover of Dr. Jacobs!" Elly said with awe mixed with loathing. The idea was frightfully clear. Taking a deep breath, she said, "Then were you or Dr. Jacobs involved in Gina's death?"

"Hmm, maybe Mark wanted to kill her, but he was too much of a coward." Annette paused and then continued. "Gina was such a whore. She had all those men in her pussy! I hated her, but I despised Allen more."

"Then who killed Gina?!" Elly asked with trepidation.

"It was an accident. I really intended to get my philandering ... And you aren't going to have a chance to tell anyone anything, my dear sister," she said. Her voice had the quality of claws on glass.

Elly assertively pushed her chair back and abruptly stood up. "Who is going to stop me, you and your flabby body? I can easily outrun you."

"Sit down. I know something about you. If you tattle on me, I can tell all too," Annette snapped.

"What do you know that would interest the cops?" Elly said with self-confessed confidence.

"I saw you do it."

"What do you mean? What did you see me do?"

"I saw you kill Allen! First you hit him over the head, and while he was defenseless, you slit his throat," Annette screamed in defiance.

Elly stared at Annette in disbelief. In a quiet voice she said, "You were there. You must have murdered him, because before you said it, I didn't know how he died. Yes, I hit him over the head in self-defense, but he was *alive* when I left him. You must have been hiding somewhere, watching. When I was gone, you came in and put an end to his life!"

The situation had changed. Elly felt doomed like a mouse caught in a trap. Her mouth was dry and her body ached to flee, but her feet seemed rooted to the kitchen floor.

Annette arched her back. Her otherwise pretty face was contorted by the monster within. She sprang to the counter and grabbed her favorite butcher knife. Whirling around, she lunged at Elly with a tonal growl. Pinning Elly to the wall, she said, "Ha, they're dead, and you will soon join them. Gina was an accident, but she died so easily. Allen was the one I really intended to poison, but he gave the vial to Gina. How gallant of him. But it served her right. She was a flirt. He was in *love* with her, and I could not tolerate it anymore. I felt so satisfied. No one knew who did it! Allen was the real problem. Although he suffered with Gina's death, he was still alive and slathering after you. This time I was really going to get him—and I did.

"I set you up with him, hoping you would kill him. But you didn't, so I took off all my clothes and put on one of those flimsy patient gowns. He was a pigeon waiting for the carver. I took such pleasure in grabbing his hair and yanking back his head. The skin was tough and leathery, not at all like a fillet of tenderloin. It was hard to make him bleed a lot, so I really had to gouge him. He was an ugly sight when I got through with him—*no* comparison to what you are going to look like."

The attack came with surprising swiftness. The knife slashed through the air. With agility, Elly dove to the left to avoid the blade. Picking up her book, she slammed it down hard and fast in an abortive attempt to harm Annette. Narrowly missing her, the knife sliced past Elly's shoulder and stuck in the table. With maniac strength, the aggressor whipped the knife into the air for another slash. Lunging sumo wrestler fashion, Elly came at Annette, frantically flailing her hands and arms. This action threw Annette off-balance, and the blade merely cut through Elly's sweatshirt. Elly caught Annette's hand with the knife and twisted it until the knife fell.

Annette became a dynamic mass of anger. With fingernails and teeth gnashing, she lashed out with all her fury. Elinor grabbed that well-groomed golden hair and held on tight, forcing Annette's head back. Annette howled in pain. With her left hand, Elly tried to punch repeatedly at her attacker's abdomen, but her left arm was too weak. Annette kicked and screamed obscenities. They each struggled for the upper hand. They lost balance and tumbled to the floor. In the confusion, Annette latched on to Elinor's head and smashed it down as hard as she could on the tile floor.

A void of blackness enveloped Elly. Her body slumped unconscious in a heap on the floor. Annette felt for signs of life. There was a pulse, and she was breathing. Exhausted and panting, Annette couldn't resist smiling. "You stupid bitch, I'm going to enjoy your death!"

Slowly, Annette got to her feet. Her legs felt weak. She wobbled as she crossed the room to where the knife lay. It felt so powerful in her hand, but then the tile floor caught her eye as well. *Do I want to create a bloody mess that I have to clean up? And it might get on my cabinets too!* This thought sobered her as she lowered herself into a chair. *I have got to think clearly.*

With trembling fingers, Annette dialed the phone. The far-off phone rang and rang, but no one answered. "He must be at the university," she whispered to herself. Panic like a growing cancer stirred her. "I must, must control myself. The other number is here someplace," she murmured as she rustled papers frantically, trying to find the number. At last she found it and dialed.

"Mycology office. This is Bob Huntley speaking" was the answer.

"I need to talk to Professor Jacobs. It's an emergency!" she croaked in a hoarse voice.

"Madam, could you give me your name, please?"

"I need to talk to Dr. Jacobs. This is Annette Pace. Do you remember me? It is very important that I talk to Jacobs," she said in a stronger voice.

"Mrs. Pace, you were on the last myology field trip. Yes, I remember you. I was being careful because the police called earlier and he is avoiding them," Bob said apologetically.

There was some clicking as the call was transferred. The moment passed like hours. Finally Mark Jacobs's reassuring baritone voice came on the line.

"Mark. How sweet it is to hear your voice. I need you so much!

"It's Elinor. We had a fight, and she is lying on my kitchen floor. I need to ... I want to put her in the car and take her up the coast and help her. Or, shall we say, she is going to jump off the cliff and commit suicide against her will!"

The words chilled him as if ice had been poured down his back. He was speechless at first. "Steady, Annette. Let me have some facts. Is Elinor alive now? Tell me about her state," he said carefully.

"She was knocked unconscious. There is a cut on her head and some bleeding. If I don't do something quick, she will come around and try to ... Mark, can't you come and help me?" she pleaded in a voice that was strident. She was filled with a cocktail of anger and dread.

Mark, in his panic, rummaged in his pocket for his pills. "We have to get out of the city. It would be better if we were in separate cars. Tie her hands, then try to rouse her. Get her into the car, and drive to that lodge we stayed at in Jenner. I'll meet you there."

"But what do I do if she won't wake up?"

***

In the cafeteria of the Hall of Justice, Todd was getting a midmorning snack and coffee for his friend and partner.

"Has Elinor called in today?" Jim asked in an effort to be friendly.

"No. She has some tests today, so at this point there doesn't seem to be much to worry about. I wish those lab results were back," Todd replied.

"We should have them tomorrow at the latest. I imagine you want to clear Elinor as soon as possible. I will do all I can to assist you.

"By the way, we got the most extraordinary call last night. Mark Jacobs, the transvestite, wanted to press charges against Gary Williams for breaking and entering, but he rambled on about duress and extortion too. No violence was mentioned. He said we could find

Gary at Jacobs's house in Tiburon. The team went out, got Gary, and locked him up.

"When I came in this morning, I couldn't wait to see what this turkey had to say. He went on and on about how innocent he was. It seems Gary feels framed. He says Jacobs confessed to Gary about having killed Gina a week ago, and he thinks that's why Jacobs is pressing charges now."

"Do you think Gary was blackmailing Jacobs?"

Jim shook his head. "I don't know. I called Jacobs at the university this morning, but he wasn't available. No one has seen him."

Todd couldn't help but imagine the scene. "Jacobs is a never-ending bag of surprises. Let's have him picked up for questioning again.

"By the way, I would like to take a second look at that device you showed me yesterday. I wish I had one on Elly at this moment. We had a very constructive talk last night, and I don't think she is avoiding me. I am beginning to worry."

"Ha! I knew you would come around. I'll get you the information right away."

"Did they find any drugs when they picked up Gary?" Todd inquired with obvious interest.

"The officers didn't have a warrant last night. I sent a request for a search warrant over to the court this morning. We can make a second trip out there this afternoon. They said it shouldn't take long for the warrant, but I am still waiting."

"When did you start the process?"

"It was only forty-five minutes ago; I'm just really impatient. The team is all assembled to go, and it is just hard to wait," Jim confessed.

"Well, let me know how it turns out. I think I'll go back to my office and see if Elinor has called. I find it hard to be patient."

Once he was back in his office, the time seemed to drag by. Todd found it difficult to concentrate on the paperwork before him. There was no message from Elly even though it was long past noon. He decided to wait until one o'clock, and if he didn't hear from her by then, he would make the first phone calls. The reports on his desk didn't help. One involved a woman brutally battered and found in a ditch. Another was concerning an abducted teenager who hadn't been located.

Impulsively, at 2:50 p.m., Todd called Elly's apartment. The machine dutifully answered. Todd left a message, but it didn't arrest his anxiety.

At three, there was still no word from Elly. Todd called the university. The woman who answered his call was painfully lacking in any ability to help him. They didn't seem to keep any information on the attendance of students. She advised him to contact the individual instructors.

Trying to find the instructors was frustrating beyond his ability to bear. By four, Todd had decided he had to find Elly himself. The problem was how to begin. He made several calls with no results. The last call he made was to Annette Pace's residence. There was no answer.

***

The little gray sports car careened around the corners with squealing tires. Annette was driven by a nervous, maddening sense of tense fear and anxiety. Bent on escape, she cut into the busy early afternoon traffic with total disregard for other vehicles. Horns blared, brakes locked, and the smell of burning tires punctuated the damp and heavy air.

Frantically the silver-gray Alfa Romeo engine roared as the car lurched through the traffic. Narrowly missing a pedestrian at an intersection, Annette in her fury plunged ahead. Commuters dodged, weaved, and pulled off the road to avoid collision.

A tollgate operator would recall later that he'd seen the car. It had come through the toll area at sixty or seventy miles per hour. The speed limit was forty-five, but this car swerved through the cars and changed lanes without a care. As the car reached the top of the bridge, it became trapped behind a lumbering garbage truck. The driver angrily laid on the horn, but the garbage truck never changed its lumbering pace. A slim space opened up, and the Alfa dove in. Horns blared. The sound of more screeching brakes punctuated the stormy conditions and swelled up from the annoyed cars that were trying to safely cross the bridge. More cars blocked the path of the Alfa as Annette drove in front of the garbage truck. The blast of sheering, tearing metal was deafening as the bumper of the Alfa was hooked. *Screech* went the numerous brakes. The silver mass leaped into the air. It seemed to pause, and then it tumbled out of control, hit the guardrail, and lurched over the side. In free fall, it plunged in silence and fell the two hundred twenty feet into the dark, deadly bay with a wind-torn splash. The water spray below the bridge was observed by a coast guard boat, whose occupants were the first to report the accident.

On the bridge, traffic came to a halt. The garbage truck driver stumbled from his rig in a daze. "I couldn't stop in time. It wasn't possible. She just drove in front of me." He sobbed incoherently to no one in particular.

Many drivers braved the driving rain and got out of their cars to run to the railing to look over. They were subdued, and they whispered quietly as they mingled. These witnessed observations would last a lifetime. Some would call up the scene in dreams, and others would gossip about it over dinner, but it was shattering to all.

***

The news was broadcast on all the networks. Still at his office, Todd was too busy to notice. He was trying to get a warrant to enter Annette's house as it was locked tight and no one had answered.

Maria Fuentes paged Todd. It was late in the day. She wasn't sure he would answer, but she had to keep trying.

"You had better be telling me that the goddamned warrant is here, Maria," he said angrily.

"I don't have news of your warrant, sir, but please don't hang up. I have some other information for you. A car with license plates registered to Allen and Annette Pace met with a fatal accident this afternoon. We don't know who was in the car, but there appears to be no survivors." Maria paused to let the gravity of the message sink in. The car went over the railing on the Golden Gate. They are sending divers down now, sir. I just wanted you to know."

"Oh God, no!" That was all he could utter. His mind raced. He paused and then said, "Call Jim at home and tell him about the warrant I've been trying to get. Give him the message you just gave me. Tell him I'm going out to the bridge to get a handle on what's happening. Ask him to go out to Annette's house. I can't bear to." His voice trailed off, and he hung up without a closing salutation so as to maintain his control.

CHAPTER 19

As Night Fell

Maria put down the receiver on her end. Grabbing her coat, she ran to Todd's office and caught him just as he was leaving.

"Let me drive you, Todd. That way you can concentrate on what we are going to do next. I can also help you by taking notes for you," she said earnestly.

"You are quick. Have you called Jim already?" Todd said, surprised to see her.

"I wanted to catch you before you left. Can I call from your office phone or on the call radio in the car?" she said, trying to disguise the fact she was worried about him most of all.

"You're right. The car phone is the best. Thank you for wanting to come. I appreciate your company. This trip out to the site is going to be more depressing than interesting."

They walked in silence. It was starting to rain again. Maria made her call to Jim as soon as they were in the squad car. Jim had just put his youngest son to bed. It was 7:55 p.m., and he agreed to do the search of Annette's house. He sounded tired, but he perked up once Maria told him the whole story. The news about the car on the bridge had aired, interrupting the game he was watching. That annoyed him, but now that he had more information, he was intrigued.

"Sure, no problem. I'll take care of the warrant and everything on this end. We will keep in touch," he said to support their efforts.

The traffic was still heavy. Two lanes of the Golden Gate were closed, and traffic would be backed up for many hours before it got better. The rain didn't help, but it did make the drivers more cautious. No one wanted to be the next fatality that night.

Patiently they worked their way through the mass of cars by driving in the left lanes, which were closed to traffic, and only using their lights when they neared the fateful site on the bridge.

Todd got out of the car and crossed over to the railing. The cold, driving wind caught his unzipped coat and almost ripped it off. The wind was coming from the Pacific Ocean toward the bay, he noted. It probably increased the chances of this type of accident since the car went over the east railing, driven by the easterly wind.

"What was the exact time of the accident?" Todd asked the CHP officer who was working the site after he had introduced himself.

"We have placed it at 16:50. Nasty. We don't get these very often, but they really shake up the commuters," the officer answered.

"Do you have any idea of the wind velocity at the time of the accident?" Todd asked, searching to understand what had happened.

"That is a good question. There have been gusts of up to seventy miles per hour today. Personally, it is my opinion that if a gust of wind occurred at the time of the initial collision, then we can blame the wind for tossing this vehicle over the side of the bridge. It might not have been a fatal accident otherwise," the CHP officer mused.

"Have any of the witnesses said how many persons were in the vehicle and possibly their gender?" Todd asked in a mechanical monotone.

"We have one witness who thinks there was only the driver in the car. Then another was unsure, so I would say there is a good possibility that there could be two people. None of the witnesses were sure of the sex of the driver or the passenger. With the rain and cold, the windows get frosted over and visibility was poor. The radical way this driver was driving is the underlying cause. I think the driver got distracted and was driving with the wrong attitude. Possibly alcohol or other drugs were involved."

The words cut through Todd like a knife. He had seen too many needless deaths due to drunk driving and drugs. Now it was ... No, he must think positively. Maybe Mark was in the car. If he only knew where Elly was. *I wish she would call.* Then the thought slowly evolved. *Maybe she can't call.* Turning to Maria, he barked an order: "Call all the hospitals and ask if they have admitted Elinor DeMartini or anyone matching her description."

***

Pitching in the swelling, turbulent waters, the heaving barge with a crane maneuvered toward the worksite near the bridge. Large flood lights illuminated the area as if it were the middle of the day. In smaller craft, the local television crews were circling like vultures. Todd stood on the pitching deck of the coast guard cutter, trying to make sense of what he saw. Beside him was the first officer, Lance Norman. Their communication was fractured by the cold wind and sea spray. The engine noise was also deafening.

"Do you think the divers have found anything yet?" Todd yelled at the top of his lungs.

"We have confirmation, sir, that they have located what they think is a car. We are coordinating our efforts with that crane over there, which is going to raise the vehicle. The divers are positioning the hooks, and then when the divers are safely out of the way, the crane will start raising the vehicle. The process is taking so long because the water is very deep here—and turbulent. We have had to send down several teams of divers because they can't stay at that depth very long," Lieutenant Norman explained with effort in a hoarse voice that was hard to hear.

As they advanced closer, Todd could see the divers in the water next to a smaller coast guard boat. Carefully the cutter inched its way toward the scene and drew up parallel to the smaller craft with a distance of about twenty feet between them.

It took several hours to work through the tedious process of attaching the hooks to the submerged mass that they thought was the vehicle. The boats and barge pitched in the rolling waves. The coast guard officer had warned Todd that the object they were bringing up only had a 30 percent chance of being the vehicle they were looking for.

They were in luck, however, when the crane strained to raise the object. It was a very tense moment. There was a spontaneous "*Whoop*" heard from the workers when the car was identified by its license plate. The Alfa had lost its proud form. Dangling at the end of a cable, it looked like a crushed toy.

With the result ensured, a wave of nausea enveloped Todd. He gulped air to keep down the contents of his stomach. He made a hasty retreat to empty his guts over the side of the ship with the wind so that the vomit would not come back at him.

Carefully the car was lowered onto the deck of the barge. It was covered with debris from the sea bottom. No one was eager to approach the death trap to observe the carnage within. Todd excused himself on the grounds that he was suffering from mal de mer.

Slowly the barge and the coast guard boats made their way back to the dock at San Francisco. Todd had radioed ahead for the coroner and a car transport to meet them at the mooring when it was confirmed that the vehicle had been found.

It was after midnight when Todd got back to his apartment. When he was at his office before coming home, there was still no call from Elly. In his apartment, he listlessly flopped on the bed, but he couldn't sleep. Time seemed to be the worst enemy. The hours crawled by with his restless tossing. He could not get Elinor out of his head.

December 8

At noon the next day, Todd called the coroner's office. He learned that the Alfa only contained one body. Annette's mangled remains were confirmed by her dental records. It was still theoretical that a passenger might have been in the car and fell out during the fall. They would have to wait until a body washed up on the shores of the bay.

December 9

The sun had set, and the next day bloomed clear and bright. A solemn shell of a man looked at a partially destroyed document that sat on his desk. Jim had brought what remained of the notebook to Todd for his opinion. "It's a miracle that any of it survived in the debris inside the Alfa. Here in the middle, some of the writing can be seen," Todd remarked.

"Do you confirm that the writing is Gina's? Can we speculate that Annette possessed this notebook all the time?" Jim asked.

"Possession is pretty condemning. There isn't much else to go on. When we searched Annette's house, it looked like a fight had taken place. Here are some pics. You can see the disarray. We found blood in the grout in the tile floor. Not a lot, not enough to sample. It was evident when we put chemicals on it. That tape recorder you asked us to find wasn't anywhere.

"One bit of good news is that the tests came back. They indicate that the blood in Allen Pace's office was Annette's. We also have Clair Minix's testimony, which strongly suggests that Annette had the time to commit the murder," Jim said with a smile.

"How about Mark Jacobs?" Todd asked.

"Sorry, no sign of him anywhere."

When the phone rang, it jarred both men. Todd rushed to answer it.

"This is Maria. I have a Doctor Jameson on line five who wants to talk to you, Todd."

Anxiously Todd got the doctor on the line.

"I have a patient here, found in the brush at China Beach. We are speculating that she fell off a cliff or something because of her injuries. She was delirious when she first arrived and didn't possess an ID; however, we did find a tape recorder on her. Now that she is more coherent, she is asking for Todd Markam. She says she has something important to tell you. All she told us about herself is her name. She identified herself as Elly DeMartini. Do you know this person?"

"Yes!" Todd could barely contain his excitement. "Is that General Hospital? I will be right down."

**

Jim decided to accompany Todd to give him moral support. At the hospital, they found the doctor without a problem.

"She is suffering from shock and hypothermia. We have set her ankle and patched her up. She has a mild brain concussion. We needed to warm her up. Her hypothermia is our most critical concern. She is lucky that the hiker found her when he did.

"The tape recorder, she wanted to give you is in the safe in the administrator's office."

A nurse led them to an enclosed heat-controlled room. Hidden under a mound of heated blankets, surrounded by a forest of stands with bottles and tubes, Elly's pale face, marred by scratches, was all but lost amid the paraphernalia. Dark curls peeked from the wrappings on her head, but her smile glowed as brilliantly as ever. It was certainly Elly!

"Hi!" she squeaked weekly.

"You are such a beautiful sight. I was so afraid I would never see you again," Todd said as he sat down on a chair near her bed. His hand tentatively reached for her hand to see if she was real.

Realizing he was in the way, Jim decided to brave the hospital bureaucracy and get the tape recorder from the safe. He knew they wouldn't give it up easily.

Leaning close to Elly's ear, Todd whispered, "Don't be afraid to tell me what happened. We have some convincing evidence that Annette killed Allen."

Elly struggled to rise up. "You've got to catch her. She—" Elly's voice cracked and was lost in her swollen throat.

Gently Todd eased her back onto the pillow. "It is okay. You just rest. Annette isn't going to hurt anyone again. She met with an accident, and she is dead."

Todd sat by Elly's side for many minutes, waiting for her to relax and rest after the shock of the news wore off. He rose up to leave and leaned over her still form. "I'm going to go and listen to the tape if it is available. Dear Elly, I need a partner to play with on those exotic beaches, so, my love, I want you to rest and get strong again," he whispered in her ear.

She smiled weakly in response and nodded her head.

He kissed her forehead and left the room.

***

By the end of the day, Elly's voice was clearer and she was strong enough to tell her story.

"I found the rest of Gina's diary that was previously lost. It was among Annette's recipe books in her kitchen. She was very strange that morning when she found me with the diary. She was threatening me with a butcher knife. Then I remember I was on the floor with this terrible pain in my head, and she was talking to someone on the phone. Annette tied my hands with a silk scarf, but she is lousy at knots. When she started dragging me, I pretended I could barely walk. I wanted to see what she would do. She tried to push me into the car. We argued. I finally gave in, but when she went around to her side, I jumped out. We had this terrible chase. I don't know how I did it, but I finally got far enough away from her that she couldn't catch me. I was exhausted. I don't know how I did it. Then she came after me in the car. I had to jump off the cliff. It was my only escape. I stumbled down it and then fell and rolled until I passed out.

"I was cold and wet, my ankle was broken, and I had no strength left. I must have passed out again. I woke up here. They told me a hiker found me. Have you listened to the tape? She killed Gina and Allen. She wanted to kill me, too! Mark Jacobs is her accomplice, I think. What are your ideas?"

"Yes, the tape is excellent. I know it was hard for you to keep it safe during the mauling you experienced, but you were wonderful. Let me think about Jacobs. He certainly could be an accomplice as he has the knowledge." Todd sat back and rubbed his chin for better concentration. "You may have a point there. Yes, you may even be right," he started slowly. "Actually, we are still looking for him. But you don't have to worry about that. For you, the nightmare is over."

CPSIA information can be obtained
at www.ICGtesting.com
Printed in the USA
LVHW040512171120
671899LV00018B/398/J

9 781664 142107